footprints
in the sand

Lucy's side of the story...

He came out with one of those exasperating
male invitations – you know the kind – totally
non-committal, so you've no idea whether they're
asking you out or not.

footprints
in the sand

Lucy's side of the story...

CHLOË RAYBAN

Collins

An imprint of HarperCollinsPublishers

First published in Great Britain by Collins in 1999
Collins is an imprint of HarperCollins*Publishers* Ltd
77-85 Fulham Palace Road, Hammersmith,
London W6 8JB

The HarperCollins website address is:
www.**fireandwater**.com

1 3 5 7 9 8 6 4 2

Text copyright © Chloë Rayban

ISBN 0 00 675303 5

The author asserts the moral right to
be identified as the author of the work.

Printed and bound in Great Britain by
Caledonian International Book Manufacturing Ltd
Glasgow G64

with grateful thanks to
Nick Price for his help with the windsurfing

Chapter One

'Mu-um! Have you read this?'

My mother looked up from her reading with one of her intentionally vague expressions.

'Umm – guide book, yes – no... Not sure. Think so.'

'You can't have. It sounds ghastly. Listen to this...'

I put on my official travel guide voice and read:

'The island's relative fertility can seem scraggy and unkempt when compared with its neighbours. These characteristics, plus the lack of spectacularly good beaches, meant that until the late 1980s very few visitors discovered Lexos. The tiny airport which cannot accommodate jets still means that the island is relatively unspoilt. Not that the island particularly encourages tourism – it's a sleepy peaceful place populated mainly by local fishermen.

'Unusually for a small island, Lexos has abundant ground water, channelled into a system of small lakes. These make for an active mosquito population...'

Mum cut in. 'Well, it sounds fabulous in this – listen. "Lexos – undiscovered paradise of the Aegean." Smashing picture too.'

I leaned over her shoulder. She was leafing through a glossy tourist brochure. She thrust the cover under my nose.

'It's only a pot of geraniums and a bit of blue sea. It could be anywhere.'

'Well, I'm intending to enjoy this holiday Lucy – whatever.'

I sat back in the airline seat and put my Walkman on. 'Undiscovered' – *typical*. I reckon she'd done this on purpose.

Neither of us had actually said anything, but we both knew it was going to be our last holiday together. By all rights I would have gone inter-railing with Migs and Louisa – three girls off round Europe together, what a laugh. That's what I'd intended to do. But just when we'd got all the arguments over our itinerary sorted out, Mum had this phone call...

Dad was getting married again.

I don't know why it got to her so much, they'd been divorced for years – five years at least. Everything had settled down. She'd seemed perfectly happy. But after the call she got this sort of thin-lipped look on her face, like I remembered from way back, when they separated.

'You know what you need – a really good holiday,' I said.

'Yes, you're right. I do. I know I do. Why don't we go somewhere right away from it all?' she said.

'We'. I hadn't actually fixed anything with Migs and Louisa. I mean, we hadn't booked the tickets yet.

She looked at me, all kind of bright-eyed and expectant. So I nodded and left it at that. I hoped she'd forget about it. But then, a day or so later, she came up with this plan. She wanted us both to go to the Greek islands just around the time Dad was due to get married. I had no intention of going to the wedding anyway. I didn't like Sue, Dad's 'partner' much. And Mum seemed so set on the idea, so I hadn't the heart to refuse.

But I didn't expect it to be *this* far away from it all.

Lexos was really off the beaten track. We flew to a larger island first – Kos. And then we had to travel on by ferry. Dad said I'd love Greece. It was the furthest I'd ever been from England. He said it was the first place where you actually felt the influence of the East. Dad was really into the East. He'd gone overland all the way to India and back when he was young, and he'd kept a ratty kind of embroidered Afghan coat in the loft. I used to dress up in it when I was little. It smelt like a dead goat.

But he was right about Greece. It did have a sense of the East. As soon as I got off the plane I could feel it in the warm dry heat of the sun, soaking into me.

We hired a taxi to take us from the airport to the ferry port, and the driver played this kind of clattering Eastern music on his radio. We drove past little whitewashed churches with strange round domes, and all the old women were dressed like witches in long fluttering black dresses. They held scarves up to their faces to keep out the dust. And the air smelt different. Hot and perfumed with herbs and pine and something sweet and kind of musky. And now and then there was just the odd whiff of dead goat smell. Maybe that was what made it feel Eastern to me – by association with the coat.

The boat trip took hours. We had to queue to board with all these backpackers who looked as if they'd been in Greece all their lives. I couldn't help noticing that some of the guys were gorgeous. Their skins were a deep bronze and their hair and clothes bleached as if they'd been left out in the sun for months. I felt really self-conscious with my white skin and my brand new jeans and T-shirt – and I was with my mother too. Pretty humiliating.

Mum said we should go up on the outer deck in case it got rough. By the time we got up there, there were no seats left, so we had to sit on the deck and lean on our suitcases. But she was right. It did get pretty rough.

Apparently, there'd been this massive storm the night before. The wind had died down but the sea was still recovering from its effects. After about an hour of being tossed around I started to feel really sick and my head ached. I must have looked sick too, because this old Greek lady leant over and handed me half a lemon. I didn't know what I was meant to do with it. But she held it to her nose and sniffed and nodded. And I did the same and I felt a bit better. Mum said it was a traditional Greek cure for sea-sickness. So I nodded and sniffed and smiled at the old woman and she laughed and nodded back. We kept up this nodding and sniffing and smiling routine for the rest of the trip.

I'll never forget my first view of Lexos. Some paradise! But, quite frankly, in the state I was in – any bit of dry land was as good as any other. As we drew nearer, the truly dire condition of the port came into focus. Boy, was it run-down. The buildings were mostly rough squareish boxes of concrete and grey breeze block. Most of them had odd bent ribs of rusty iron sticking out from their flat roofs as if they'd meant to build another storey on top and changed their minds. I think my first impression must've registered on my face because Mum was desperately trying to stay positive.

'Oh look Lucy, there's a palm tree,' she said, as her eye lit on the sole acceptable item in the panorama. I was beyond a reply.

I wasn't actually sick until I got on shore. And then I was, dramatically, behind a cactus. Cheers! Welcome to Lexos, I thought to myself as I took sips from the bottle of water Mum sympathetically handed to me.

After we'd sat at a café for a while and I'd drunk a lemonade, I started to feel a bit better.

'Well, I hope you don't think we're going to stay here,' I said as I recovered the faculty of speech.

'Oh, it's not that bad,' said Mum, looking fixedly in the direction of the palm tree.

'Mum – it's ghastly and you know it.'

'Let's get back on the boat then,' she threatened, pointing to where the last boxes of freight were being loaded into the hold. 'It'll be leaving in a minute.'

'Ha ha, very funny,' I said. 'I'd have to be anaesthetized before you'd get me back on that.'

'Feeling any better?'

'Mmm... the lemonade helped.'

'Well, if you're up to it, I reckon we ought to find the Tourist Office and see if they can suggest somewhere to stay.'

We trekked miles in search of it. Mum kept spotting all these little signs with 'I's for Information on them which seemed designed to take us on a scenic tour of the town. I'd never been anywhere so Third World. The roads were cracked and pot-holed and smelt of donkeys, and the few bars or restaurants we came across just had men sitting outside who stared at us. The whole place felt vaguely threatening.

'I don't like it here,' I said.

'Oh don't be silly, Lucy. Ports are always like this. It'll be fine when we get out into the country – you'll see.'

We must have been walking round in circles because when we eventually found the Tourist Office, it was located more or less where we'd disembarked from the ferry. It was in a forbidding grey concrete block next door to the Customs Office. It had bars over the windows and looked like a prison. But there was a sign outside with the same jolly tourist picture showing the pot of geraniums that we'd seen on the front of Mum's brochure. I cracked up when I spotted the slogan written underneath: *You'll learn to love Lexos.*

'What's so funny?' demanded Mum. I think she was losing her cool by this time.

But when she caught sight of the poster she started giggling as well. 'Do you think they give indoctrination sessions?'

'Vee haf vays of making you luf us...' I said.

The people in the Tourist Office brought out a plastic folder full of pictures of hotels and guest houses. I could see Mum getting hot and bothered trying to calculate how much the prices quoted in drachmas worked out at. She was never any good with noughts. I helped her with the maths and made a few acid comments about the pictures.

They all looked incredibly dreary. I'd wanted to go somewhere like Corfu or Skiathos, somewhere with a bit of life. Clubs maybe. The places they had on offer looked as if they were all in the back of beyond – and I couldn't make out any guests under the age of about *fifty* in the photos.

I kept giving Mum meaningful glances and turning the page.

'Well, if you're going to be like this, Lucy,' whispered Mum, 'we'll never find anywhere to stay.'

I felt hot and my head ached.

'How can you possibly tell what a place is like from a photo in a book?' I whispered crossly. 'Think of what that poster does for this island.'

Mum glanced at the poster with a sigh and then turned to the girl behind the desk, saying apologetically: 'I'm sorry. I think we'd better come back later.' She raised an eyebrow in my direction. I loathed it when she did that.

We trailed back to the café where I'd had the lemonade and Mum ordered two more.

'Look,' she said when we'd both cooled down. 'Let's hire a taxi and get away from the port. Ports are always dreary. I bet we'll find a gorgeous beach with a taverna just along the coast. All we've got to do is look around a bit, that's what Dad and I used to do when we came to the islands in the seventies...'

She paused for a moment, and just a shadow of that thin-lipped look came back on her face. I remembered photos in our album of Mum and Dad, young and tanned and carefree on hired mopeds, bumming round the islands. Mum in a ridiculous daisy-printed mini dress and Dad with long hair and John Lennon sunglasses, both totally relaxed and happy together. Looking at the pictures, you'd think that feeling would last forever. Weird how things can change like that.

'Maybe you're right,' I said, picking up my backpack before she could get all emotional and embarrassing. I suddenly felt guilty about being such a pain.

'I know I'm right,' said Mum, sounding more like her old self.

'You're always right,' I teased.

'Come on,' she said. 'Let's make a move then. We're bound to find somewhere you'll love.'

We bought cheese pies and honey cakes from the bakery for our lunch, and once I'd eaten I felt loads better. Then we tracked down what seemed to be the one and only taxi on the island.

I think Manos, the driver, must have come from a very large family. At any rate, he had an awful lot of cousins, and we must have visited most of them that afternoon. We started at a five-star hotel. It was a great big pink stone barracks of a place which smelt like a hospital. It did have a pool... but it was empty. Mum turned that down with the excuse that it was too expensive. So Manos must've come to the conclusion that we were flat broke, and he took us to his poorer cousins. One had a flat to let that reeked of calor gas and drains. Another had a room with a large decaying double bed and a fridge standing in the middle of the bedroom. And worse still, when Mum said we wanted a place on our own, he took us to what he called 'a bungalow' which was a kind of prefab with a compost heap for a garden and a goat tethered outside.

As the sun dipped towards the horizon I was fast losing faith. I hadn't seen a single decent beach yet.

'What we really want is a *taverna*,' said Mum. 'A nice, clean, cheap *taverna*, near a beach.'

'Oh, *taverna*,I' said Manos – and he sucked through his teeth as if the very concept of a *ttaverna*, was new to him. Then he swung back into the driving seat and shifted noisily into gear. 'OK, if you want *taverna*, I take you.'

It was a long drive along a winding cliff road to the other side of the island to find this taverna. I don't think Manos was in a very good mood. He obviously didn't have a cousin who owned a taverna, so he wasn't going to get his cut, or free drinks, or whatever it was he usually received as commission.

Mum had her eyes closed for most of the journey, which was a waste because she was on the cliff-side and the views must have been staggering. The sun was going down and it was the most magical sunset. All gold and blue and mauve with puffy little clouds turning candy-floss pink.

It was almost dark when we crunched to a halt in a cobbled square. We climbed out of the taxi. Manos beckoned to us and led us up over a rise.

We were on top of a headland, looking out over the most amazing view of the sea, which had turned a livid copper colour in the low sunlight. We could see for miles, right over to the misty shapes of the neighbouring islands.

Some kind of building was outlined against the sky. It had a corrugated iron roof which looked on the point of caving in and a battered sign surrounded by coloured light-bulbs, most of which didn't work, which read: TAVERNA PARADISOS.

'Perfect,' said Mum.

Chapter Two

A fat man with a sagging belly, who I took to be the owner, was lounging on the terrace, wearing a dirty vest and boxer shorts. He had a bottle and a glass beside him, and I reckoned he had been indulging in the contents for some time.

I shot Mum a warning glance, but before it registered, she was already asking if he had a room free.

He leapt to his feet with remarkable agility for a man his size,

'You want room? I have good room. How long?'

'Oh I don't know – a week? Ten days maybe?'

'Best room! Best price! Private facilities,' he said.

'Oh, that's nice. Can we take a look?'

He ushered us across the terrace as if he was showing us around the Ritz.

I followed. Mum had really lost it this time. The place was awful. It wasn't what I had in mind at all. It didn't have a pool or anything, and by the look of it we were the only guests he'd had this side of Christmas.

He was already unlocking a door with a big metal key. The floor was plain concrete. It didn't have a carpet or lino. All there was by the way of furniture were two narrow beds, a three-legged table on the point of collapse and a fly paper hanging from the bare lightbulb. It even had dead flies on it – that was *so* gross.

'We can't stay here,' I whispered to Mum.

She frowned at me. 'We can't keep searching all night. It'll be dark soon,' she hissed back.

'You no like?' asked the taverna owner, looking sulky.

'How much is the room?' asked Mum.

He came out with a figure that was way below anything we'd seen that day. I could see Mum working out the sum in her head and for once – would you believe it? – she must've actually come up with the right answer. She raised an eyebrow at me.

'No, it's fine, we'll take it,' she said.

I shot her another furious glare.

The taverna owner walked out with a satisfied look on his face, leaving us alone together.

'I can't believe you said that.'

'Oh honestly Lucy, what do you want to stay in? One of those ghastly air-conditioned tower blocks full of people on package tours?'

'Well maybe I would. At least we'd get MTV – this place hasn't even got a room phone.'

'Dear, dear, how on earth are we going to order room service?' said Mum breezily, plonking her suitcase down on a bed.

I sat down on the other bed. It was hard as a board.

'Come on Lucy, don't look like that. It's incredible value. It'll look lovely with the sun on it in the morning – you'll see.'

'Huh!'

'Well, I'm going to pay the taxi driver and order us some nice cold drinks. We can have them on the terrace and watch the last of the sunset.'

Big deal! I thought as Mum went off with a determined look and her purse in her hand.

The taverna owner served the drinks. He seemed to do everything around the place – show the rooms, check the passports. He even swabbed down the table, brushing the crumbs right into my lap.

When we'd finished our drinks, Mum asked him about dinner.

'No eat here tonight. No food. Restaurant down in the village.' He waved a hand in the direction of the cliff-side.

We were both dead tired after the journey. We'd been up at five that morning in order to catch the plane. Mum took one glance at the unlit and perilous-looking steps that led down to the harbour below and said:

'We don't want much. Just an omelette will do.'

So he served us reluctantly. We sat at a table with a greasy oilcloth on it. The oilcloth was grudgingly covered by a paper tablecloth which was held in place by a long stretch of what looked like knicker elastic. He wasn't up to much as a waiter – he just slammed the plates down on the table and refused to cook me chips although they were on offer, chalked up on the board which served as a menu. I wondered if he was always in such a bad mood.

When we'd finished our meal I was still hungry.

'Ask him if he's got a yogurt or something,' suggested Mum.

So I went to the kitchen to ask. When he opened the fridge, I saw it was jam-packed. He had plenty of food. He just couldn't be bothered to cook it. That's when Mum called him 'the Old Rogue'. And the name kind of stuck.

There wasn't a lot to choose from by way of entertainment after dinner. Not even enough light to read by. We had the choice of either sitting and looking at the view on the left of the terrace or the view on the right. Both were equally dark. So we went to bed. Outside, I could hear the thumps and clatter of the tables being cleared. And then the lights went out on the terrace and silence descended on the place – *total* silence. God this place was bo-ring!

Was it an earthquake? Was it a landslide? God knows what it was! The shock had woken me and I was sitting bolt upright.

'What on earth was that?'

Mum was awake and dressed, perched on the bed opposite looking equally stunned.

'No idea.'

The last of the landslide was followed by a deep, guttural *chug-chug-chug* which echoed through the room. Mum went out to investigate.

A minute or so later she returned. 'It's OK. It's only a dredger.'

'A what?'

'They must be doing some work on the harbour. Making it deeper or something. It's a rusty old thing – amazing they've kept it going.'

'Sounds healthy enough to me. How long d'you think it'll keep that racket up?'

'Oh, I don't know. Why don't you get up? It's a lovely morning.'

'In a minute.'

I turned over and tried to get back to sleep on the rock-hard mattress. My pillow felt as if it was made of concrete. My right ear was flattened and sore. I doubted whether it would ever regain its normal shape.

I was just dropping off when it happened again. Another deafening landslip of gravel cancelled out any further attempt at sleep, so I climbed out of bed and stomped over to the bathroom. You could hardly call it a bathroom, it was about the size of an airplane lavatory. I paused in the doorway... Hang on. Where was the shower?

'Mu-um?'

'What?' She was rubbing sunscreen into her legs.

'I thought the Old Rogue said we had a shower.'

'We have. The tap's under the towel thingy.'

I went back into the bathroom. On closer inspection, I discovered that the 'shower' was just a rusty sort of sprinkler sticking out of the ceiling. When I turned the tap on, water gushed out all over the loo, all over the basin and then drained away through an evil-looking hole in the floor. And what's more – the water was stone cold.

'Yuuukkk!' I said as I climbed out of the icy flood

and found a dry bit of floor to towel myself down on. 'That was just about the most gruesome experience I've had in my entire life.'

'You'll soon get used to it,' said Mum. 'You find showers like that all over the islands. Labour-saving – it washes down the bathroom too.'

'I think it's disgusting.'

'Oh Lucy, don't be such a killjoy. It's lovely outside. He's laid breakfast on the terrace. What do you want? Tea or coffee?'

'Tea, I suppose. And orange juice.' I'd had a Greek coffee at the airport. The cup was half-full of muddy-tasting dregs.

'See you out there, then.'

When I emerged into the sunlight, Mum was already seated at a table in the shade making the best of the 'breakfast'. We each had a plate with couple of slices of dry white bread, a sliver of margarine and some red jam. When Mum asked for orange juice, we were each presented with a Fanta.

'Well I suppose we can't expect much at the price we're paying,' said Mum when the Old Rogue was out of earshot.

'Now you can see why we're the only ones staying here,' I remarked grimly.

Anyway, after the guy had made it clear that breakfast was over by swabbing down the table all around us, we decided to spend the morning exploring. Armed with swimming things and suntan lotion, a book for Mum and my Walkman, we set off in search of a decent beach.

The nearest beach was in the long bay lying to the right of the headland. But the sand was an unwelcoming black colour and you could see by looking down from the terrace that there was a wide band of weed along the shore which you'd have to swim through to get to open water.

'Don't even think about it,' I said to Mum.

'But it's nice and close.'

'Nice! Imagine what could be lurking in that weed. Crabs or jellyfish or *sea urchins.*'

At the mention of sea urchins, Mum agreed. I'd trodden on one once and had all these little prickles stuck in my foot which had to be taken out one by one with Mum's tweezers. It was agony.

'What about the harbour?' I suggested.

'Let's go down and see.'

So we tried the bay on the left. A flight of rough irregular steps wove its way down through some poor little tumble-down houses. At the bottom there was a pathetic fringe of shingle edged by some rotting fishermen's shacks. Nets were stretched out on the tarry stones to dry. The air smelt of weed and gently decaying fish.

'Oh, isn't this wonderful!' said Mum brightly. 'Look Lucy, real fishermen!'

I looked. Some rather depressed-looking whiskery Greeks were sitting barefoot on the beach mending nets.

'Look at their boats! Oh, it's all so unspoilt.'

23

I thought the place could do with a bit of spoiling actually, but I didn't comment. I suppose the boats were pretty. They were a fading weathered sea-blue, like those trendy kitchen cabinets you get in Ikea – but this weathering was obviously genuine. One of the fishermen was rowing his boat out to sea. He stood up in it and rowed in the direction he was going, leaning forward on the oars in a really weird way.

'We can't swim here, it's all fishy and tarry,' I pointed out. My new sandals were rubbing a blister on my foot and it was already really hot. I was longing for a swim.

'There's probably a beach in the next bay,' said Mum. 'We just need to clamber over those rocks.'

The rocks were dark and evil-looking and I didn't hold out much hope of there being a nice white sand beach the other side. But I clambered after Mum anyway. It took about half an hour to get round to the next bay. And once we got there, predictably enough, we found there was yet another headland to negotiate. I was lagging behind and my blister was rubbed red and raw.

When, at last, we rounded the further point, I could see that there were only more jagged rocks. To top it all, this bay wasn't as sheltered as the fishing harbour – the sea looked dark and angry as it lashed against the rocks. It didn't even look safe to swim in.

I was getting really fed up. The Greek sea Dad had described to me was calm, blue, crystal clear – so clear, he said, you could see fish swimming beneath you, twenty metres down.

Mum was up ahead of me, trying to see round into

the bay beyond. I tried shouting to catch her attention but my voice was lost in the sound of the sea.

I sat down crossly on a rock and took my sandal off to examine the damage. The blister was throbbing. I dabbled my foot in the water to cool it.

'Lucy! Come on!'

'I've had enough of this,' I shouted back.

'What?'

She turned and started picking her way back over the rocks. 'What's up?'

'I'm hot and I'm thirsty and I've got a humungous blister,' I shouted.

Mum joined me on my rock. 'It doesn't look very inviting, does it?'

'No.'

'But having come so far...'

'Look. Anyone in their right mind can see there's no way there's going to be a decent beach anywhere round here.'

'Perhaps you're right. Maybe we should go back.'

'At last!'

I climbed to my feet and tried to ease my foot back into my sandal, but it was too painful.

'Oh Mu-um! I don't believe this!'

'What is it?'

'Tar. I've got it all over my new shorts.'

'Oh Lucy.'

'Oh Lucy' – it was the way she said it. Mum had her tired voice on. I could tell she was really fed up too.

We made our way back over the sun-baked rocks. I was forced to limp with one sandal on and one foot bare, and I could feel the sole of my bare foot practically griddling on the hot stone.

'I think we should treat ourselves to a really nice lunch to make-up,' said Mum, trying to cheer me up in the most obvious way as the harbour came into view once again.

The 'restaurant' the taverna owner had mentioned was nothing but a few blue-washed tables and chairs set out in a sloping lopsided way on the beach. The whole place was salt-encrusted and fishy, and by the look of it, salmonella was generally the dish of the day.

But by the time we reached it, I was past caring about food. I just sank down gratefully on one of their rickety rush chairs.

'All I want is a drink,' I said.

'Oh Lucy.'

'Well, do you seriously want to eat here?'

'There isn't anywhere else. Not without climbing up all those steps again.'

I just sat on my chair not speaking. By all rights, I should be stopping off somewhere glamorous with Migs and Louisa – somewhere clean and civilised, sitting at a café in Venice maybe, eating a nice squidgy slice of pizza, with loads of dark and gorgeous Italian boys chatting us up.

'Well, the dredger's stopped anyway,' said Mum.

'I thought something was missing.'

'Oh come on Lucy, what are you going to have?'

I sighed. 'What's the choice?'

'Umm...' Mum peered at the menu, which was all in Greek.

'I bet it'll be fish, fish, fish or fish.'

'There's nothing wrong with fish.'

'I loathe fish, as well you know.'

'You used to love fish fingers.'

'That was *ages* ago.'

'I think we'll have to go into the kitchen and choose,' said Mum, after a minute or so. 'They won't mind, everyone does that in Greece.'

The kitchen was dark after the bright sunlight outside. It took a moment for my eyes to adjust, and when they did, I found I was face to face with a glass-fronted fridge.

I was right, the choice was fish. There were loads of them, all shapes and sizes, staring back at me. This fish wasn't cut up into neat white rectangles like it was back home. And it didn't have batter or breadcrumbs on it. It had heads on, and tails on, and looked as if, ever so recently, it had been swimming around alive and well, unaware that the day's swim was going to come to such a nasty end.

There was a large lady in a witch dress standing behind the fridge, grinning at us. A gold tooth gleamed in the darkness.

'I don't fancy anything if you don't mind,' I said with a grimace.

'Oh Lucy. Don't be such a wimp, darling, it looks simply delicious. It's probably just come out of the sea.'

'Can't I have chips?'

'Only chips? Well, if you must. But we didn't have

much to eat last night.'

'Chips'll be fine.'

So I had chips and a Coke and Mum had fish and some wine. We sat at a table in the shade not far from the water's edge. I think the wine must've been pretty strong because after a glass or so, Mum kept going on about what a brilliant place it was. She came out with all this 'unspoilt' stuff again and droned on and on about how we were getting back to the 'real Greece' and how time stood still in this kind of place. It was all that 'alternative lifestyle' nonsense that Dad sometimes came out with. I reckon the olds had been brainwashed with it when they were young.

All I could see was that we were sitting on a grotty beach that had several centuries of discarded fish-bones and rotting fish heads mixed in among the pebbles. And that there were feral-looking cats hanging around which seemed horribly mangy and possibly rabid. And that the sea looked weedy and oily and fishy and had bits floating in it...

'Oh look at those children. It must be paradise for them here. It's like going right back to nature...' said Mum, absent-mindedly filling her glass again.

I looked. A couple of unhealthily chubby little boys were wading in the rust brown sea. They had a plastic bag with them and they were emptying it into the water a few metres out. A load of bloody-looking fish guts fell from the bag. As they did so, a shoal of tiny fish surrounded them and the water boiled around their legs as the younger fish eagerly devoured the

28

remains of their elders. The boys squealed with delight and tried to catch them with their fingers.

'Yeah, what's that phrase? Nature raw in tooth and claw?' I agreed.

The trek back up the steps to the taverna seemed to go on forever. By the time we reached the top, we were both hot and cross and headachy.

'Bags first in the shower,' I said.

'Don't be long then. I think I'm going to melt.'

I turned the shower on and nothing happened. When I tried to flush the loo it made a hollow cranking noise and no water came out.

'That's it,' I said. 'That's the final straw. I'm not staying here any longer.' I was near to tears.

'Oh Lucy. Don't tell me the water's off.'

'Try for yourself.'

I lay down on my bed as Mum tried a range of clanking and cranking, but she had no more luck than me.

'See?'

She sat down on her bed. 'Do you really hate it here?'

'Don't you?'

'Well, I suppose it is a bit primitive...'

'Primitive! It's positively Stone Age. I'm hot and I've got a headache and there isn't even any water.'

'Maybe we should have looked further.'

'Hmmm.'

'And I really wanted us to enjoy this holiday...'

'So did I!'

'I know that next year you'll be off somewhere with your friends... It could be our last together...'

'I know, I know...'

'Listen. If you absolutely hate it here, we could move on...'

'But you keep saying you really like it.'

'Not if you're not happy...'

'Well, it is a bit cut off...'

'I suppose I could get on a bus this afternoon and have a look round. There must be other places.'

'Nowhere could be worse than this.'

'Well, we could be nearer to a decent beach.'

'Want me to come with you?'

'No point in us both going out in this heat. You rest that headache, get a plaster on your blister. Have a sleep.'

'Thanks Mum.'

Chapter Three

It was cool in the room. The shutters had been closed all morning to keep the sun out. I lay back and shut my eyes. I heard Mum bustling around the room, collecting her things. As she went out through the door she said: 'Oh, and Lucy – don't go out in the sun again. Not till after four. It's scorching. You'll get burned.'

'Mmmm. OK. Bye.'

I lay gazing into the semi-darkness, chasing the tiny squiggles you get in your eyes as they darted back and forth across the gloom. They're stray cells apparently, being washed back and forth over the eye. I'm fascinated by all that stuff. Mum calls it gruesome. She's not exactly scientific. I reckon her science education must've ended with the life-cycle of the frog. When I told her I wanted to be a vet she nearly freaked out. She claimed I'd got the whole idea from some series I'd seen on the telly and it would wear off. But it is what I want to do – really badly.

My head had stopped throbbing. I listened to the noises outside. The dredger must've knocked off for the day and I could now hear all the other sounds of the village. Hens somewhere not too far off. And a donkey braying in the distance – a long cascade of eeyores, like mad hysterical laughter. Then the soft sound of the wings of pigeons as they landed on the roof and started scrabbling and cooing.

I was starting to feel bored. What a waste of all that sunlight out there. I climbed off the bed and went to the door. It wasn't *that* hot. Mum was just being over-protective, as usual.

My shorts were hanging on the balcony rail. I could at least try and get the tar off. There was a pump in the vineyard – maybe that worked. I took the shorts and some soap and went and cranked the handle. Sure enough, a gush of water came out.

The shorts were brand new from Gap. They were the first pair of shorts I'd ever had which didn't make my bottom look big. I'd been really pleased with them. But after five minutes or so of scrubbing with the soap, I'd made the tarry marks bigger and darker, if anything.

'What you doin'?'

I jumped. The Old Rogue was standing with his hands on his hips watching me, frowning. Maybe I wasn't meant to be in his vineyard.

'There's no water in the bathroom. I was trying to get these marks off.'

He held out a hand. 'Let me see?'

He took the shorts and made some tut-tutting noises. Then he carried them over to where he had a can of what looked like kerosene. He slopped some on and rubbed the marks. Then he brought them back to the pump, and with a lot of huffing and puffing, soaped the stains and rinsed them out.

'See – good – like new,' he said.

The tar had disappeared as if by magic.

'Thank you, that's brilliant.'

'*Parakolo.*'

'Parakolo?'

'No worries.' His face broke into a smile. He wasn't such an Old Rogue really.

'How do you say "thank you" in Greek?'

'*Efharisto.*'

I messed it up the first time, and he repeated the word syllable by syllable.

He was tickled pink when I got it right.

I hung the shorts on the balcony rail to dry in the sun and leaned beside them gazing out to sea. It was a really intense blue – like a mirror-image of the sky, but deeper. There was a lone windsurfer skimming across the bay. My eyes lazily followed it. I've always wanted to windsurf. Plenty of girls do. There was a gravel pit not far from home where they gave lessons. But Mum said they were too expensive. That's the thing about your parents divorcing. You soon discover that two different homes cost a lot more to run than one did. Even though Mum worked too now, we never seemed to have anywhere near as much money as we used to.

Leaning further over the rail, I saw that there was a kind of shack on the beach that I hadn't noticed before. It had a pile of windsurfers beside it and a sign which said that they were for hire. Civilisation!

Once my shorts were dry, I'd take a closer look at that beach. Maybe, somewhere along that stretch of sand, I could find a big enough gap in the weed to risk a swim.

Half an hour later, I was down on the beach. I cast an eye along the stretch of sand, looking for bathers or sunbathers, but it was deserted. Or was it? At the very far end, almost too far away to see, there seemed to be a few rough tents and towels maybe, hanging between the trees – signs that backpackers had taken up occupation. I thought of the bronzed boys on the boat. Just maybe this wasn't such a bad place after all.

I drew level with the shack. The sign advertised pedaloes as well as the windsurfers, but I couldn't see any. The shack was locked up, and on closer inspection, I found a piece of paper was stuck on the window giving the opening times for hire. It was closed between one o'clock and four.

I took off my sneakers and found the black sand was burning hot, so I had to do a hurried hop, skip and a jump down to the water's edge. The sea felt deliciously cool. Just the right temperature, in fact, and the weed didn't look too bad close up. There were plenty of gaps to get through.

I hesitated. I was longing for a swim, but a swim is always all the more delicious if you get really hot first. So I spread out my towel quite near to the water's edge, stripped off to my bikini and stretched out. Not much point smothering myself in sun-lotion – I was going in the water any minute.

I had a compilation tape made by Migs' brother in my Walkman. It was brilliant, he'd put all my favourite tracks on it. I quite fancied Nick actually. He was quite a bit older than us, going to University next year, so he was hardly likely to take much notice of a friend of his kid sister. But he was always nice to me for some reason.

I lay on the sand soaking in the delicious warmth of the sun, with my eyes closed listening to the tape and having some rather censorable thoughts about Nick...

I woke up to find the tape had come to an end. How long had I been asleep? I'd left my watch back at the taverna. I looked guiltily at the height of the sun. It had moved round quite a bit. My skin didn't look burnt in the bright light – maybe I hadn't slept for too long. It would be just my luck to end up looking like a slab of coconut ice – all pink one side and white the other. Maybe I should have that swim. But now the sun was lower, the sea didn't look half so inviting. I wondered again what was lurking in the weed. Perhaps a better idea would be to turn over and get my back to catch up with my front. I turned over on to my stomach, and as I turned, I caught sight of the windsurfer again.

I watched the little pink and blue sail gliding effortlessly in the steady breeze. It must be so quiet out there, with just the sound of the sea and the wind. The windsurfer hesitated and the sail dipped, then quick as a flash it was up again and the board started off in another direction. The surfer was tacking like a sailing boat, and as he turned and took another tack, I realised he was obviously heading for my beach. I propped myself up on an elbow and slid on my sunglasses to cope with the glare.

As the surfer came closer I could see it was a guy –
and quite a nice guy too, as far as I could tell from this
distance. It was going to be tricky to tack in to the shore,
and I was interested to see how neatly he could do it.
As he drew nearer, I became even more interested. He
must've been here some time because he had a great
tan and I couldn't help noticing, not a bad body. That's
the thing about windsurfing – at least that's what Migs
always said. 'It tones guys up in all the right places –
pecs, six-pack, you name it! Take it up Lucy – and then
you can introduce us to all your friends.'

The windsurfer changed direction again, and for
an instant he paused and the sail dipped into the sea.
In those few seconds that he waited, poised and
about to pull the sail up, I got a full view of him. Oh
no, this just wasn't fair. He was absolutely gorgeous,
sunbleached hair, nice jaw-line – yes, definitely – he
was very, very yummy.

He was pretty close to the shore now and I could
tell he'd caught sight of me. To my delight he did an
epic wobble and nearly fell off. Wicked! I'd really put
him off his stroke.

I just managed not to laugh. Instead, I turned over
and put my headset back on and pretended to ignore
him. I didn't turn the tape on though. Through the
phones I could hear him beaching the board and
dragging it up on the sand. I sneaked a glance. A pair
of nice strong feet and ace legs deliciously flecked
with golden hairs strode past me. He carried the sail
up the beach and then he went back for the board.
Closer up he was definitely very good news indeed.

I lay pretending to be absorbed in my music as he

stowed the board and then made off up the beach in the direction of the taverna. Our taverna. Maybe he was staying there too...

Brilliant! I sat up and started to gather my things together.

Once back at the taverna, I was half-expecting to find my bronzed windsurfer sitting there, having a drink after his sail, maybe. I ran my fingers through my hair and just prayed I hadn't burnt myself red as beetroot. But he wasn't on the terrace. I caught sight of him walking down the path between the vines with a towel round his neck. So he was staying here. Excellent!

Then I suddenly had an awful thought. Oh my God, what if Mum had found somewhere else to stay? Nightmare! Oh curses and damnation! Why had I been such a pain about wanting to move on? It wasn't such a bad place. I mean, one beach in Greece is very much like another, isn't it? And the taverna was so cheap. A real bargain. There might even be some money left over for windsurfing and I could start to learn and...

But Mum wasn't back yet. Did that mean she was still searching – *fruitlessly*? Or was she held up looking at rooms – fixing up the details – oh pl-ease!

I went into the bathroom wishing there was some magical method of thought-tranference by which I could bring her back. Our shower was working again and wonders will never cease – the water was actually *hot*.

I had a really good shower and washed my hair. My skin stung as the hot water ran down it. I had overdone it. I just prayed it wouldn't all peel off before I had a chance to tan. I'd have to be really careful tomorrow.

After my shower, I dressed in my most favourite T-shirt and the pair of jeans that made my legs look longest and went out on to the terrace.

The sun was dipping towards the horizon and promising a pretty spectacular sunset. The evening light shone through the vines, casting dancing shadows across the terrace. The faded blue tables and ancient wicker chairs looked kind of rustic and picturesque.

I sat down at a table nearest the sunset. Even the dredger looked somehow glamorous in this light. The low sun had lit up all its rust, turning it a dramatic burnt ginger colour.

The Old Rogue came out of the kitchen wearing a clean vest.

'You want drink, yes?'

'Yes please. Orange.'

'*Portocalada*?'

'Is that orange?'

'Yes. Greek for orange.'

'*Portocalada*?'

'Yes, good!' he smiled. He was in a much better mood today. He held out a hand. 'Stavros,' he said. 'What is your name?'

'Lucy.'

'Lucy – very nice.'

He was a long time bringing my orange, but when

he came back he was carrying a plate as well, with what looked like crispy fried onion rings with a slice of lemon on them.

'For you, on the house,' he said.

'Oh thank you. What are they?'

'*Mezze*,' he said. 'Good – eat!'

I tasted one. They were hot and crispy and delicious.

'Good, yes?' he said, watching me.

'Very good,' I agreed.

He was going to be ever so disappointed if we moved on. We'd really be letting him down. I smiled and nodded and sipped my drink and indulged in a silent prayer that Mum had found nothing but chicken-pens and and five-star rip-offs on her search.

Stavros waved an arm towards the sunset.

'Beautiful, yes?' he said proudly as if it was his very own sunset 'on the house'.

'Fantastic!' I agreed.

'Best sunset view in the island,' he said, and he made his way off back to his kitchen.

It really was, too. A narrow band of cloud was hovering above the horizon, splitting the sunlight into great golden shafts like you see in old-fashioned religious pictures. It was incredible. I mean, Stavros was right. This headland must be the very best place in the whole island to watch the sunset.

As I sipped my drink I heard footsteps on the gravel. I steeled myself to confront Mum. But it wasn't Mum. It was *him*... the windsurfer. He did a double-take when he saw me – almost dropped the package he was carrying.

'Hi,' he said.

'Hello,' I said, in what I hoped was a suitably cool and laid-back voice.

Then he made off down some steps behind the taverna and I heard a door slam. He *was* staying here. There was no question about it.

There was no way I was going to move on now. My mind raced. How was I going to persuade Mum to stay? Well, there was the sunset for a start.

I climbed down the few steps from the terrace and on to the headland to get an even better view of the last moments. It was only a few metres to a rocky outcrop that stood at the furthest tip. Standing there was like standing on top of the world. I was sandwiched between sea and sky, and the two of them were putting on a performance that was like the biggest firework display and the most dramatic laser show ever.

The clouds were tinted violet and the sun had turned into a great molten ball of fire, sliding down the sky. As the last liquid orange glob of it slipped down into the inky sea I heard Mum's voice, calling:

'Lucy... Lucy!'

She was back.

Making my way across to the terrace, I prepared myself for a forceful introduction to a change of plan.

She dumped her bag down on the table. She looked hot and tired. She didn't look as if she'd had a lot of luck!

I slid on to a chair opposite her.

'Phew, what an afternoon!' she said. (I felt sure she hadn't found anywhere.) But then she leaned forward with a triumphant look on her face.

'It's all settled. I've found a fabulous place. You'll love it.'

Chapter Four

'I can't understand why you've changed your mind like this,' said Mum. 'You couldn't wait to get out of the place at lunchtime.'

'Yes, I know but... I went down to the other bay this afternoon. The beach is much nearer and it's quite nice really.'

'I hope you didn't sit in the sun.'

'Don't fuss, Mum. I had a closer look. It should be fine for swimming. There are plenty of channels through the weed.'

'But the beach I've found hasn't any weed at all.'

'Really?'

'I've left a deposit on the room. Said we'd arrive by lunchtime. If we get up early and pack before breakfast, we can settle up with the Old Rogue and be there by mid-morning.'

'He's not really an old rogue. He's actually quite nice. His name's Stavros. He brought me some hot crispy onion rings, free with my drink.'

'This new place has got a proper water heater and everything. We have to share the bathroom, but at least we can have decent hot...'

I leapt on this shred of hope.

'Oh, we don't have to share a bathroom, do we?'

'It's only with one other room. And that room may not even have people staying...'

'But I had a hot shower here this afternoon. It was fine...'

'Is the water on again? Thank God for that. I'm feeling really anti-social.'

She got up and reached for her bag.

'Mum, do we have to go?'

'What do you mean – *have* to go?'

'Well, it's not really so bad here, is it?'

'Lucy, what's going on? I've been half-way across the island in a stuffy bus, searching in the broiling heat. And all because you said you absolutely loathed the pl...'

Mum paused. An arm leaned over and took my glass and empty plate away. It wasn't the Old Rogue's arm. It was a nice bronzed one, flecked with golden hairs.

'Hi,' he said. 'Welcome to the Paradisos. My name's Ben. Can I get you anything?'

Mum looked up and smiled at him.

'I'd love a glass of white wine. Chilled white wine?' she said.

'Coming right up.'

He turned and gave me a half-grin and walked away, disappearing into the kitchen.

Mum sank back into her chair and looked at me wryly. She raised an eyebrow. 'Oh I get it now,' she said. 'A lot can happen in an afternoon, can't it?'

Half an hour or so later, Mum was sitting on her bed wrapped in a towel. She'd perked up a lot after her shower.

'It's not like that, honestly. I haven't even spoken to him,' I protested.

43

'Does he work here or what?'

'I don't know. I wish you wouldn't keep going on about him. Wanting to stay here has nothing to do with *him*.'

Mum wasn't buying that. 'Oh, I suppose it's the view of the bay that's the big attraction.'

'Maybe it is. There was another fantastic sunset. You missed it.'

'Lucy, you get sunsets everywhere. You said yourself, there's absolutely nothing for you to do here.'

'Yes there is.' I racked my brain for inspiration. 'We could hire a pedalo.'

'I saw the pedaloes on the beach, in pieces. They're wrecked.'

'Well, we could hire donkeys then.'

'Correction, donkey. There's only one – one of us would have to walk.'

'You've already made up your mind, haven't you?'

'I've paid a deposit. For two whole nights. And the beach there is far nicer.'

'How much have you paid?'

'Umm – two nights, about fifty quid.'

'Why did you have to go and do that?'

'It was the only way to secure the room.'

'Well you could've checked with me first.'

'I think you've forgotten, Lucy. It's because of you we're moving.'

I could tell Mum was losing her cool. She was right of course, it was because of me.

I tried a new angle. 'But you said you really liked it here.'

'I did, yes. But, I don't particularly want to waste fifty quid. Do you?'

'It's only fifty quid.'

'Only!'

'No, I suppose not.'

We had a meal down at the port again. It was a warm evening so we sat at the water's edge. The fishermen were setting out in their boats. Each had a tiny lantern in the bows. They rowed out really quietly and you could see their lights reflecting in the water going further and further out to sea. It was so still, their voices came over the water to us as if they were sitting at the very next table.

The lady at the taverna had cooked a cheese and spinach pie. I think maybe she'd been expecting us to come back – she looked really pleased to see us.

Mum said her fish wasn't nearly as nice this time. And she noticed the bits floating in the water. She kept going on about them.

'It's only weed,' I said.

She looked at it darkly. 'You can never be sure.'

When we got back to the taverna Ben wasn't around.

He wasn't there next morning either. We packed up first thing and Stavros brought us breakfast. I kept expecting Ben to turn up. I'd felt sure he'd be around and I'd purposely worn my favourite T-shirt – the one that didn't have a flattening effect. But he must've gone off somewhere – windsurfing perhaps. I scanned the bay for a glimpse of his pink and blue sail as I listened to Mum explaining to Stavros why we'd changed our plans. It was really embarrassing.

'But you say you stay one week – two weeks maybe? Why you change your mind?' said Stavros in a grumpy voice.

'I'm really sorry. But you know, my daughter...' Mum glanced apologetically in my direction. 'You know what they're like, young people!'

She was making out it was my fault. That was so unfair!

Stavros frowned and shrugged his shoulders. 'I make the bill,' was all he said.

I felt terrible. And he'd been really nice to me.

'How could you blame it on me?' I hissed to Mum.

'Well, what was I meant to say? There was no water yesterday. And honestly, look at the breakfast...'

The dredger started up at that moment, drowning out her voice.

'Oh yes,' said Mum in the direction of the dredger. 'Thanks for reminding me – that too.'

I spread my bread carefully, hoping that maybe, given time, Ben might turn up.

'Hurry up Lucy. We'll miss the bus.'

'I'm not really hungry.'

'Well, leave it then, I don't blame you. Perhaps we could have a proper breakfast when we get there.'

'Mmmm.'

I shrugged my backpack on and followed Mum to the bus stop. We didn't miss the bus. It was standing waiting in the square. It wasn't full up either. There were two seats free at the back.

I sat staring miserably out of the window. The bus took off with a lot of honking at some chickens that had wandered into its path. The sun gleamed on the little white dome of the chapel. A dog which was lazing in the sun raised its head and then flopped back again, basking in the warmth. The donkey brayed in the distance. Mum had been right – it was all *so unspoilt*.

I didn't see him until the bus had practically turned the bend in the road. He was running along the goat track. He ran effortlessly, as if running was his natural way of moving. God it wasn't fair. He was *so* gorgeous.

The place Mum had chosen was miles away. Right on the other side of the island. My heart sank as each kilometre went by. Every one of them taking me further away from Ben. Why on earth had she wanted to go so far? There was no way we'd meet up if we were on opposite sides of the island.

The bus was full of local people – old ladies mostly with bundles and crates who got dropped off at remote bus stops in wind-torn villages in the interior. They were dismal-looking places. There was one in particular where an old granny in a tattered black dress was standing on a corner, screaming something at the passers-by. I wondered what it could be like living in a place like that, year in, year out, until you got really old with absolutely nothing happening – ever. No wonder she was in such a state.

I was really fed up by the time we reached the place Mum had found. The bus dropped us off right beside it. It was a modern brick building, set back from the road standing on its own, in a dusty olive grove. It didn't even have a view of the sea or anything.

Our room was on the first floor. It led off a communal corridor that was open on one side to the wind. The bedroom seemed small and dark. As Mum drew up the roller blind a white box of a place came into focus. It had a horrid tasteless lino floor.

'You see, it's all lovely and new and clean.'

'But there's nowhere to sit. No terrace or balcony or anything.'

'There are some garden chairs in the olive grove.'

I looked out of the window. There were a few broken plastic recliners standing in the dust.

'So how much is this room?'

'Well, it's a bit more than it was at the other place.'

Mum was already unpacking and trying to hang things in the wardrobe, battling with those beastly hanger things that come off in your hand.

'So if we went back now, it'd come to the same thing in the long run, wouldn't it?'

'Lucy, I've paid for two nights, so we're staying here now. Don't be difficult.'

'But it's daft to spend our holiday staying somewhere we don't like.'

'I like it here.'

'No you don't. I can tell you don't.'

'I'm not going to waste fifty pounds. You haven't even looked around yet. You'll love the beach. *White sand.*'

'Really?'

'Oh for goodness sake, don't look like that. Come on, let's have some breakfast – you're probably hungry.'

We had breakfast sitting on the broken recliners in the olive grove. Unfortunately, it was a much better breakfast than we'd had at the taverna. Mum kept going on about how much better it was. I made a point of not eating much.

'I hope you're not sickening for something.'

'The butter tastes funny.'

'No, it doesn't.'

'It's got a kind of rancid goat taste.'

'Oh honestly Lucy, don't exaggerate.'

'But if we really don't like it here, we could go back *after* the two nights you've paid for, couldn't we?'

'I don't want to spend my *whole* holiday moving from place to place like a bag lady.'

'Now you're exaggerating.'

'Well, it's a bore all this packing up and moving around. I came here to relax.'

She slid the back of her chair down and stretched out with a sigh as if to demonstrate her commitment to the place.

A wasp settled on the bowl of jam.

I made more fuss than absolutely necessary about

the wasp, and went back to our room to change for the beach.

The beach was about ten minutes' walk away. We had to cross a stretch of green swampy marshland to get there. There was a wobbly bridge made of planks which crossed a stagnant-looking stream clogged with reeds.

Below us, standing waist deep in the dyke, was an old man cutting reeds. Up on the bank was another fellow who had a sackful of wet reeds and an old chair frame. Oh, local colour! Mum was going to *love* this. Sure enough, she'd spotted them.

'What do you think they're doing?' she asked.

'How should I know?'

'Let's go and see.'

The chap on the bank was doing something tediously rustic with the reeds. He'd twisted them into long strands. You could see where he'd already woven some of them back and forth to make a new rush seat for the chair.

Mum went into 'reverie mode' at that point.

'It's just so timeless, isn't it? You know – I reckon they've been making chairs like that since... since...' She paused. 'Since chairs were invented,' she finished.

'How long ago is that?' I asked with a yawn.

'Oh I don't know – couple of thousand years – more probably.'

'That must explain why they're so uncomfortable.'

'Oh honestly Lucy,' said Mum, forging on ahead again.

I followed, scuffing up the sand. 'Well, it must.'

'See?' she said when we reached the beach. 'Isn't it lovely?'

It was white sand. Acres of it – deserted – not a soul to be seen.

'Why isn't there anyone here?'

'I don't know. Aren't we lucky, we've got it all to ourselves.'

'Mmmm.'

I smothered suntan lotion on and lay down on my stomach before Mum could get a good look at my red skin. I wasn't going to let on, but the skin on my front was still pretty sore from the day before.

Mum stretched out on her towel and took out her book.

'The sun's pretty high, so just half an hour and then we can have a lovely cooling swim before lunch,' she said.

I put a tape in my Walkman and turned it on. Anything to try and put myself in a better mood.

Mum made her usual fuss about the volume. ('Sounds like people clashing saucepans around – can't understand why you like that stuff, Lucy.') So I turned it down a bit. Some holiday this had turned out to be.

It was barely half an hour before Mum started fussing about sunburn, so I agreed to a swim. Or should I say a paddle? We had to walk out about a kilometre before the water got up to our waists. No wonder no-one came to this beach.

'But there's no weed,' said Mum, still trying desperately hard to stress the finer points of the place.

'And we're not likely to drown, that's for sure,' I commented sarkily.

We had a very half-hearted swim, constantly encountering sandbanks and running aground. And then we went back for lunch and a siesta.

Once back in the room Mum fell asleep almost immediately, but I lay awake staring at the ceiling and silently plotting ways to talk her round. Outside, I could hear the steady rhythmic chanting of the crickets. It really wasn't fair. There were all those crickets outside, thousands of them by the sound of it, packed tight as bodies on a beach on a hot Bank Holiday, sounding as if they were having the time of their lives. While I was here in positive solitary confinement – except that I had Mum for company. I was starting to feel like those hostages you read about. Locked up with just one other person till they drive you barmy. If this went on much longer, I reckoned I'd start having delusions.

I wondered what Ben was doing. Ben – short for Benjamin, I supposed. I could imagine him now, serving people drinks maybe, at the taverna. A vision of him came into my mind, so vivid it was almost real, of him standing there last night in the gloom...

The low sun had turned him a kind of over-the-top all-over golden colour. I'd had to look away. He'd stood there waiting to take my glass, and when I looked up he was already walking off – but then he turned back slowly and smiled at me. I'd gone hot

and cold and tingly all over. It was *how* he'd smiled.
I mean, I've got to notice these things. There's a
certain way guys look at you when they fancy you.
Kind of eyes halfway between open and closed,
trying to look as if they're not looking, if you know
what I mean. We *had* to go back. I'd get around
Mum somehow.

And then I had a dreadful thought. What if
someone else had come and taken our room? What
if all the rooms in the taverna were booked up?
Maybe there was some other girl staying in my
room. Who was older. And had a nicer nose...

I stabbed at my pillow and turned over. Oh why
had I been such an idiot wanting us to leave like that?

Fate didn't intervene until that night. I didn't hear
the first one. I woke with a hot itchy feeling on my
leg. Switching on the light I discovered that I had the
most a gigantic mozzie bite.

'Oh no!' There was a whole row of them all the
way up my leg.

'Hmm – what is it, Lucy? Why's the light on?'

'We can't stay here! I'm getting eaten alive!'

'What?'

'Mosquitoes. Look at them! We'll get malaria!'

'Don't be silly – you don't get malaria in Greece!
Hand me that magazine – I'll swat it. And put the
light out!'

'How can you see to swat it with the light out?'

'Well if you don't put the light out, more will come
in.'

'Too late,' I announced.

There were already six or seven of the creatures circling round the lightbulb.

'Oh my God.'

I turned the light out.

'Oh damn and blast, one's bitten me now.'

'Didn't we bring any mozzie spray?' I whispered to Mum.

'No need to whisper. They can't hear you, you know.' Mum sounded really cross.

'But didn't we?'

'Didn't think we'd need it. And besides, that stuff's so bad for you.'

Mum was such a fanatic about chemicals and things. I could hear her raking through her bag.

'What are you looking for?'

'Bite stuff – can't see a thing.'

'I'll put the light on then.'

'No! Oh bother, think it must've fallen out on the beach.'

'But I'm itching to death!'

'Put some lick on it. And cover yourself up or you'll get bitten again.'

We both covered ourselves in sheets, including our faces. I lay in silence, hearing the mosquitoes circling overhead like heat-seeking missiles searching for a target. My bites itched like mad, and I could hear Mum turning over restlessly. Hers were obviously as bad as mine.

After half an hour or so, I turned on to my side.

'Mu-um?' I whispered.

'Hmmm?'

'Not asleep, are you?'

'What does it sound like...?'

I lifted the corner of her sheet.

'There weren't any mosquitoes at the other place.'

'Maybe there are now.'

'No, it's the fresh water. You know where the swampy bit was, by the beach? They only breed in fresh water. We did mosquitoes last term.'

'So all that education wasn't wasted after all.'

'You have to admit – you liked the other place better, didn't you?'

There was a moment's silence and then she answered: 'Well, yes, OK. I suppose I did.'

'So what's the big deal about staying here?'

'There's no big deal.'

'You mean we could possibly go back?'

I could sense Mum staring at me through the darkness.

'You're really *keen* on that place, aren't you?'

I blushed in spite of myself. I was glad it was dark.

'Well it was just – *so* much nicer, wasn't it?'

Mum leaned over and gave me a hug through the sheet.

'After two days, yes. Why not? Better give the Old Rogue a chance to calm down first.'

'Really, honestly, truly?'

'Well it's what we both want, isn't it?'

'*Now* she admits it.'

There was another, longer silence.

'Can't we go back tomorrow?'

'Oh Lucy. I don't know. Maybe.'

'We could have another swim at that *brilliant*

beach of yours first.'

'It's not *that* brilliant.'

'Mum, it's ghastly and you know it.'

Chapter Five

So we went back the following morning. Mum
didn't even seem to mind about losing the money
she'd paid for the second night. And she didn't want
a swim either, so we left straight after breakfast.

We saw the bus coming as we finished our coffee
and had to run for it across the olive grove.

The bus driver waited for us, grinning and
honking his horn in a teasing manner. Mum and I
flopped down in the front seats.

'Two please, to Paradiso,' said Mum.

'To Paradiso!' said the bus driver. 'You go back?'

He winked at me. It was the guy who'd driven us
here. It was such a small island he obviously
recognised all his passengers. It was a nice feeling
actually.

'Yes,' said Mum.

'Ahhh! Paradiso. Paradise! Yes?'

'Yes – I know.'

He leaned forward and switched on his radio full
blast, and we set off with the sun glinting through
the trees and the music clattering in our ears and the
sea dreamily blue in the fresh morning light.

We drove back through the villages we'd passed
on the way. Maybe it was the direction of the sun or
something, but in the morning light, those villages
looked completely different. Between the
whitewashed houses, there were flowering plants

brightening the place up with totally improbable splashes of colour, colour that plants simply don't have back home. All the mad old ladies had disappeared and been replaced by younger women who had baskets of bread on their arms. And there were loads of children around, and contented-looking cats and well-fed dogs. And even the men sitting outside the cafés smoking and chatting had a kind of festive look about them, as if they were on holiday like us. I wondered how it could all look so different.

'Maybe we should have rung first. What if he hasn't got a room free?' Mum interrupted my train of thought.

'Oh no, I'm sure he will have.'

'I think we should stop off at the next village and check. It'll be a waste of time going all that way back if he hasn't.'

I'd been dreading this. What if the rooms were let – they couldn't be! No way! The very idea of not getting back to the Paradisos after all this effort – it was unthinkable!

'Mum. Who else in their right mind would want to stay at the Paradisos?'

'Yes, I suppose you've got a point there.'

It was about twelve by the time we reached the square above the taverna. The bus juddered to a halt, and with a gentle sigh of the power brakes, the doors swung open.

The dog was still basking, but he'd moved out of

the sun and into the shade. The donkey was still there – I could hear it braying a hilarious greeting in the distance. The sun was so bright on the chapel, you couldn't see the flaking paint. Even the shop with its dusty display of out-of-date *Hello* magazines and battered sun-hats looked somehow welcoming.

The driver climbed out of the bus and hauled our luggage on to the cobbles.

'Ahhh,' he said, stretching out his arms as if encompassing the view of the bay. 'Paradise!'

'Mmmm,' agreed Mum. 'Isn't it just.'

We were about to start the trek with our luggage, back down the goat path, when a figure shot out of the shadow of the chapel.

'No,' he said. 'I carry bags for you.'

It was a skinny boy of about fifteen or so. He was wearing peculiar old-fashioned trousers made of cheap material and one of those tourist T-shirts they gave out free at the Tourist Office with the picture and the slogan on it – the one we'd cracked up about. *You'll learn to love Lexos*.

He took Mum's suitcase out of her hands and made a grab for my backpack.

'No it's OK,' I said. 'I can manage.'

But Mum said: 'Let him, Lucy.'

The boy lifted Mum's suitcase on to one shoulder and flung my backpack over the other. He put out a hand for the beach bag I was carrying too. But I shook my head, he was smaller than me. As we followed behind him, I thought Mum was being

59

really crazy. We were on a really strict budget, it didn't allow for luxuries like porters.

The poor kid was so puny too – I wondered how he could support the weight of luggage from both of us. But he went at quite a pace on the rough track as if he was used to it.

Carefully selecting a clean place, he put Mum's suitcase down at the top of the steps that led to the taverna and placed my backpack beside it.

Mum was scrabbling in her purse. She came out with a one thousand drachma note and handed it to him. I frowned at her. Typical – she was getting all mixed up with the noughts again.

The boy took the note and hesitated.

'Yes, take it, thank you. That's fine,' said Mum.

He cast a wary glance towards the taverna entrance and then made off.

'Mum!' I exclaimed. 'That was worth over two pounds.'

'I know,' she said. 'Didn't you see? He looked half-starved.'

'Yes I did. I don't know why you let him take our stuff in the first place. Honestly, two pounds for carrying a suitcase fifty metres? I thought we were meant to be on a budget. If you're going to give hand-outs to every Greek...'

'He wasn't Greek. He was Albanian.'

'How do you know?'

'His accent. It wasn't Greek.'

'To every Albanian then...'

'Lucy... Don't you read the papers? Those people – they don't have anything.'

'Oh honestly, Mum.'

'Honestly what?'

'You exaggerate. He's probably got a job. He may even work at the taverna...'

An awful thought struck me. What if Ben had left? What if that boy had got Ben's job? Maybe he'd been sent to wait at the bus stop and drum up trade for the Old Rogue – Stavros.

'Come on, we'd better go and see if we can get our room back,' said Mum.

I brushed my hair out of my eyes and followed Mum with a thumping heart. Stavros was sitting alone at a table on the terrace. Ben was nowhere to be seen. The minute Stavros caught sight of us he leapt to his feet.

'You come back!' he said, waving his arms about in a wild greeting. 'You no find other place nothing like Paradisos – no?'

'No,' said Mum. 'I mean yes, we've come back. I hope you have a room free?'

'I have room, your room yes? Best room in the taverna. You like, eh?'

'Yes,' said Mum. 'We like very much.'

'You like views – quiet, peace, eh?'

The dredger let loose a joyful welcoming cascade of gravel.

'Umm, quite,' said Mum suppressing a smile.

'Oh they not work long. They go. Very soon,' said Stavros with a dismissive wave towards the bay. 'Bad for business.'

'We really don't mind,' I said.

'Siddown,' said Stavros. 'You have drinkses. On the house.'

I sat down and cast a searching glance towards the kitchen. At any moment Ben would come out with a tray in his hand and give me that wicked smile of his. I waited.

'Whaddya want?' asked Stavros.

Ben didn't come out. Stavros went to get the drinks himself, and I realised with a sinking feeling that Ben wasn't there. But maybe he was out windsurfing. He must get some time off during the day.

Ben didn't come back while we were having lunch either. And he still wasn't there when we took our bags to our room and started to unpack.

Mum threw the shutters open wide while we did so.

'Lovely,' she sighed.

I gazed past her. There was a really good view of the bay but I couldn't see a windsurfer out there.

'It really is such a nice room,' said Mum, unzipping her suitcase.

'Mmmm.'

I stood at the window, scanning the sea for a glimpse of a pink and blue sail. The sea was a milky blue in the harsh midday sun. Maybe the sun was too hot for windsurfing. The dredger had fallen silent – the workers must've knocked off for the day.

'I wonder what happened to that English boy,'

mused Mum. As if she'd read my mind.

'What English boy?' I asked innocently.

Mum stood holding up her sundress and examining it for creases.

'The one we had to come back for,' she said, without looking at me.

'Oh Mum, *honestly*.'

'Well, I hope we haven't come all the way back for nothing.'

Chapter Six

She was like that. She'd always been like that. She knew instinctively the kind of boys I fancied. It was *so* maddening. I'd do everything to cover up. I'd send out a massive smoke-screen of negative comments or drop red herrings about some other boy who wasn't even in the running, but I never fooled Mum.

I lay there on the bed while we were meant to be having our siesta, thinking about it. She always looked kind of crumpled when she was sleeping – but she wasn't bad-looking really for a mum. One of the best in my class at school, as a matter of fact. How was it that someone who was such a brilliant judge of who *I* liked could have made such a mistake in her own life? I mean, she must've been in love with Dad once. Weren't you meant to know if you really loved someone? And if you did, wasn't it meant to last? And if it didn't last... was it really love in the first place? It was a terrible circular argument which went round and round in my head and never seemed to have an answer.

As I tried to get off to sleep my mind kept swinging back to Ben. I could imagine him right now, sitting outside under the vines, having lunch maybe at the table by the kitchen door. Or sitting with a drink in his hand, in silhouette against the sunlit sea. Maybe he was there now. I strained my ears for the sound of a chair scraping on the concrete or the chink of a knife on a plate. There wasn't a sound. Where was he? Maybe he had left? I couldn't just lie there doing nothing. I had to find out.

I crept to the door and peeped out. The sun was beating down from practically overhead. It was the hottest time of day and very still. I had the feeling that the whole village was asleep. Even the chickens were quiet.

Ben wasn't on the terrace. Nor was Stavros – I could hear his steady snoring coming from a room beyond the kitchen. I went back and lay on the bed again. Oh curses and botheration. I picked up my book and tried to concentrate on reading.

I must've fallen asleep. I woke with my face crushed uncomfortably against the book. Mum was still asleep. I glanced at my watch. It was four o'clock. If I left her sleeping I could have a look for Ben in peace, without her interfering.

I tiptoed out of the room and across the terrace in bare feet and picked my way down the long flight of steps that led down to the beach.

The pile of windsurfers was neatly stacked. The shack was locked up and the sign advertising that they were for hire was leaning up against the door. I tried to make out whether the pink and blue sail was rolled up with the others. Did he always use the same sail? I stared at the boards, wondering if his was among them... They all looked identical to me.

That's when I caught sight of them. Footprints in the sand. Large strong footprints with a fine curve inwards where the foot arched. They looked like male footprints. They were deeply imprinted as if whoever they belonged to had been carrying something heavy. I went up to one and tried my foot in it. Yes, by their size, they were definitely male.

They led down to the water's edge. And beside them, where the water met the sand, something heavy had been placed down – like a windsurfer's board.

With a rush of conviction, I felt sure the footprints were Ben's. Who else could they belong to? The Albanian boy's feet would be far too thin and puny – and as for big flat-footed Stavros…

I studied the sand for more clues. There was a slight graze in the sand where the windsurfer had been launched. He was out there somewhere, I knew it.

I made my way slowly along the beach, scanning the horizon for a glimpse of pink or blue. No sign of a sail. So I sat down on a rock in the shade, under the very furthest tip of the headland where it jutted out into the sea.

And I waited…

Waves don't actually move towards the shore. That's an optical illusion. The waves move through the water but the water stays where it is. Or at least that's what I'd learned in Physics. Over the next hour or so I had quite enough time to study this puzzling phenomenon. And I added a P.S. to it. Whatever was on top of the waves didn't move into the shore either – neither plastic bottles, nor bits of weed, *nor* horny windsurfers.

I was about to give up and head back to the taverna when a flash of colour caught my eye... Was it a sail? Was it really pink and blue? At a distance, with the sunlight on the water, your eyes can play tricks on you. I blinked as the sail dipped, and then as it raised again and the windsurfer tacked away – I was certain. It *was* Ben's.

It took him forever to tack back into the shore. As he drew nearer I felt really shy for some reason. And it occurred to me that I couldn't just appear out of nowhere. It'd look as though I'd been watching – waiting for him. I drew a little further back in the shadow of the cliff.

He reached the shore, climbed neatly off the windsurfer and drew it up behind him on the beach. I decided to wait where I was – hidden until he'd dismantled and stacked all the equipment. I reckoned he'd go back to the taverna and then, after a suitable pause, I'd be able to wander up nonchalantly – as if I'd just come back from a walk or something.

But he didn't stack the windsurfer right away. Instead, he seemed to be looking for something on the beach. He crouched down and peered at the sand. Maybe he'd dropped something.

No, he'd given up. He went to lock up the shack and then he came back to where he'd been searching before. I watched as he moved a few steps in my direction. He seemed to be following something. Yes, he was definitely tracking something along the sand.

Oh my God! My footprints! That's what it must be. And they led right to where I was sitting.

I felt myself go hot and cold all over with

embarrassment. This was just so cringe-making. I wondered frantically if I could try and edge my way round the other side of the headland. But on the far side, there was nothing but open sea and a sheer cliff – no chance of making a speedy escape. I was going to have to brave it out.

He was really close now. I could see a gap in the footprints where the sea had washed some away. Please, please – let him give up right there. But no such luck. He was looking for where they continued.

He'd found them. In seconds he was bound to catch sight of me. There was nothing for it. I took a deep breath and stepped out of the shadows.

'Looking for something?'

He stopped dead. For a moment he seemed at a loss for words. That's when I suddenly realised that he must be just as embarrassed as I was. I decided to make the most of the situation.

'Yeah... a flip-flop,' he said.

I tried to keep a straight face. 'A flip-flop?'

'Mmm.'

'Want some help?' I asked innocently.

'Help?'

'Finding it.'

'Oh yeah, thanks. Why not?'

'Right. What colour was it?'

'Umm. Blue.... Blue and white.'

So we both set out on a search for this fictitious flip-flop. I concentrated my efforts on the area around my rock. He backtracked a bit down the beach. But I could tell he was sneaking glances at me.

'So you came back?' he called over from where he

was splashing around in the shallows.

'Mmm. Mum liked it here. So I had to give in, in the end.'

'Ohh?'

I clambered over some rough shale to where there was a rock pool. And believe it or not, right in the middle – there was a blue and white flip-flop. It was old and tarry, looked as if it'd been in the pool forever.

'I've found it!' I said.

'*Have* you?' (He sounded *ever* so surprised.)

'Yep. But I don't think I can reach it.'

He joined me and we both stood gazing down at the flip-flop.

'You could probably reach it if you climbed down,' I suggested. 'Your arms are longer than mine.'

'Yeah, guess so.' But he didn't seem in too much of a hurry. Instead he asked: 'You staying back at the taverna?'

'Yes.'

'How long for?'

'Not sure. Depends...'

'On what?'

'Oh I don't know. Mum's always getting ideas. She'll probably want to go off and delve about in some boring old ruin or something.'

'There's an interesting site on the next island.'

'Is there?'

'Well, it's not up to much – mainly Roman but...'

'Whatever you do, don't tell Mum about it.'

He grinned. 'You going back to the taverna now?'

'Mmm... sun's going down.'

'Maybe I'll walk back with you.'

'Aren't you going to get the flip-flop?'

'Yeah, guess so.'

I watched as he clambered down the slippery side of the pool and picked it out. It was so *gross*. Must've been in there ten years at least. It was all rough and perished and had disgusting slimy algae growing all over it.

'How can you tell it's yours? You'd better try it on,' I suggested wickedly.

He turned and looked at me through half-closed eyes and caught my expression.

'Here catch,' he said, making as if to throw it to me.

I flinched.

But he didn't really throw it. Instead he turned and hurled it as far as he could out to sea.

'What a waste,' I said.

He laughed.

'Yeah, well. What's the use of one flip-flop, anyway?'

Chapter Seven

He didn't walk all the way back to the taverna with me. He stopped at the foot of the steps and said in a kind of embarrassed voice:

'You go up first.'

'And he's got manners too!'

'No, it's not that. Stavros, the guy who runs the taverna – he says I'm not meant to socialize with the guests.'

'We were only walking up the beach. I'd hardly call that socializing.'

'No, he's like that. Doesn't even want me talking to people.'

'That's a bit heavy. How are you meant to communicate?'

'I take all the orders in sign language.'

'Sure.'

'Go on. Go ahead. I'll give you five minutes, then follow.'

I walked up the steps, only too conscious of him watching me. I mean, he was trying to pretend he wasn't, but I could tell he was. I felt kind of flattered and embarrassed at the same time. I came to the top of the steps to find Mum was up and sitting at a table on the terrace, reading.

She looked up from her book.

'Where've you been? You look pleased with yourself.'

I flopped down on a chair beside her.

'Just for a walk down the beach. I'm really thirsty. Do you think we could order some drinks?'

'Did you see anyone?'

'Anyone? Like who?' I ignored Mum's expression and got up and went over to the kitchen.

I poked my head around the door but Stavros wasn't in there. 'Do you think Stavros'd mind if I helped myself from the fridge and paid him back later?'

Mum wasn't listening. She was looking over at Ben, who was standing at the top of the steps, silhouetted against the low evening sun.

'Someone trying to do me out of a job?' he asked.

'Hello,' said Mum. 'We thought you must've left.'

(How could she? She'd made it so obvious we'd been talking about him. I could have killed her.)

'I had a few things to do in town. Then soon as I got back, the wind was absolutely perfect...'

'For windsurfing? So it *was* you we've been watching, out in the bay with the pink and blue sail...'

'Yeah. Must've been.'

'Please, do you think I could have a drink?' I interrupted Mum before she could give him a total run-down of every single movement we'd seen him make.

'What can I get you?'

I thought I'd impress him with my Greek. '*Portocalada*?'

'Coming up.'

'And I'd love a cold white wine,' said Mum.

'Oh, and could we have some of those yummy onion rings as well?'

'Onion rings?'

'You know the ones Stavros does, all hot and crispy with a slice of lemon?'

He grinned. 'Those aren't onion rings.'

'What are they then?'

'*Kalamari.*'

'Kala – what?'

'Squid.'

'*Squid*? Oh that is so *disgusting*!'

'No it's not.'

'It is. Yukk – to think that I ate *squid*!'

Mum and Ben cracked up. Don't you just hate that, when you've made a real fool of yourself and other people laugh at you – kind of *indulgently*? They both seemed to think it was a *great* joke.

'So what are you doing here? Working in a place like this?' asked Mum, when Ben returned with the drinks.

'The money's not much, but I took the job because Stavros said I could use the boards for free in the afternoon.'

'You're pretty keen, aren't you?'

'On windsurfing? Yeah, I'd do anything, if it meant that I could sail.'

I wished Mum wouldn't go on like this. Why does she always have to talk to boys – to show so much interest. It was so un-cool. I pretended not to be listening and looked out to sea.

'You weren't very friendly,' commented Mum when we returned to our room.

'Well, you were. Far *too* friendly,' I retorted.

'He seems a nice boy.'

'He's all right, I suppose.'

She looked at me assessingly. 'All right. Enough said. Let's eat down at the harbour tonight. I wouldn't want to cramp your style.'

'What d'you mean – cramp my style?'

'I'm obviously being a real embarrassment to you.'

'I don't know what you're talking about. Do you want to shower first or shall I?'

Chapter Eight

I woke early next morning and lay in bed savouring the deliciousness of a totally relaxed body. I was on holiday and I could enjoy the luxury of being able to drift in and out of sleep. The bed might be hard, but wasn't a hard bed meant to be good for your back? And during the night, the pillow and I had come to some kind of mutual agreement. If I made a big dent in it, it was even vaguely comfortable. But more importantly – Ben was somewhere out there, maybe on the terrace right now – just the other side of that door.

The very thought of him had me wide awake. I leaned over and reached for my watch. It was only seven. But I simply couldn't lie in bed any longer. What a waste of the day. I climbed out of bed and peered between the shutters. And what a day! Everything looked fresh and newborn in the pale early sunlight.

I slipped on my clothes and left Mum asleep. I'd go down to the beach, have a swim maybe before breakfast.

Ben wasn't on the terrace. And he wasn't in the kitchen. I couldn't see him in the vineyard. And when I got down to the beach, he wasn't there either.

I slipped off my sneakers and paddled along the

edge of the water. The sea felt pretty cold this early in the morning. I'm not absolutely wild about swimming, anyway. I mean I can swim all right – a good few lengths of a standard swimming pool. But I loathe all the business of inching my way into cold water. And I'm not too keen on going underwater either – I hate the way it goes up your nose and into your ears. And then, in the sea, you're never quite sure of what you might meet. All those *kalamari* maybe – trying to get their own back with their slimy tentacles twining round my legs. I shuddered. A swim really wasn't a good idea at all. It would be a much better idea to have a walk.

I retraced my way back up the steps and started wandering along the track that led from the taverna through the olive grove. If it happened to be the track I'd seen Ben running down the other morning – so what? That had absolutely nothing to do with it.

The bay was so quiet. The dredger hadn't started up yet and you could hear for miles. The donkey braying a slow cascade of sad eeyores. Chickens somewhere with a cock crowing triumphantly from time to time. The sea very faint and distant beneath it all. And through everything and everywhere the constant, steady, rhythmic chanting of the crickets.

Then alongside this sound I heard a distant approaching *thud, thud, thud...* of sneakers on the dusty track. I heard him long before he came into sight. I considered turning back, but he'd rounded the bend before I had a chance.

He slowed to a trot and drew level with me.

'Hi. You're up early.'

'Mmm. Seemed such a waste of time. You know – staying in bed.'

'Here look. Hold this a moment?'

He handed me a parcel. I could feel the bread inside through the paper. It was still hot.

He brushed the hair out of his eyes with the back of his hand and leant down to tie a shoelace. He was quite sweaty actually from running, you could see a damp mark on the back of his T-shirt. It showed the shape of his shoulders, the muscle on him. And it gave off a faint and delicious whiff of warm male into the air.

'Fresh bread! Smells good, I'm starving,' I said and broke off a bit of crust and nibbled at it.

'Don't! Stavros'll kill me.'

'Blame it on me.'

'I can't. I'm not meant to speak to you, remember?'

'Crazy.'

'Look, this is for your breakfast. If you come back now you can have it while it's still hot.'

I'd turned anyway. I was already walking back with him.

'Where were you going?' he asked.

'Just wanted to see what was along the path.'

'Another village.'

'Oh, right.'

We continued walking in silence for a while. And then he suddenly stopped and said: 'Listen.'

'What?'

'They've stopped. The crickets. One moment they're all going for it like crazy, giving it everything they've got, chirping or whatever they do. And then

77

suddenly, they all stop. All at once. Why do you think they do that?'

While we listened they started up again.

'I don't know.'

'Maybe there's one of them – like the boss. A kind of bumped up orchestral-conductor cricket who's in charge.'

'No, I think it's more likely to be because of predators.'

'Predators?'

'Yes. If you really listen, there comes a point when they're all starting to go quiet. Imagine you're a cricket and you suddenly become aware of it. You don't want to be the last one to chirp, or you'll get noticed and nabbed... by a predator.'

'You think?'

'Mmm.'

'Then why do they start up again?'

He was right. This is where the theory fell down.

'Maybe it's a mistake. Perhaps some inexperienced cricket kind of can't stop himself. You know, like when you're singing at school and you come in at the wrong moment and all eyes turn on you...'

'And then all the others feel – like it's safe to join in?'

'Exactly.'

'No. I think you're wrong. It's nothing to do with predators.'

'What is it then?'

He looked embarrassed for some reason.

'There it is again. They've stopped,' he said.

We were both standing listening for the first one to start up again, concentrating hard and kind of staring at each other – you know the way you do when you're listening. He was looking me straight in the eyes.

People talk about a glance being electric. It's an understatement. This was more like nuclear fission. I reckon if someone had put a quark between us, we could have split it.

And then a single cricket started up, nearby, breaking the spell.

'There it is,' said Ben, looking away. 'It's in that tree.'

'So you see what I mean?' My voice kind of shook.

'Yeah. When there's only one, you can kind of *home in* on it.'

He came a step closer as he said this.

'Mmm.'

I took a step back.

I felt sort of odd as we walked back down the path. I went on ahead. Mum was still in bed when I got back. She looked up from her pillow and smiled that Mona Lisa smile of hers. You know, sometimes I wonder if she's psychic.

'What happened? Have the clocks gone forward and no-one's told me?'

'I just felt like getting up early, that's all.'

'That's not like you.'

I sat down on my bed. 'I was going to have a swim actually, but the sea felt a bit cold.'

'You? Having a swim, before breakfast!'

'I don't see why not.'

'Come on Lucy. Normally, this time of the morning, you're in a persistant vegetative state.'

'It's so lovely here, that's all.' I brushed my hair out of my eyes and concentrated hard on staring out of the window. 'Why aren't you up anyway?'

'I felt lazy.'

'Slug!' I said. It was her favourite nickname for me when I was vegging out. 'Do you want breakfast in bed?'

'Mmm. Bring me a lettuce leaf.'

'Ben's just brought bread, hot from the bakery. He ran all the way.'

'Oh did he now? How do you know?'

'I met him...' I'd fallen straight into her trap. 'I met him, by chance, on the goat track.'

'In that case I'd better get up,' said Mum. 'Wouldn't want to waste all that effort.'

Ben brought us a really nice breakfast. Fresh bread with butter and honey. Proper breakfast orange juice and coffee.

'There you are,' I said to Mum, triumphantly. 'That's a much better breakfast than we had at the other place.'

'Mmm, things have certainly changed for the better round here,' she agreed. And she cast a half-amused glance in Ben's direction.

I ignored her comment. Instead I turned my attention on to a group of cats who were sitting at a polite distance, eyeing our plates. There were three of them – almost full-grown kittens. Young cats at the age when they're at their hungriest.

By the way they sat together so peacefully, I could

tell they were a family. They were obviously weaned –
their mother was lying some way off, contentedly
washing. She was one of those cats nature had made
a complete mess of – mainly white with asymmetric
blotches of tabby on her. Which was odd because all
the kittens were perfect specimens – one pure white,
another a tiger-striped tabby and the third a picture-
book ginger cat.

I was trying to work out how a mother cat like that
could have such an unlikely litter. I'd been doing this
project on genetics for Biology. I had six white mouse
females and two white and two brown mouse males,
and I was attempting to make a graph to demonstrate
how many different coloured mice came out of each
generation. I was halfway through the project when
one of my brown mice, Benjie, had escaped and
spent a night of bliss with all the white females and
totally thrown all my calculations.

But what intrigued me about the cats was how
something as seemingly superficial as fur colouring
could be passed down absolutely perfectly like that,
through a real mess of a mother.

'Penny for them?' said Mum.

'I was just wondering how such perfect kittens
came from such a dreadful-looking mother.'

Mum looked at me sideways. 'It has been known.'

I suddenly had an awful feeling that this was a
really tactless comment. I mean, Mum's really nice-
looking. She's not fat or anything, she's got a really
nice figure for her age and she looks great when she's
not got her glasses on and she's happy and dressed
up and going out.

'Oh Mum, honestly. Don't be daft. You are the best-looking Mum in my class. Everyone says so.'

'Oh do they?'

'Yes.' I was about to add that I bet she'd find a really great new man soon, but something stopped me – it didn't seem the right time somehow.

'Well it's nice of you to say so.'

That thin-lipped look of hers had come back again. I thought of her and Dad. I thought of the wedding photo that used to be in a frame in their bedroom. The one she'd put away somewhere and said she couldn't find. She'd looked oddly unreal in it – not like Mum at all, dressed up in white like that. And now Dad was marrying someone else. It gave me a really bad sick feeling inside every time I thought about Dad marrying Sue.

And it must be beastly for Mum – much, much worse. I remembered that electrical feeling in the olive grove. She must've felt like that once. How could she live without it? I mean, seeing young people around like Ben and me, it must really rub it in. I made a resolution to keep whatever happened between us well out of her way. It would be kinder really.

Chapter Nine

Ben was working on the beach when we went down for a swim. Stavros was sitting by the shack reading a paper and smoking cigarettes, giving Ben the occasional grunted order. Honestly, it wasn't fair – he seemed to expect Ben to do all the work.

That morning Ben had to uproot all the parasols that were planted along the beach and lug them up the steps. They were terrible old things, spotted with black mould and with half their ribs broken. Mum and I had taken one look at them and decided we'd be better off without one.

I felt really self-conscious lying on the beach doing nothing while he worked like that. I listened to all my tapes and had a few swims. I was feeling a bit bored really. Eventually Ben disappeared up the steps with the last load of parasols and didn't come back again.

Stavros seemed to have fallen asleep in his deck chair. I wondered what Ben was doing up at the taverna. I made an excuse to Mum that I was going up to our room for my book.

Ben's door was open and I could hear him moving around inside. I tiptoed over to it.

'Hi!'

I peered around the door and got the shock of my life.

But I wasn't as scared as the boy inside. It was the boy who'd carried our suitcases. He was crouching in the shadows, looked even shabbier than when I'd last seen him – looked as if he'd been sleeping in his clothes. By his expression, I assumed he was up to no good.

'What do you want?' I asked.

He didn't answer – he just stared at me, terrified.

'What are you doing in there?' I demanded. I wondered where Ben was. Maybe I should shout or scream. But the boy looked so scared I didn't have the heart to.

'Please lady – is my room,' he said.

'No it's not. It's Ben's room.'

'*Was* my room,' he corrected himself. 'When I work here.'

'You worked here?'

'Yes, before him – the English boy.'

'So what are you doing here now?'

'I look for my knife – my knife is here, I know,' he continued. 'Don't tell. Please?'

He was edging his way out of the room, trying to get past me.

'How do I know you haven't stolen something?'

'No...' his eyes blazed. He flared up: 'It is he who is thief. He take my job!'

'Who... Ben?'

'Yes... He sleep here... Eat here, no pay. He speak good English. Stavros like. He give him my job.'

'But that's awful.'

He shrugged.

'I go now. Don't tell,' he whispered.

I decided to give the boy the benefit of the doubt. It seemed a very odd excuse for a burglar, so I moved aside to let him pass.

'I hope you find your knife,' I said.

He nodded, slipped silently across the terrace and disappeared from sight through the vineyard.

I went to my room and looked for my book. My mind was racing. Would Ben do something as low as that? Do a poor boy out of a job? I remembered the gleam in Ben's eye when he said: 'I'd do anything, if it meant that I could sail.' Boys were like that. They could be obsessive about things like sport. But he'd seemed such a nice guy. Maybe the Albanian boy had made up the story. But what a strange thing to make up.

My book wasn't on the rickety table and it wasn't underneath the bed either. I had a half-hearted rake through my backpack but it wasn't in there. Maybe I'd put it in the bag with the swimming things after all.

I went back to the beach. Stavros had gone off somewhere, his deckchair was empty. And Ben was nowhere to be seen.

I flopped down on my towel feeling really hot and confused. My book wasn't in the beach bag. Irritatingly enough, Mum was totally absorbed in hers.

'Have you seen my book?'

'Hmm what? – no.'

'Bother – must've left it at the last place.'

'Oh honestly, Lucy.'

'It was only a paperback.'

'Still.'

I stretched out again, turned my tape over and listened to it with one eye on the flight of steps, expecting Ben to appear at any moment. Sure enough, after a few minutes, I heard his footsteps coming two at a time down to the beach.

He glanced over, grinned at me and then made for a deckchair. I watched as he got in a muddle with the back bits, trying to adjust the chair to a more comfortable angle. He didn't *seem* the kind of person who would do a half-starved boy out of work. But how could you tell? I didn't know what to believe.

I watched him assessingly as he got out a book and started reading. He turned a page and laughed to himself. No, he really didn't look capable of doing anything mean or underhand.

I cast a glance up at the taverna to see if Stavros was looking down. He wasn't, so I got to my feet and wandered over to Ben.

'What are you reading?'

'*My Family and Other Animals.*'

It was my book. He'd nicked my book. And he didn't look in the least bit guilty.

'Where did you find that?'

'Someone must've left it on the wall.'

'They did – *me.*'

'Oh, look, sorry – take it – I had no idea.'

He stared up at me with those wonderful grey-green eyes of his and smiled that gorgeous open smile. He was just such a babe. How could I suspect him of anything...?

'No honestly – you borrow it. I've hardly started it,' I backtracked.

'No really – take it back.'

'No, I don't want it. I'd like you to have it. Mum's brought plenty of other books.'

'Is it any good?'

'It's about this boy living on a Greek island and the animals he finds and his family and it's really funny.'

'Sounds great.' He was looking at me like that again. I was convinced now – there was absolutely no way this guy could be anything less than perfect.

'Just let me have it back when you've finished,' I said.

'Thanks.'

We kind of ran out of things to say at that point and I stood there feeling awkward. And then I caught sight of the Albanian boy again. He was running up the beach with a dog. They were playing some kind of game – he was just a kid. I remembered his face as he begged me: 'Please don't tell. '

The nagging doubt came back like an evil shadow in the corner of my mind.

'Do you know that boy?' I asked.

'What boy?'

I pointed him out.

'Oh him, yeah – kind of.' (He was being dead suspicious about him.)

'Is he Albanian? Mum says he is.'

'Yeah, she's right.'

'He's always hanging around. Hasn't he got anywhere to live?' I prompted.

Ben frowned. 'Search me. Why do you want to know?'

'He carried our suitcases. He's really thin and he

looks dead poor.' (I was really laying it on.) 'I just wondered...'

'There are loads of Albanians around. The Greeks use them as cheap labour.' (This sounded *really* heartless. Maybe Ben *had* pushed him out of his job!)

'No-one's using him,' I said pointedly. 'He doesn't seem to have anything to do.'

'No.' Ben looked uncomfortable. He cast an anxious glance up at the taverna. He obviously wanted to drop the subject.

'Oh, I'm sorry, I forgot. I wouldn't want to get you into trouble,' I said, giving him a very straight look.

He *totally* misinterpreted the look. Would you believe it? He took it as a come on. The arrogance of the guy!

He came out with one of those exasperating male invitations – you know the kind – totally non-committal, so you've no idea whether they're asking you out or not.

'I was thinking of trying out a club in the next bay tonight,' he said. 'It's not much of a place but it might be good for a laugh.'

'Really?' I said. And waited for him to be more specific. Typically, no more was forthcoming – so I added: 'Well have a good time. Let me know what it's like.' And turned and walked back to Mum.

Mum propped herself up on one elbow. 'What was all that about?'

'I lent him my book, that's all.'

'I thought you'd lost it.'

'So did I, but he had it.'

'So what are you going to read?'

'I don't feel like reading anyway.' I stretched out and turned on my Walkman.

I was fed up with this tape, I'd heard enough of it.

I watched Ben through half-closed eyes. He turned another page of my book and shook his head and chuckled to himself.

I would have liked to go out to a club as a matter of fact. Oh bother, bother, bother, bother, bollocks!! Why is life *so-oo* complicated?

Chapter Ten

I stood in the shower allowing the water to wash through my hair and down my body. I was thinking about *men*.

Why did it always have to be like this? You meet a boy and you think he's the greatest thing that ever happened to you. And then, as you get to know him better, you find out what he's *really* like. And he's never anywhere near as great as you thought he was. At least, that's what had happened with all the boys I'd fancied before. But I'd thought Ben was different. It was just so-oo bugging!

I stood there cursing myself for not taking him up on the offer. That's if it *had* been an offer. How was I going get to know what he was like if I was never alone with him? I had Stavros on one side and Mum on the other, like a couple of jailers. I should've said I'd go along with him tonight. I didn't have to stick with him all evening. Now it was too late.

Or was it? Maybe if I hung around later, when he was leaving, I could just casually disappear with him. That's if we could give Stavros the slip *and* I could get Mum to agree. Mum was dead funny about clubs. There were certain ones she wouldn't let me go near.

'Are you using *all* the hot water in there?' Mum's voice came through the door.

I turned the shower off.

'No – I 'spose not.'

'Good. Then you can rinse these out,' she said, handing me our swim things. I rinsed the salt water out of them and then went out on to the balcony to hang them up.

Ben was out there, kind of hovering. Was he waiting for me? I shot him an uncertain smile. He raised a hand but he didn't say anything. My mind was going round in circles. I had no idea where I stood.

Mum wanted to have dinner at the harbour again – I reckon she'd got addicted to fish. I said I wanted one of Stavros's omelettes, but she said if we ate another one we'd get terminally egg-bound. So she won in the end.

I wasn't wildly hungry, and after eating half of my spinach pie, I thrust it aside. Mum ate all of her meal and then ordered another glass of wine.

'What's wrong?'

'These chairs. They're really uncomfortable. Don't you hate the way they cut into you?'

'Mine doesn't.'

'Maybe you're better padded.'

'Thanks a lot!'

'How long do you want to sit here?'

'Oh I don't know. There's nothing else to do, is there?'

'No, I 'spose not.'

'Well, is there?'

'Apparently there some sort of club in the next bay.'

'Club? What sort of club?'

'Oh I don't know – open air. They have music and stuff.'

'What sort of music?'

'I don't know.'

'Lucy, I hope you haven't come all this way to have your eardrums blasted by some sort of heavy metal...'

'Heavy metal's really passé, Mum...'

'Well some sort of amplified rubbish.'

'Do you really expect me to just sit here, doing nothing every night?'

'How did you hear about this club, anyway?'

'Ben mentioned it.'

'Oh, *Ben*.'

'Mmm.'

Mum looked at me with her head on one side. 'Oh dear. I suppose it is a bit boring for you, isn't it?'

'A bit.'

'Well, why don't we go then?'

'We?'

'Yes, why not?'

'You don't want to come, do you?'

'Well you can hardly go on your own, can you?'

'But you'd hate it. There's bound to be really loud music...'

'No I wouldn't!'

'But Mum...'

'Come on Lucy. You said I ought to break out a bit. You never know, I might meet some dark romantic Greek – remember Shirley Valentine?'

I reckon the wine had got to her again. This was totally unlike Mum. She was already calling for the

bill. She really seemed keen on the idea of the club
for some reason.

I followed her back up the steps to the taverna,
racking my brains for some way to put her off. Ben
wasn't around any longer. I wondered if he'd already
left. Mum was unlocking our door – she seemed really
excited about going out.

'What shall I wear?' she asked, searching through
the stuff she had hanging from the peg on the wall.
She took down her sundress.

'You can't wear that.'

'Too creased?'

'No-one wears dresses to clubs.'

'Well if you think I'm going to dress up like some
teenager... Maybe I should wear these...'

She brought out her really gross patterned
leggings. I'd loathed them from the start and now
they were years out of date.

'No, wear the dress if you like. I'm sure no-one'll
notice. It'll probably be really dark in there. And
smoky,' I added, still hoping to put her off.

'Rubbish. I thought you said it was in the open air.'

'Well open air-ish. Anyway – how are we meant to
get there?'

She raked in her purse and drew out the card of
the taxi company. 'We'll call Manos – good thing I kept
his card.'

My heart sank even further.

Chapter Eleven

Manos picked us up from the square. Mum had put make-up on and she wasn't wearing her glasses. It was a nice sundress, not flowery or anything, a kind of dark terracotta colour – it suited her. In fact, she really looked quite good.

I was wearing my jeans and my non-flattering T-shirt. I lingered in the room as long as possible, putting on my make-up in slow motion. I was hoping against hope that Mum would have some last minute doubts and decide she didn't want to come.

But no, there was a series of hoots from the square and Mum announced that the cab had arrived. Manos was leaning against his car, smoking a cigarette, waiting for us.

'You go out?' he said to Mum.

'Mmm – we thought we'd try a spot of nightlife.'

(A spot of nightlife! Pl-ease, Mum.)

'Very good,' he said as he opened the door for her. 'VIP Club. First class. Five star.' And he turned to me with a grin and a wink and added: 'Lots of young people. Co-ol.'

'Oh good,' I said with a grimace. 'That'll be nice.'

I could really picture myself, sitting at a table with Mum, being the last word in 'co-ol'.

It must've been round about nine pm when we drew up outside the club. As the cab slowed to a stop, Mum suddenly said: 'Oh look Lucy. Look who's over there.'

I shrank into a corner, trying to make myself invisible. But it wasn't Ben. It was the Albanian boy. He was leaning over a wall and people were gathering around.

'What's he doing? I can't see without my glasses.'

'Umm – he's got some sort of fruit. I think he's trying to sell it.'

Mum groped in her purse. 'Take this, buy us some, whatever it is.'

I left Mum to pay the fare and went over to the boy.

'Hi!'

'Hello lady,' he said.

'Not lady. Lucy,' I said.

'Lu-cy,' he said with a shy smile and he pointed to himself. 'Ari.'

'Hi Ari... What have you got there?'

'Fragosika. Taste good. Have some.'

They were the fruit of the prickly pear – the cactus I'd seen growing wild all over the island. He must've been out gathering them in spite of their lethal prickles. I'd no idea they were edible.

Deftly he split one open and held it out to me.

'Oh, so you found your knife?'

'I get it back, from the English boy,' he said in a superior manner. By the way he said it, he obviously didn't think much of Ben. Or maybe he was just trying to stand up for himself, the way boys do.

Sometimes they were so difficult to understand.

He wrapped the fruit in a leaf and I carried it over to Mum. She was standing peering through the entrance to the club – it looked deserted.

'There you are,' I said. 'We're way too early. It's not even open yet. We'd better go back to the taverna.'

But Manos was on Mum's side. 'The club is open, yes. Look, very nice. Co-ol.'

'He's right. There are some people dancing in there,' agreed Mum.

I leaned over her shoulder and peered into the gloom. There was a lone couple on the dance floor. A really fat lady and a little bald man who came up to about her cleavage. They were slow-dancing to a Frank Sinatra number.

'Oh, it looks really gross. Let's go back.'

'No, don't be silly. We might as well have a drink now we've come,' said Mum. 'At least the music isn't too loud.'

'Quite!'

'Come in ladies. Ladies free tonight,' said a voice. A Greek guy popped up out of nowhere, making over-the-top welcoming gestures. This offer sealed my fate.

'See?' said Mum. 'We might as well stay for a drink while we're here. Come on Lucy. It'll be a laugh.'

She was already negotiating with Manos to come and pick us up at eleven pm. I stood there helplessly as he nodded and shook hands and then drove off into the night.

Mum and I were shown to a table like royalty. I managed to steer her away from one right beside the dance floor and chose another further back in the shadows.

I unwrapped the fruit and she helped herself.

'Mmm, delicious,' she said, 'We used to eat these when we were in Greece. I'd totally forgotten the taste.'

'You and Dad?'

'Mmm.'

The fruit was red and sweet and kind of gritty. As I ate it, that photo of Mum and Dad on the mopeds flashed through my mind. I decided to make the best of the evening – for her sake.

She lashed out on the drinks. She ordered a really exotic cocktail for herself and something called a 'Tropical Dream' for me – a mixture of different kinds of fruit juice with grenadine. They came complete with a cringe-making display of cherries and umbrellas.

'Oh, isn't this fun,' said Mum, sipping from her straw.

Another couple had risen from their table and joined the first lot on the dance floor. The music suddenly switched from Frank Sinatra to Abba and the four of them began to wiggle random parts of their bodies in a grotesque imitation of dancing. I caught Mum's eye and we both cracked up.

'So which one do you fancy?' I asked her. 'The little bald one, or the big one with the paunch? Oh no – hang on... Here comes the talent. Wow, you're going to be totally spoilt for choice now.'

A group of middle-aged Greek blokes had come in through the gate. They didn't have any women with them.

I nudged her. 'What are you going to do if one of them asks you to dance?' I whispered.

'Dance of course,' said Mum, taking another long sip of her cocktail. 'Why not?'

'Oh Mum – honestly.'

I remembered the last time I'd seen Mum dance – that was embarrassing enough. The thought of her dancing to an Abba number, making an exhibition of herself and possibly Ben turning up... It didn't bear thinking about.

But the blokes didn't seem too interested in Mum. They'd ordered a big bottle of ouzo, and one of them went over to the guy who was putting on the tapes and said something in his ear.

Abba came to an abrupt stop right in the middle of *Dancing Queen*, and then the clatter of Greek folk music filled the air.

Mum settled back into her chair with a sigh. 'Oh this is more like it. This is the real Greece,' she said.

There was a lot of toasting and cheery laughter coming from the men's table, and then a group of them got up.

'They're going to dance,' said Mum. 'You watch.'

It was a really old man who started. Must've been at least seventy, but he moved with incredible agility. The others paused and clapped as he raised his arms and bent his knees and swayed to the music. The guys formed a circle round him and stood cheering and hissing – but in an appreciative way, not like people hiss back home. And then another of the men joined in, bending and swinging and leaping. One by one the dancers wove themselves into the circle, all in perfect time with the old man who was still going strong in the middle, dancing like a fellow half his age.

'Incredible, isn't it?' said Mum in my ear.

'Mmm – why aren't there any women with them?'

'This is a man's dance.'

I looked around. Come to think of it, there didn't seem to be any Greek women in the club at all.

'Where are all the women, anyway?'

'At home, with the children.'

'That doesn't seem fair.'

'I suppose it's not much different from blokes going down to the pub in England.'

'That's never seemed fair to me either.'

That's how it had started with Dad. He used to go to the pub to meet friends, leaving Mum behind with me. And then he was out more and more. Eventually, he hardly came home in the evenings at all. And then they broke the news to me that they were separating...

Maybe all males were like that? Like it was some sort of unwritten law of nature, or something. Most male animals went off and left their females stuck down holes or up trees or in nests or wherever, to bring up their young. Apart maybe from... was it male sticklebacks? Or was it sea-horses? I reckon, whatever the species, males had it all their own way. I don't know why Mum had just accepted it. I wasn't going to let what happened to *her* happen to *me*.

Mum tugged at my arm. 'Hey, look Lucy – isn't that Stavros?'

'Where?'

I made out his great sagging body standing at the edge of the dance. As we watched he joined in.

'Well,' said Mum. 'Would you believe it? The immovable object has actually moved.'

Stavros was obviously the star turn. As soon as he joined in, the others stepped out of the circle to allow for a solo. They were laughing and clapping and urging him on. The music got faster and faster with the bazouki clattering at a frantic tempo. Sweat was running down Stavros' face, but however fast the music went, he kept up with it. His great body was flying around the circle now as if he was about to take off like a spinning top... and then suddenly with one leap he landed and the music stopped dead on the beat.

He put up both arms for applause. A great roar went up from his audience. He turned and bowed, his face red and beaded with sweat but triumphant.

The men had finished dancing and were returning to their table. But Mum was beckoning to Stavros.

'Oh no Mum, don't, please...'

But it was too late. Stavros had spotted us. He came over immediately. 'Good evening. *Kalaniktasas*! You like watch dance, eh?'

'You were wonderful,' said Mum. 'Can I buy you a drink? What would you like?'

'No no, I buy you ladies...'

'No, I insist.'

'Well, after dance... Maybe a beer. Thank you. May I siddown?'

'Of course.' Mum handed me her purse. 'Lucy, go

and get Stavros a beer and something for yourself, darling.'

Great! Wonderful! That did it. Now, if Ben *did* turn up I'd have both of them to contend with. Stavros on one side keeping his beady eye on us, and Mum on the other being cringe-makingly encouraging. I took her purse and made off for the bar.

It took ages to get the drinks. More people were arriving by the minute and a queue had built up. Younger people had started to seep through the doors. Sun-bronzed guys who looked like nicely laid-back backpackers, and cool-looking girls who *weren't with their mums*.

When I got back to the table, Mum and Stavros were deep in conversation.

'Sorry I was so long.'

Mum peered at her watch. 'Oh my God. Completely forgot the time. The taxi should be back!'

I barely had a chance to gulp down my drink before she was on her feet saying goodbye to Stavros. He was in a great mood – he even kissed her hand! And he insisted on escorting us right across the club and out through the doors to where Manos was waiting outside in the taxi.

As we crossed the dance floor a really cool track came on and the lights were dimmed. All the older people seemed to have dematerialised and there was actually some talent on the dance floor. Typical, wasn't it? Just when the place was starting to get a bit of life, I had to leave?

I sat in the taxi feeling really pee'd off.

Ben hadn't even bothered to show up. Don't you just hate that? When a guy says he's going to be somewhere, and you wait around half the night expecting him to arrive – and he doesn't?

So much for our great night out!

Chapter Twelve

'What were you and Stavros talking about?' I asked Mum in the car.

'Oh he was telling me about Ben.'

'Really? What about him?'

I waited for her to go on, but Mum was scrabbling in her purse. 'I do hope I've got the right change. How much do you think I should give as a tip?'

I pulled out a hundred drachma note. 'That should do it.'

'Do you really think that's enough?'

'*Yes*. What was he saying about Ben?'

'Oh, I said I thought it was a bit unusual having an English boy working for him.'

'Yes?'

'And he told me how he'd turned up without any money. He'd had all his possessions stolen on the beach. Everything! He was absolutely penniless. Couldn't pay his bill.'

'Poor Stavros! That must've really got to him!'

'No, but the thing was – Ben came back the next day. He'd borrowed the money and insisted on paying Stavros back. Now how many boys do you think would do that?'

'Not many.'

'Not any.'

I went to sleep feeling really good. I'd been right about Ben all along. Why had I ever had doubts? He was a good guy – and a babe – a *total* babe.

The next morning I went out with my camera. Dad had given me this brilliant one for my fifteenth birthday. It had a zoom and everything. I think it was a bribe really. When he first started going out with Sue, he missed three Saturdays in a row which we were meant to spend together. I suppose he thought the camera would make up.

I lingered on the terrace. What I really wanted were some pictures of Ben, to show Migs and Louisa. I could impress them with the talent on my holiday if nothing else. He was down below on the beach messing around with the windsurfers. I homed in on him, focusing the camera so he looked really close. He was stripped to the waist and he had such a *yummy* body. These pictures were really going to put my rating up at school...

Mum came up behind me.

'What are you taking?'

'Nothing!'

'That's going to be interesting.'

'I thought I saw some dolphins in the bay.'

'Dolphins! Where?'

'Quite a long way out...'

'Oh damn and blast! Where are my glasses?'

I ranged the camera over the sea, peering through the lens. 'But I think they've gone now.'

'Did you got some shots of them?'

'Umm... not sure.'

'Are they still out there?'

'No, they've definitely gone.'

'Oh well, you can take some nice views of the bay to show Dad, anyway.'

I focused in on the shack.

There was a new sign today, chalked up on a board:

Windsurfing lessons
Instructor: Ben Bernard

Now *that* was a thought!

'Mu-um?'

'Mmm?'

'How much money have we got left?'

'Oh I don't know...' Mum yawned and settled down on a chair in the shade. 'Why?'

'I just wondered...'

'Ye-es?' (She obviously recognised my tone.)

'Since this place is so much cheaper than the other place, we must have some money over.'

'I don't think I want to hear this.'

'Yes you do – you know you're always trying to get me to try new things?'

She raised her eyebrows and smiled at me. 'Like kohlrabi?'

'Well, kind of...'

'Come on, out with it. What've set your heart on this time?'

'I just wondered whether the budget would stretch to a windsurfing lesson?'

Mum propped herself up on one elbow.

'Windsurfing? Do I sense an "ulterior" here?'

'No! You know I've always wanted to learn. And it would be much cheaper here than at the gravel pit back home.'

'Well, I suppose that's true.'

'Thanks Mum!'

'I haven't said yes yet.'

'But you're going to, I can tell.'

'Well, as long as it's not too expensive. Check it out with Stavros. And don't commit yourself to anything until you've agreed it with me – please!'

Stavros said a lesson was ten thousand drachmas. Which I calculated was really good value compared with back home.

I bought Mum an orange juice and took it to where she was sitting reading.

'Ahh – I see you've brought a bribe. What's the damage going to be?'

'Ten thousand drachmas.'

'Sounds extortionate!'

'No, that's under twenty pounds. It's a real bargain.'

'Is it?'

'Please Mum. It'd be much more expensive back home. I'd have to hire a wetsuit and everything.'

'OK, you've talked me into it.'

'Thank you, thank you! Can I go and tell Stavros?'

Stavros was predictably delighted and ambled off to find Ben. I was glad I'd bought a swimsuit; much better than my bikini for windsurfing. I had a brand new white one with high-cut legs – made my legs look really long. A real windsurfing lesson – and with Ben as my instructor. I could see myself now, skimming across the water – and Ben shading his eyes, watching me from the shore, kind of amazed and impressed at the same time. And then maybe he'd surf out to join me – and we'd glide out over the water side by side...

Ben materialised at the top of the steps just as I was imagining him coming across the water, leaning towards me and our lips *just touching*...

'I hear you want a lesson,' he called out.

'I'll probably be hopeless.'

'What time?' he asked.

'When it suits you.'

'How about in half an hour? That'll give me time to get a board set up.'

He swung round and I caught sight of his eye. It was all red and puffy – looked as if he'd been in a fight.

I moved closer. 'What happened to your eye?'

'Had a bit of a disgreement over the ownership of a certain possession,' he said.

I stared at him in disbelief. *The knife*. The Albanian boy's knife. Surely he couldn't have had a fight with *him*? He was half Ben's size.

'That's awful. Who with? What happened?'

'It's a long story, see you on the beach – OK?'

I stared after him as he loped down the steps in his

usual way, two at a time. He seemed dead keen. I wondered if he got the money for the lesson or whether Stavros pocketed it. By all rights it should be the Albanian boy – Ari – who was working here right now. And the money would have gone to him. All those doubts flooded back into my mind again.

I went back to our room to change. Mum was standing holding my camera.

'How do you work this zoom thing?'

'You're not going to take photos, are you?'

'Why not? Could be a – historic moment. Your first windsurfing lesson.'

'No – please. I'll feel really self-conscious.'

'Your dad'll want to see this. Go on or you'll be late.'

'Well, if you must...'

Ben had the board out on the sand. He'd built a kind of mound and had it balanced on top.

'Hi,' I said. 'Where do we start?

'Right here,' he said, pointing at the board.

'What? Not even in the water?'

'It's better this way. Step on and get the feel of it.'

This was a bit of a let-down, but I supposed he knew what he was doing.

It was really difficult to balance on the board. I thought I was doing quite well. But then Ben started wobbling it from side to side – there was no way anyone could be expected to stay on while he did that. I reckoned he was doing it on purpose.

I started to lose patience with him.

'I'm sure I'd be much better on the water,' I pointed out.

'No, it's better to master the basics on dry land.'

A few more wobbles and I landed hard on my bum on the sand. It really hurt. This wasn't fair. I'd seen people windsurfing – they had a bar thing to hold on to. It must be a lot easier in the water. I reckoned he was just trying to make it as difficult as possible to prove how superior he was – you know the way boys do.

'Oh, this is crazy. I've had enough. Let me try in the water.'

He put on this doubtful look, as if I was a hopeless case or something. 'Well, if you really think you're ready.'

'Yes, I do as a matter of fact.'

'Well, I don't.'

'Look it must be much easier when you've got that bar thing to hold on to.'

'It's called a wishbone. And it's not easier. It's much harder, as a matter of fact.'

'It can't be.'

'It is. You have the wind to contend with as well.'

'Well, I just know I'd feel more confident on the water.'

'You wouldn't, you know.'

'You can't know how I'd feel. I'm the one who should be able to judge if I'm ready or not.'

'Well if you want to be like that. Go ahead, try. See for yourself.'

'Thank you.'

❧

He put the board in the water but he kept it tethered to the shore by a rope. It was really difficult to get on. Personally, I think the board he'd chosen was extra slippery. I fell off three times before I even got to kneel on it. He just stood on the shore, watching me as if I was the dumbest thing on two legs and telling me to stand up. It wasn't easy. In fact, it was practically impossible. I was barely on the board before he started going on about the wind direction. How was I meant to know which way the bloomin' wind was coming from?

Then, just as I'd got upright and had the board kind of round the right way, he shouted out that my feet were in the wrong position so I wobbled and fell off again.

With difficulty I hauled myself on to the board again and managed to stand up straight in spite of my wobbling knees. He wasn't even impressed. He just kept on shouting technical stuff about getting the rig into the lee of the wind, or something.

'I am!' I shouted back.

'No you're not. You're about five degrees off.'

'How can you tell?'

'By the way the board's acting. And you should be able to tell by the feel of it.'

'OK, I've only just started – give me a chance.'

'I am. Why don't you come back on the shore like I suggested in the first place, and learn to keep your balance?' (Oh, now he was being *really* condescending.)

'Why don't you just let me be?' I shouted back. 'I can't concentrate with you criticising the whole time.'

'I'm not criticising, I'm trying to teach you.'

(Bollocks!)

'If you'll just leave me alone, I know I'll be able to do it,' I said between gritted teeth.

'Look Lucy...' he started. He sounded just like Dad in one of his bad moods. It put me right off – I fell off backwards for around the twentieth time.

'Don't you "Look Lucy" me!' I retorted.

'Look, the thing is, I don't think you're really trying to do what I...'

'*Trying*!' (This just wasn't fair.) 'I don't think you really know how to teach windsurfing,' I shouted back to him.

'How can I teach you, when you won't listen?'

'How can I learn when you're telling me three different things at once?'

'OK – have it your own way. I won't say another word.'

He stood on the shore with his arms crossed, just willing me to fail. I could tell he was getting a real kick out of this.

With dignity, I climbed on to the board again. I carefully stretched up to my full height. Good. There you are – simple! I eased the board round until it was sideways to the wind. This was it. Any moment now I'd be away, skimming across the water. I was a natural. I hoped Mum was ready up on the terrace with the camera poised.

'Right – cast the rope off. I'm ready,' I announced.

'No way!'

'*Let go*!' I insisted. If he didn't let go of the rope it would stop me before I'd even started. The sail was coming up out of the water now – *beautifully*.

'Oh Lucy, be realistic...'

What was he waiting for? The sail was billowing out in the wind.

'Who's paying for this lesson?' I snarled.

'Who's giving this lesson?' he replied. 'Look, you haven't got the faintest idea...'

'Stop being so bloody superior,' I shouted back.

'Superior? Right! OK. Have it your own way – here goes.'

As the sail caught the breeze – *bliss* – I started to move. I cast a knowing look in his direction. Huh! I was right all along, you see.

SPLASH!

Water was filling my eyes and ears and rushing up my nose. I thought for a minute I was going to drown. I surfaced coughing and choking.

He was standing there laughing. He wasn't the least bit repentant. He'd made me fall off. He'd kept hold of the rope. It had stopped the board in its tracks, just as I'd got under way. No wonder it had flung me off. And now I had weed – horrible green slimy yucky weed – dripping down all over me. Oh yes, very funny, I'm sure.

'*You did that on purpose.*'

'No I didn't.'

'You pulled on the rope. You must've done.'

'No I did not!'

'Liar!'

'Look Lucy...'

I was wading out of the water now. A fine lesson this had turned out to be. I'd never felt so humiliated in all my life. I felt tears of anger starting up in my eyes. 'You enjoyed ever minute of that, didn't you...?'

I thought I was due for an apology. But no... Instead, he ranted on about me doing everything wrong. Me! This was totally out of line. I just blew my top.

'If you weren't so *bloody arrogant*, you might be able to teach...'

'If you weren't so bloomin' *pig-headed* you might be able to learn...' he shouted. He was standing in the water now, fiddling with the board with his back to me.

'*Pig-headed! Who's talking*?'

'Oh Jeesus – women!'

He strode out into the water and said in a really sarcastic way: 'Come on. You can at least learn how to get the board out on to the shore.'

That really did it.

'You can get the damn thing out of the water yourself,' I said, and I left him to it.

Chapter Thirteen

I went back to the taverna fuming. If I'd had a decent instructor I'm sure I would've been OK. Ben had been putting me off right from the start. I reckon it was his was of proving his male superiority – how *pathetic*.

'How did it go?' asked Mum.

'You were watching, you should know.'

'Oh, don't be like that Lucy – you can't expect to be brilliant right from the start.'

'As far as I'm concerned you can take all the windsurfers that have even been made and build a giant bonfire and set light to them – and you can put Ben on top.'

'It'd make an interesting alternative to Guy Fawkes.'

'Hmm.'

'Don't sulk, darling.'

'I'm not sulking. I wish you wouldn't say that.'

'Would you like a nice cool drink?'

'Not if he's serving it.'

'Oh *really* – don't be so childish.'

'I'm going for a shower.'

'Good idea – maybe you'll feel better afterwards.'

'I'm feeling absolutely fine, thank you.'

'Good.'

The shower didn't work. The water was off again. Typical! And it was broiling. It was the hottest day we'd had yet. I stomped back on to the terrace feeling really angry.

'There's no water.'

'Oh well, I expect it'll come back on later.'

I was feeling hot and cross. Ben would come up to the terrace any minute. I didn't want to have to face him right now.

'Let's go somewhere else for lunch. Can't we go to another beach?'

'What, in this heat?'

'It's not that hot.'

'Oh Lucy, honestly. Don't be such a pain.'

'Pain! Pain! I'm only asking for a bit of variety for once. We've been stuck here for days.'

'Look. I just want to finish my book and have a nice quiet siesta.'

'You can be really boring and middle-aged sometimes.'

'Thank you.'

'Well I'm not staying. I'm going to the next beach where there's some life.'

'On your own?'

'Why not?'

'Well, I don't know. I suppose you could go on the bus.'

'Thanks.'

'I'll give you some money for lunch and you can get some more factor ten, we're almost out. And we need another film for the camera and you could see if you can find a *recent* newspaper...'

'Anything else? I'll have to dash – the one o'clock bus is due soon.'

'Oh, and Lucy – don't go out in the sun before three, will you?'

'Don't fuss!'

It was a relief to get away from the Paradisos. It was a relief to get away from everyone. Talk about claustrophobic! No wonder we were all getting on each other's nerves.

When I arrived at the next beach it was like another world. Civilisation! The people sitting at the pavement cafés were wearing clothes with a bit of style to them. One of the cafés was even serving cappuccino. And there were proper beach loungers and parasols for hire. I walked along the front looking in the shops.

I did all Mum's chores – even found a one-day-old *Times* for her. Then I considered lunch. A glance at the menus told me that all the restaurants were really pricey, so I bought myself a sandwich and a Coke and decided to splurge the rest of the money on hiring a lounger.

I ignored Mum's advice about the sun. She was really pathetic about sunbathing. Everyone on this beach was incredibly tanned – I felt really self-conscious being a mere kind of pale beige. At this rate I'd go home looking as if I hadn't had a holiday at all. I'd put the afternoon to good use and remedy the situation.

I rubbed plenty of sun lotion on and stretched out on my lounger.

I spent a nice *civilised* afternoon, in comfort, watching all these hunky windsurfers sailing in the bay. They had amazing gear. I reckoned Ben was a bit of a loser. He only had one of Stavros' funny old hired boards and he didn't use a harness or anything. I bet it was easier windsurfing with a harness. I reckon if I'd had one this morning, it would've been a doddle.

Ben had been *so* arrogant. I could hear his voice now: '*Oh Lucy, be realistic*'. Huh! I turned over and forced myself to stay a full half-hour on my front. By tomorrow I was going to look so brown and so beautiful he wouldn't know what had hit him!

Without Mum to interfere, I spent four whole hours out in the sun.

I was on my way back in the bus when my skin started to tingle. OK, maybe I'd overdone the sunbathing – but at least I'd have a tan to show for it when I was back at school. But by the time I reached the taverna my skin felt as if it was on fire. I stalked over the terrace, hoping not to meet Mum, and shot into our room. She wasn't around. I stripped off and went into the bathroom and turned the cold tap on.

My body! I gazed down in horror. I was a horrible combination of strawberry and vanilla stripes. Steeling myself, I let cold water run down my body. 'Yow!' I didn't actually sizzle, but pretty nearly.

'You in there, Lucy?' Mum's voice came through the door.

'Mmm.'

'Well don't use all the water. Gosh, what a scorcher! It must've been practically up in the forties today. Hope you weren't out in it.'

'Mmm...'

'Hurry up darling. I'm melting out here.'

There was nothing else for it. I covered as much of myself as I could with a towel and re-emerged.

'Oh my God.'

'What?'

'Lucy – you're scarlet!'

Mum really let rip after that. She went on about wrinkles and skin cancer. As if sunburn wasn't bad enough in its own right.

I plastered myself all over with aftersun but I couldn't face going out for supper. Mum brought me some food on a tray. I spent a pretty miserable night. I couldn't bear anything on top of me, not even a sheet. My whole body felt as if I'd accidentally been cremated.

The next morning I woke with my skin feeling tight and sore, and horror of horrors – my nose was already peeling! I hate anything that draws attention to my nose. And to have a peeling nose – that is the very *worst*.

'I think I'll stay in the room today,' I announced to Mum.

'Oh don't be silly, Lucy.'

'Well, look at me.'

Mum looked and tried to keep a straight face. 'Can't you cover it up with make-up or something?'

'I've tried. It made it look worse.'

'Well, if you're worried about bumping into Ben, he's not around.'

'Why should I care what Ben thinks? Where's he gone?'

'I don't know. He wasn't there at breakfast. Maybe

he's got the day off. Now where did I put the passports?'

'Why?'

'Stavros is giving me a lift into the port. I've got change some more travellers' cheques. Do you want anything?'

'Apart from a new nose, no, I don't think so.'

'I'll get you some calamine and I'll see if I can find some magazines and...' Mum's eye lighted on my camera. 'And maybe I can get your film developed.'

She was trying everything she could think of to cheer me up.

'Thanks.' I took the film out of the camera and handed it to her.

'Anyway. This'll give you a nice opportunity to write your postcards.'

'Great.'

I heard the *phut-phut-phut* noise of Stavros' three-wheeler disappearing into the distance as I emerged tentatively on to the terrace. There was no sign of Ben. I leaned over the balcony. I couldn't see him on the beach below either. And I couldn't see his sail on the bay. The coast was clear.

I sat at a table, staring at the postcards, wondering what to say.

I'm a windsurfing failure. I've alienated the only fit guy around and I've got terminal sunburn.
Wish you were here!

The chair was cutting painfully into my sunburned legs. I wandered over and leaned on the balcony rail again. The cats were back. The three of them were lounging on the terrace as if they owned it.

They watched me with their six round eyes. Clearly, they considered everyone and everything in this village had been put there for their benefit. I'd noticed over the past week that there was a kind of pattern to their day.

They'd start out on the harbour side of the village, which caught the morning sun. Breakfast was anything they could steal from the cottages. Then by mid-morning they moved on to the more serious business of lunch. I'd heard them searching through the taverna rubbish bags. By dinner time they'd descend to scout round the restaurant in the harbour. But there was a lot of competition down there. There were always at least a dozen hungry full-grown cats hanging around the back of the restaurant, ready to fight for the scraps. These young cats didn't really stand a chance. This morning, the three of them were obviously hoping to steal breakfast from the Paradisos.

I decided to make the whole thing official by collecting all the bread left from breakfast and putting it on a plate for them.

As soon as the plate touched the terrace, three lithe bodies leapt to it. I crouched down watching them. Can you imagine any self-respecting British cat eating dry bread? I added what was left at the bottom of the yogurt pots, and after a quick check to make absolutely sure no-one was around, I gave them all the milk I could find in the kitchen. Well, the milk looked a bit iffy anyway.

The cats wolfed down the meal, then without the

least sign of gratitude they wandered off. I could see them leaping from wall to wall, winding their way down to the harbour until they became tiny moving dots on the beach and disappeared from sight.

My postcards were still lying on the table in the shade of the vines. With a sigh, I decided that I had better get down to the job.

I loathe writing postcards. Unless I can think of something really witty to say, they're just a chore.

I worked through the easy ones – the duty cards to aunts and uncles and the various people who'd sent cards to me and expected ones back. They only needed to be told tedious things about the food and weather.

I'd got to around my fifth when suddenly a voice behind me said: 'Hi.'

I nearly jumped out of my skin. It was Ben. So he was here after all.

Well, I wasn't going to be the first one to climb down. I replied in an off-hand manner:

'Hello. What are you doing here?'

'I work here – remember?'

'I thought you'd be out *windsurfing*,' I said pointedly.

'No, I er... I er – had other things to do.'

'Oh.'

He disappeared into the vineyard and returned a few minutes later with a towel over his arm. He kind of hovered. I ignored him.

'So... How's things? What are you up to?'

'Writing postcards.'

'Yeah I know but – apart from that.'

'Nothing.'

'I'm – er – going to get a drink. Do you want anything?'

'No... thank you.' I finished a postcard and placed it on the pile.

He got himself a drink and sat at a table on the other side of the terrace.

'Lot of postcards,' he commented.

'I've got a lot of friends,' I said. I picked up the stack and tapped it on the table to make my point.

'Do you want me to post those for you?'

'No... thank you.'

'Look Lucy...' he started again.

'You're distracting me. I can't write while you're talking.'

'Oh right. OK. I won't say another word.'

'Thank you.'

He started jangling coins in his pocket.

'You're still distracting me.'

'No I'm not.'

'You are. You're rattling things and you're looking at me.'

'I am not.'

'Yes you are.'

'You can't possibly tell! Unless you've got eyes in the back of your head?'

'I can feel it.'

'Rubbish. Look here... Lucy...'

I'd had enough of this. I swung round. 'What?'

He cracked up. 'Whatever happened to your nose?'

I'd totally forgotten about it. He was laughing as if I looked the biggest freak ever.

'Why don't you just *go away*!' I said, as forcefully as I could.

'Oh come on – loosen up – I've got just as much right to be on this terrace as you have.'

I glared at him, meaningfully.

It worked. He got up from the table and walked off into the vineyard. I took up another postcard:

Dear Louisa,

It's a smashing place apart from this guy here who's really bugging me.

Ben came back after ten minutes or so. I think I was getting through to him – at last. He didn't look nearly as arrogant as he had before. In fact, he paused at the end of the path and came out with as near as damn-it an apology.

'Look, I mean... Listen, Lucy… I'm really sorry about losing my cool with you yesterday.' His voice sounded all kind of quiet and husky. As if he was really upset – as if he really meant it.

'Are you?'

I put down my pen and swivelled to face him. He had this anxious questioning look on his face. Standing there in the dappled shadows of the vines, looking like that – honestly, he was *so* gorgeous. I could see little green glints in his hazy blue eyes. Maybe I *had* been a bit hard on him.

'Mmm – really truly,' he said. (That was rather sweet.)

'Well, perhaps I was a bit...er...'

'No... no it was my fault. It's difficult enough learning to windsurf, without...'

'Well maybe, you know... I shouldn't have flown off the handle like that.' (He was right. I had been pig-headed. I'd been beastly.)

'Oh, it was understandable...'

'Listen Ben...' I started again.

He didn't seem to be listening. He'd turned a kind of green colour and looked as if he was about to make off again.

'You OK?'

'I think maybe it was something I ate last night.' It was the way he said it. He sounded really sorry for himself. I tried not to smile.

'Oh you poor thing, there's nothing worse. Look, Mum's got some tablets somewhere. They're brilliant.'

I delved into Mum's suitcase and found her stash of medicines. She'd something for everything. Typically he had no idea what he ought to take. I had to go through the instructions on the back of the packs with him and ask highly personal questions. I can tell you – any trace of arrogance he might have had totally disappeared.

'Why aren't you on the beach? Where's your mother?' he asked when he'd swallowed a couple of pills.

I explained about the sunburn and how Mum had gone off with Stavros.

'So it's just you and me, marooned here?' he said.

'Mmm.' Little prickles of excitement went up and down my spine.

'Nice,' he said, and pulled his chair up closer.

'Mmm.' I couldn't trust myself to look him in the eyes again. I knew what with my sunburn and everything, I'd go red as a Greek tomato. I could already feel a mega-blush spreading upwards.

'But you'd better not sit too near,' I said. 'Germs, you know.'

'Oh yes, right.'

I went back to the postcard I'd been writing to Louisa and drew a line through '*bugging me*'. Then I tore the postcard in two.

Chapter Fourteen

The cat's breakfast was meant to be a one-off, but the following day they were back, twining their bodies round the legs of the breakfast table, mewing for attention. They seemed to think breakfast at the Paradisos was an ongoing service.

When Stavros wasn't looking, I put another plate out for them in the vineyard. I took more bread from the kitchen this time and slopped a load of milk on top. I stood back to watch. Within minutes the plate was licked clean.

'What you doin'?' Stavros was standing with his hands on his hips, watching me.

'Poor things, they're half-starved,' I said.

'What you think happen when you gone? Everyone gone? When winter come?'

'I don't know.'

'They starve. Same every year. Only big ones live. Strong ones – good hunters – they will be here next summer. Is nature.'

'Well, somebody could feed them.'

'How many cats do you think in Paradiso?'

'I don't know.'

'Too many,' he said, shaking his head.

I stared down at them licking the last remnants off the plate. They were such beautiful cats. It was so sad. I thought Stavros was being really mean.

Things were so different here.

I gazed out through the vineyard. On the far side, a movement caught my eye. Ari was there on a bit of wasteland, sitting on his haunches flicking stones, watching us.

'Stavros – that Albanian boy – he's always hanging around. What does he want?'

Stavros looked over my shoulder. 'Him? He want work here. He want money.'

'Can't you give him something to do?'

'I did. He work here two... three months. He was no good.'

'Before Ben?'

'Yes, before Ben.' (So Ari had been telling the truth.)

'What will happen to *him* when winter comes?'

Stavros sighed and shrugged his shoulders. 'Albanians, big problem. They come here, want jobs. But there are not enough jobs. What can we do?'

I looked over at Ari again. He still had that dog with him. They both looked pretty dejected.

'Where's Ben this morning?'

'Gone to the Tourist Office for his air ticket.'

'So who will work for you, when Ben leaves?' I prompted.

'I don't know,' said Stavros. He sounded annoyed that I'd interfered, and raised both hands as if to close the subject.

He went inside, and I heard him fussing around in the kitchen. He came out with an empty bread basket in his hand.

'Now,' he said, 'there is no bread if peoples come.'

One of the cats stalked past, its stomach bulging

with food. Stavros looked at it pointedly.

'I'm sorry. I'll go and get some more.'

'No, you are guest!'

'No I'd like to, honestly. It's my fault. I'd like a walk. Just tell me where the bakery is.'

'OK,' said Stavros. 'Tell Maria at the bakery you want bread for Stavros.' He took me by the shoulder and pointed out the path through the olive grove. And then, just as I was about to set off, he said: 'Wait.'

We were standing by this massive jasmine bush. The flowers were pretty insignificant but they gave off the most incredible perfume. I'd noticed it in the evening, every time the wind came from this direction. I'd wondered what it came from. This morning in the still air, the smell was almost overpowering.

Stavros leaned over and broke off a few twigs, and then he wound another stalk very carefully round them to make a little bunch.

'Give this to Maria,' he said. 'And say "*Yassos*" from Stavros.'

'"*Yassos*"?'

He nodded.

'What does it mean?'

'It means,' said Stavros, 'God bless you.'

And he smiled and patted me on the shoulder. He was an old softy really.

The bakery was about a kilometre away. The path that led there went up over the headland and then wound down through terraces of ancient olive groves. I found it easily – I only had to follow my nose and the delicious fresh bread smell led me straight to the door.

Maria was as round and brown as one of her loaves.

'*Kalimera*,' she greeted me.

I held out the flowers. 'They're from Stavros, he says "*Yassos*".'

'Ah,' she said with a big smile. 'You stay at the taverna?'

'Yes.'

Then she leaned forward and said: 'Ben is nice boy – yes?'

'Yes,' I said. I could feel myself blushing.

She took the flowers and put them in a jar and stood it on the window sill. I could smell their perfume trapped in the confined space mixing deliciously with the smell of hot bread.

'Say "*Yassos*" to Stavros,' she said. 'And tell him, the answer was "Yes".'

'It was "Yes"?'

She nodded, smiling. 'Yes, the answer was "Yes"!'

I was intrigued. Maria was quite pretty for a woman her age – a bit younger than Mum, probably. What was Stavros up to?

'All right.'

And then she took two loaves and wrapped them in paper and handed them to me. She paused, and then took a sesame seed bun from a rack where they were cooling and added it with a smile. 'For you.'

'Thank you.'

As I made my way back though the olive grove, I nibbled at the bun. It was fresh and sweet and had a wonderful flavour of toasted sesame seeds. I hugged the warm bread parcel.

It was quite a hike up to the highest point in the track, and on the other side I rewarded myself by a jog on the easy slope down. Rounding a concealed bend, a voice hissed at me:

'Psst, English boy...'

I came to a stop. It was Ari's voice.

'No, it's not Ben. It's me, Lucy.'

He slipped out from between the olive trees, the dog panting at his heels.

'What do you want?'

'Nothing.' He looked down at the ground. Then his eyes shifted to the bread parcel. He could obviously smell the bread. The dog could too – it whined. I could tell by the look on his face that Ari was hungry. They both were.

'Does Ben give you bread?' I asked.

The boy looked at me assessingly. 'You don't tell Stavros?'

'Of course not.'

He shrugged. 'Sometimes.'

I tore one of the loaves out of the parcel and handed it to him. 'Take it. I won't say anything.'

'Thank you... Lucy,' he said. It was the first time I'd ever seen him really smile. He disappeared among the trees with the dog loping after him.

I went on slowly and thoughtfully. Quite obviously, he'd been hiding in wait for Ben. Did Ben give him bread every day?

The sun was filtering through the olive grove, dappling everything in a shifting light. As the air warmed up, the chanting of the crickets increased in volume. The dew was evaporating into the air, and with it all the suspicions I'd ever had about Ben seemed to disappear. I was sure of it now. I'd been totally unfair.

And then suddenly the crickets stopped. All together.

I paused too. There was complete silence. And that moment came back to me as vividly as if it was happening all over again...

We were standing on this very same path, not so far from where I was standing now. The look in his eyes had gone right through me. *Electric!*

Stavros was sitting on the terrace fiddling with his worry beads when I arrived. I held out the bread.

'Maria said "*Yassos*" to you,' and I added her odd message: 'She said to tell you: the answer was "Yes".'

'"Yes?"' He repeated, getting to his feet. 'She said it was "Yes"? You sure?'

'"Yes"... that's what she said.'

'"Yes?" he asked again like a zombie.

'*Yes!*'

'Yes!' He took the bread. He didn't even notice that it was one loaf short. He walked into the kitchen looking totally dazed. He reappeared with a bottle of Metaxa and sat down at the table again and poured himself a glass. He seemed to be in shock.

I went back to our room and found Mum packing the beach things.

'Stavros is behaving in the most peculiar way.'

'Is he?' She didn't seem particularly interested. 'Your photos are back.'

'What?'

'I asked Ben to pick them up since he was going into town. They're on the table.'

I stared at the envelope. It had been opened.

'You've gone through them. How could you?'

'No I haven't. I know better than that.'

'Someone has.'

'Lucy – they're only photos.'

I slid them out of the packet. There were the cringe-worthy ones of me windsurfing, or trying to. And then there were about twenty photos of Ben. Some of them were gorgeous. What if he'd looked inside? I went hot and cold all over with the very thought.

'Did you get the dolphins?'

'The what?'

'The dolphins.'

'Oh them. No. No, I didn't.'

'Lucy, you're in a really funny mood this morning.'

'No I'm not.'

I didn't see Ben until the afternoon. I was sitting on the terrace trying to concentrate on a book when he came and sat down opposite me.

'Did you get your photos OK?'

'Yes, thanks for picking them up.' (I couldn't look

at him.)

'No trouble. I was going in anyway. Any good ones?'

I risked a glance. (If he'd seen them, he wasn't letting on.)

'Aren't you going to show them to me?' he continued.

'No.'

(He had seen them. I knew he had. And he was getting the most out of the situation.)

There was a silence that lasted for about two lifetimes and then we both started speaking at the same time.

'Listen... '

'Listen...'

'After you.'

'No, after you.'

There were sounds of movement from inside Stavros' room and then he slammed his shutters closed.

Ben leaned over the table and lowered his voice: 'What I was going to say was – I should get a whole day off soon. Maybe we could do something...?'

'What did you have in mind?' I asked.

'Oh I don't know. Perhaps we could go for a swim at another beach or something...'

'Do you know one where there's no weed?' I asked.

He didn't catch on immediately, he asked: 'Does it really bother you?'

'It did the other day.'

He smiled that gorgeous grin of his.

'You shouldn't have laughed, it was cruel,' I said.
'It won't happen again. Promise.'
'In that case – I'll come.'

Chapter Fifteen

Stavros agreed to give Ben some time off without even complaining about it. A *whole* day off, which was pretty generous for Stavros. But a curious change seemed to have come over him recently. One evening, I came across him standing in the vineyard, actually *feeding* the cats. Would you believe it – he was pouring his best olive oil into their bowl.

I went back to Mum.

'You'll never guess what...'

'What?'

'Stavros is giving the cats olive oil.'

'Is he? Well, it's probably good for their coats.'

She'd totally missed my point. What I was trying to point out was how generous Stavros was being. But, for some reason, she didn't seem particularly interested. She'd been really vague and peculiar all day.

She was really restless over dinner. She came up with this plan for a boat trip.

'I was thinking we could go and see that site tomorrow. You know, the one on the next island,' she said as she started her salad.

I practically choked on an olive. 'Tomorrow?' (Tomorrow happened to be the day Ben was getting off. The one we'd planned to spend together.)

'Why not?'

'Does it really have to be tomorrow?'

'Well, I suppose it doesn't *have* to...'

'I just don't particularly feel like spending hours on a boat, that's all...'

'Well, I know archaeology isn't exactly your thing...'

'It's just that all those bits of stone and stuff look alike to me... You know, seen one, seen the lot.'

'You really are a dreadful philistine you know. It would do you good to come.'

'But why must it be tomorrow?'

Ben came out of the kitchen at that point. I could tell he'd been listening in. I cast him a warning glance.

'The boat only goes twice a week.'

'What about my sunburn?'

'Honestly darling, you could cover yourself up and wear a hat.'

'Mmm, but I'd get so hot. You know how stifling it gets at midday.'

'True. Maybe we should put it off till Tuesday.'

(No way! This was a real chance for me and Ben to get some time alone together.)

'No! You've really set your heart on it. If the weather turns bad you might miss the opportunity.'

'It looks pretty settled to me.'

'But you can never tell. A storm could flare up any time.'

'Won't you get bored here all on your own?'

'I'd be more likely to get bored looking at beastly old ruins.'

'You are impossible. I suppose I'll have to go alone.'

Ben arrived to take our plates away. 'Will that be all, ladies?'

I flashed him a triumphant smile.

'I think I've got everything I want. Thank you.'

I hardly slept that night. I kept imagining that something would go wrong. A storm would blow up, or Mum would change her mind for some reason. But I woke to find her up early, dressed and ready for her trip.

'Now promise me you won't stay out in the midday sun.'

'Do you think I'm totally mad?'

'Yes.'

'Must run in the family.'

'You're absolutely sure you don't want to change your mind?'

'Absolutely!'

I heard her footsteps fading away down the path to the square. Then I leapt out of bed and into the shower. Only an hour to get ready. What was I going to wear?

Ben nearly missed the bus. I had to stand there pleading with the driver to keep the bus from leaving. He came running down the path just as I thought I was losing the battle.

We climbed on board. The bus was really full for that time of day.

'What kept you?'

'Stavros... You'll never believe this...'

'What?'

'He suddenly announced this morning – he's getting married!'

'Married! Stavros!'

'To the lady in the bakery. Maria!'

'Oh that's just so sweet. I thought something was going on.'

We managed to grab the last two seats.

'Why are there so many people on the bus?' I asked.

'Oh I don't know. It's Saturday. I suppose a lot of people get the day off.'

'Oh right,' I nodded. 'Is it Saturday.' I'd totally lost track of time.'

Saturday. The word nagged at my mind for some reason. And Stavros getting married. There was some odd connection... Saturday... Oh my God, *Saturday*! It was the day Dad was getting remarried. I'd completely forgotten. How could I? I'd been so absolutely wrapped up in my own life, I hadn't given anyone else a thought. I should've spent the day with Mum. Today of all days.

'What's wrong?'

'I've just remembered something...'

'Do you want to go back?'

'Not that sort of thing. And it's too late now.'

'It can't be that bad?'

'No, it's OK.' I gazed out of the window. I felt terrible. All the brightness had gone out of the day somehow. I reached for a tissue in my bag.

'Lucy? What is it?' He was staring at me.

I cleared my throat. 'It's just that my dad's getting married today, that's all.' I stared out of the window again.

'Your dad? Didn't you want to be there?'

I shook my head and blew my nose.

'You don't like his new wife?'

'Not madly, but it's not that. It's just that I forgot. And now Mum's gone off all on her own to that site on the other island. I should've spent the day with her. Today of all days.'

'Maybe we could catch up with her and join her?'

'Thanks but... there's only one boat in the morning. We've missed it.'

'Oh.'

'Look, I'm sorry. I don't want to spoil your day off. Let's talk about something else.'

'If you're sure you're OK.'

'I'm fine. Really.'

'OK – first things first. Where are we going to stop off?'

I tried to think of something he'd like. You know, boy-stuff. I reckoned the beach with all the windsurfers would be right up his street.

'How about the next beach?' I suggested.

'Oh you'd hate it, it's really crowded.' (He was being really considerate.)

But I insisted. 'I wouldn't mind. I could do with a bit of life. I've hardly seen anyone this holiday.'

'The people there are real posers...'

'Great! That'll give us something to watch!'

I put on a big show of enthusiasm as we approached the beach. 'Oh great – sun loungers! Luxury!'

'You really want to hire a lounger?' he asked as we disembarked from the bus.

'Don't you?'

'Well yeah, maybe.'

'Better hurry. Or they'll all be taken.'

We found a couple free at the end of the beach which had a parasol that actually worked. I stretched out on the shady one.

'Mmm – this is heaven!'

He lay there for a while with his eyes closed, and then he turned over and said: 'Do you want me to oil your back or anything?'

I pointed out that Mum had insisted on smothering me in the stuff that morning, but I offered to oil his instead.

He had a really nice back. I took longer over it than absolutely necessary.

'Right – you're done.'

'I think maybe you missed a bit – up round my neck and shoulders,' he said with a sidelong glance.

'No I didn't.'

'Pity.'

I lay down and closed my eyes again.

That's when the people on the loungers next to us started to row. It was really upsetting actually. They weren't arguing about anything in particular, they were just having a real go at each other for the sake of it. It brought back memories of all those stupid arguments Mum and Dad used to have. Arguments which really got to me. I used to go and shut myself in my room just to get out of their way.

I tried not to listen, but it was impossible not to.

Ben noticed. He leaned over and whispered, 'Maybe we should make a move – go somewhere a bit quieter?'

'Good idea, let's move on before we have to pay for the loungers.'

We stood at the bus stop feeling at a bit of a loss.

'So where to now?' asked Ben.

'I only know one beach apart from Paradiso. The one where Mum and I stayed, when we moved on.'

'What's it like?'

'Well, it's not up to much, but it is quiet.'

'Sounds good to me.'

'There's a taverna where we can get some lunch.'

'Sounds even better.'

There were even more people in the bus this time. We had to squeeze on to the bench seat at the back. We didn't talk much. I was only too conscious of his body close to mine. He must have been too. Our bare legs kept touching every time the bus lurched. I kept wondering what would happen when we were alone together. I'd wanted to be alone with him, desperately. But now I was nervous about it. Really scared in case I messed everything up. At home, I generally went around with a whole group of friends. So it was really odd being alone with just one boy.

I think maybe he felt the same way, because while we ate our meal he was very quiet. All they had at the taverna was spaghetti – wasn't that just typical? I kept going 'slurp' with mine. I'm sure he noticed.

I was relieved when they took the plates away. 'I made a real pig of myself,' I said apologetically, stretching. 'I feel really full and sleepy now.'

'Maybe we should go to the beach and find some shade?' he suggested. 'These old olive trees don't give much shelter.'

'Good idea.'

We walked in single file down the little narrow path to the beach. Every nerve in my body was conscious of him walking behind me. I've always been paranoid about my backside. Isn't everyone? I turned once and caught him watching me. But he was smiling. He didn't look critical.

'What is it?'

'Nothing. Keep going.'

We walked along the shoreline for a while looking for shade. I kept finding bright pebbles along the waterline, washed up by the sea. He picked up a few and sent them skimming across the waves. And then he handed me one. It was a piece of serpentine, a wonderful blue-green colour – exactly the colour of his eyes.

He was staring into my eyes now, with a questioning look.

'I thought there were some trees here,' I said. 'Maybe we ought to go back to the olive grove.'

'What about those rocks over there?' he said, pointing

to the far end of the beach. 'They must give some shade.'

'Maybe – it's worth a try.'

There wasn't much shade. We had to lie really close. My heart was beating so hard as I laid out my towel, I thought he'd notice.

But he was flattening his out in a really matter-of-fact manner.

'Just enough room,' he said.

'Good,' I managed to say as I lay down beside him.

He pretended to go to sleep. But I caught him sneaking glances at me under his eyelashes. And sure enough, after a while, his arm slid round on to my towel.

He had this really innocent look on his face – it made me smile.

He started by kissing me very gently. It was nice. It was very nice. Soon he was edging over my way...

'Not enough shade?' I asked.

That was it. Both his arms were round me now, warm and strong and pulling me towards him. I've never been kissed like that in my life. It was brilliant. I mean, I've never even liked kissing that much before. As we paused to draw breath, he cast a glance in the direction of the sun.

'Can't be too careful,' he said, sliding right over on to my towel now. 'Can't be past three yet.'

Three. *Three o'clock.* I'd seen it on the invitation in that posh squiggly writing. Three o'clock was the time when Dad was getting married. It completely ruined the moment. I sat up.

'No,' I said. 'We can't.'

'Yes we can.'

'No, we mustn't.'

'Mustn't we? Why?'

'Umm, because... Umm... I don't know you well enough.'

'I was just trying to put that right.'

'Yes but... I mean, I don't think we should, erm...' I paused because I wasn't quite sure what we were going to do anyway.

'Too fast and too soon?' he asked.

'Exactly.'

'But Lucy —'

'No buts.'

I got up and rolled my towel. 'I really like you and all that, but...'

'You said no buts...' he pointed out.

'I know, but...' (He was being so nice I thought I was going to blub.)

'It's not you – it's just that it's three o'clock.'

'Three o'clock?' He looked mystified.

I explained about Dad and the invitation and how it had all suddenly got to me. He was brilliant. He really seemed to understand. He just put out his arms and said: 'Come here.'

'I'm so sorry.'

'Don't be. It's OK. Lucy – look at me.'

I couldn't. But I felt his arms around me in a big brotherly hug.

'Better?'

'Mmm... thanks, Ben.'

We took the next bus back to the taverna. I wanted to get there before Mum arrived back.

'I've spoiled your day out. I know I have,' I said as we reached the terrace.

'No you haven't.'

'Yes I have.'

'No really, honestly – you haven't.'

'So what are you going to do now?'

He looked out to sea.

I smiled – *silly question.*

I watched him as he loped in that way of his, two at a time, down the steps. He turned at the bottom and waved.

I went back to the square to wait for Mum. She wasn't on the five o'clock bus, but she arrived on the next. I watched anxiously as she got off. She looked hot and tired but not particularly unhappy.

'Hi! What are you doing here?' she asked.

'Waiting for you.'

'That's nice. But what happened? Where's Ben?'

'How did you know I was with Ben?'

'Honestly Lucy – I may be short-sighted, but I'm not blind. Where is he, anyway?'

'Out windsurfing.'

'Oh... Was your day a disaster?'

'No, not really. It's just that... Oh Mum – how could I have forgotten?'

She put an arm round my shoulders.

'Don't be silly...'

'No honestly... I should have been with you, today of *all* days.'

'No – I was glad you were going out. It was better that way... It gave me a chance to... get things into perspective.'

I could tell she was being brave about it.

'Really?'

'Come on – I'm dying for a drink and a shower.'

I got Mum a white wine while she was in the shower. She came out wrapped in her bathrobe and patted the bed beside her.

'Sit down. I want to hear all about your day. I'm sure it was much more fun than mine.'

'Not much to tell really. I made a bit of a fool of myself, I think. I kept thinking about Dad and you.'

'That's all in the past now.'

'I know but... I kept thinking it must be so horrid for you. And I was out enjoying myself. As if I didn't care. I mean, if it had been me I'd have felt... well...'

'...old and rejected and past it?'

'No! But kind of sad maybe.'

'You couldn't be more wrong.'

'What do you mean?'

'It was the one thing that kept me going – cheered me up. The thought of you two, young and happy and out together.'

'I would've been dead envious.'

'No, you wouldn't.'

'How do you know?'

'I've been there, Lucy. You haven't.'

who cry. I mean, I'm absolutely hopeless. I don't understand all this relationship stuff. My parents have always been happily married. She must have been feeling awful.

'You don't like his new wife?' I prompted.

She shook her head again, obviously trying to get a grip on herself.

'Not madly, but it's not that. It's just that I forgot. And now Mum's gone off all on her own to that site on that other island. I should've spent the day with her. Today of all days.'

'Maybe we could catch up with her and join her?'

'Thanks but... there's only the one boat out in the morning. We've missed it.'

'Oh.' I tried to sound disappointed.

'Look, I'm sorry. I don't want to spoil your day off. Let's talk about something else.'

'If you're sure you're OK.'

'I'm fine. Really.'

'OK – first things first. Where are we going to stop off?'

'How about the next beach?'

(I had in mind somewhere rather more secluded.)

'Oh you'd hate it, it's really crowded.'

'I wouldn't mind. I could do with a bit of life. I've hardly seen anyone this holiday.'

'The people there are real posers...'

'Great! That'll give us something to watch!'

The resort was crowded with weekend visitors. We had to walk the entire length of the beach to find a couple of vacant loungers. But Lucy didn't seem to mind. She stretched out on one with a sigh of contentment.

'Mmm – this is heaven!'

I stretched out on the next lounger. We lay in silence for ten minutes or so.

'Do you want me to oil your back or anything?' I asked after a while.

'No, it's OK. Mum insisted I put sunscreen on from top to toe before I left – to be absolutely sure I didn't miss a centimetre. I'll do yours if you like, though.'

'Oh thanks.' (I had a really good protective tan. Hadn't used sun lotion since I ran out a week ago – but if the girl was willing...)

Minutes of sheer bliss followed as I felt her nice soft hands running up and down my back – magic!

'Right – you're done.'

'I think maybe you missed a bit – up round my neck and shoulders.'

'No I didn't.'

'Pity.'

She lay down on her back with a little smile of satisfaction on her face and closed her eyes.

I lay back and closed mine, too. At this rate I wasn't going to get as far as holding hands with her. Now for some serious tactical planning.

A strident female voice broke in through my train of thought.

'You never think of what I want, do you?'

'What do you mean?' The male voice was huffy, defensive.

'That's just typical of you, answering with a question.

Always throwing it back at me.'

'Always! What do you mean, *always*...?'

'Always! What d'you think *always* means...?'

There was one hell of a domestic going on next door to us. I raised myself on one elbow.

It was Blondie – the girl staying below the taverna. She was pouting with this really spoilt look on her face and Lover Boy wasn't looking cool at all. Close up, he wasn't even that good-looking. And she was really tarty, wearing full make-up on the beach. You could see each eyelash caked with mascara. What a let down!

I lay back and became a reluctant eavesdropper on their row. They weren't arguing about anything important, they were just laying into each other – the way people argue just for the hell of it, just to make the other person's life a misery. So much for their great romance. It was pretty depressing listening to them, really. I stared out to sea but somehow their row had put a damper on the day.

I looked over at Lucy. She was frowning – she obviously couldn't help overhearing them either.

I leaned over and whispered: 'Maybe we should make a move – go somewhere a bit quieter.'

She nodded and reached for her clothes.

'Good idea, let's move on before we have to pay for the loungers.'

Dodging the gladiators with their obsessive sports equipment, we made our way back to the bus stop.

'So where to now?'

She shrugged. 'I only know one beach apart from

Paradiso. The one where Mum and I stayed when we moved on.'

'What's it like?'

'Well, it's not up to much, but it is quiet.'

'Sounds good to me.'

'There's a taverna where we can get some lunch.'

'Sounds even better.'

By the time we got to Lucy's beach we were both ravenous, so we ended up having lunch at this modern taverna. Not much of a place but the food was good, and it was cheap too.

When we'd finished she stretched that lovely body of hers and smiled. 'I made a real pig of myself. I feel really full and sleepy now.'

Sleepy? Some illicit thoughts about the rooms in the taverna crept in at that point, but I promise I put them right out of my mind.

'Maybe we should go to the beach and find some shade?' I suggested. 'These old olive trees don't give much shelter.'

She nodded. 'Good idea.'

A narrow little path between some reeds led down to the beach. We were forced to walk in single file, which was nice because I could enjoy watching the way she moved on those long legs of hers. Lovely, lovely Lucy.

She turned at one point and caught me watching.

'What is it?'

'Nothing. Keep going.'

When we arrived at the beach we found there wasn't much shade there, either. I skimmed a couple of stones and handed Lucy a nice flat blue-ish one, perfect for skimming. But she didn't seem particularly interested in ducks-and-drakes.

'I thought there were some trees here,' she said. 'Maybe we ought to go back to the olive grove.'

'What about those rocks over there?' I said, pointing to the far end of the beach. 'They must give some shade.'

'Maybe – it's worth a try.'

There was just the right amount of shade beside the rocks – just enough for two beach towels laid out side by side. And by my reckoning, as the sun moved round, the area of shade would get quite a bit smaller.

Lucy spread her towel out and I spread mine beside hers.

'Just enough room,' I said casually.

'Good,' she said and stretched herself out.

I lay down beside her and pretended to try to sleep. Sleep! Nothing could've been further from my mind. And I could tell by the occasional glance I sneaked at her that Lucy wasn't particularly sleepy, either. I slid an arm up over my head and brought it casually round to rest on her towel.

She opened her eyes and smiled. (Encouragement!)

I moved a little closer. She still didn't object, so I moved a lot closer. And then I moved closer still.

I was just getting to the really good bit of getting to know her, and I'll tell you, Lucy was a very kissable girl. And she seemed to be enjoying it. In fact, everything was going absolutely brilliantly. I even started, very gradually, to make headway on to her towel.

'Not enough shade?' she asked, which I took to be a real come-on.

'Can't be too careful,' I cast a glance up in the direction of the sun. 'Can't be past three yet.'

With that, all of a sudden, Lucy sat up. Oh this wasn't fair! I hadn't got anywhere near the getting-out-of-hand bit yet.

'No,' she said. 'We can't.'

'Yes we can.'

'No, we mustn't.'

'Mustn't we? Why?'

'Umm, because… Umm… I don't know you well enough.'

'I was just trying to put that right.'

'Yes, but… I mean, I don't think we should, umm…' (Girls really find this hard to articulate for some reason.) Like an idiot I helped her out. 'Too fast and too soon?'

'Exactly.'

'But Lucy—'

'No buts.'

She was getting to her feet and rolling her towel. OK, OK – I knew I'd blown it.

'I really like you and all that, but…' she was saying.

'You said no buts…'

'I know, but…' She seemed really upset for some reason.

I stood up and dutifully rolled my towel.

'It's not you – it's just that it's three o'clock.'

'Three o'clock?'

Her lower lip wobbled. 'I know it's stupid but that's when Dad's getting married. I saw it on the invitation. And then when you said three – I thought of Dad and Mum and how they came to Greece and...'

'Come here,' I said.

'I'm so sorry.'

'Don't be. It's OK,' I said, catching her round the waist. 'Lucy – look at me.'

She didn't, so I put my arms around her and hugged her close. Not a sexy hug, just a big reassuring hug.

'Better?'

'Mmm... thanks, Ben.'

I didn't try anything more for the rest of the afternoon. We just talked and got to know each other a lot better. Not exactly the way I'd planned but... Still, there would be other times.

Lucy was anxious to get back and wait for her mother, which I guess was understandable in the circumstances. We arrived back at the taverna early, shortly after four.

'I've spoiled your day out. I know I have,' she said.

'No you haven't.'

'Yes I have.'

'No, really, honestly – you haven't.'

'So what are you going to do now?'

I stared out to sea. It was a brilliantly clear day and there was a perfect twenty knot cross-shore wind.

That's what I needed. A really good sail.

Chapter Seventeen

I went much further out than I should have done. Even further out than the guys from the next beach. I was a lot more disappointed by the way the afternoon had turned out than I had let on to Lucy. It had all been going so well. She'd totally turned me on. And I could tell she felt the same. And then – nothing...

I guess I was taking my frustration out on the water. And the sea seemed to respond with a series of angry little waves that were intent on flinging me off the board. It was like a battle of wills – each time I slapped into a wave and survived upright, I felt a surge of adrenalin. I'd started to work the whole thing out of my system when, quite unexpectedly, I shot out of the lee of the island.

The wind was a lot wilder out in the open sea. There was a series of totally uncharacteristic gusts which caused some pretty hairy moments. Scared me into turning back. That first return run was faster than I've ever sailed before. As I hit wave after wave, the board was practically lifting out of the water. And then it happened...

There was a sickening *crunch* and I was flung head-first into the sea.

As I surfaced, I caught sight of the damage. The mast hadn't simply dislodged itself, the mast foot was actually split through, so there was no way I could get it back in place. I cursed myself for being so casual. I'd noticed the pressure cracks each time I'd set up the rig, but I hadn't considered them more than superficial. No, let's be honest, I'd ignored them. This was the best board Stavros had and I hadn't wanted to compromise.

I swung myself up on the board and sat astride, wondering what to do. I waved both arms in the direction of the other windsurfers but none of them seemed to be looking my way. The only thing for it was to start paddling back towards the shore and hope that, by some freak of luck, a boat would come by and give me a tow.

I remembered all the things the manuals told you – crystal clearly – how you should always carry flares. Who did? How I should have been surfing with others or at least have someone on the look-out for me. In fact, I remembered, chillingly, there was only one person who knew I was out here – Lucy.

Would she have the sense to realise I hadn't come back, or would she be too bound up with her mother? I lay on the board and paddled with my arms as hard as I could, but it hardly seemed to move. I knew I must be moving but I was so far out, my progress was almost undetectable.

I yelled as hard as I could but my voice didn't register in the vast expanse of sea. The wind was building up now and, intermittently, I lost sight of the land between the waves. A shudder of ice-cold panic went right through to my guts. I could die out here from exposure. The only thing to do was to stay with the board and pray for rescue.

How could I have been such a damn fool?

※

Two hours later, it was pitch dark and I was still paddling. My shoulders were at breaking point and my mouth was so dry I could barely swallow, but I was still inching the board forward, painful stroke by stroke, trying to keep sight of the lights on the shore.

You read things about people who survive against all the odds – hour after hour, clinging to tiny bits of wreckage, or for days on life rafts. But then you hear about other people who disappear without trace, in boats which accidentally drift into shipping lanes, or lone swimmers whose bodies are never recovered. I tried to keep my mind on the positive stories as I paddled doggedly on.

The one thought that kept me going was that one of those lights, the highest one, must be the taverna. And somewhere up there was Lucy. And that when I did get back, I'd feel the warmth of her and the closeness of her against my body again – like I had on the beach. Lovely, lovely Lucy.

And this thought renewed my strength. She must be thinking of me. She must be wondering where I was – worried that I hadn't come back. She *must*.

※

It wasn't until an hour or so later that the first glimmer of hope came. The light was so tiny, I kept thinking I was imagining it. I'd been peering into the darkness so long, I thought my eyes were playing tricks on me. But it really seemed to be moving. Then it detached itself from the other lights. Yes, it was moving. It must be a boat – a fisherman perhaps, coming out to check his nets.

I yelled into the wind again.

No answer came back and so I yelled again, harder. I could see the light clearly now. I shouted again. And then I heard a distant barking – a dog. I knew that bark – it was the stray dog which went around with Ari.

'Ari!' I yelled.

And then his answering voice came over the water to me.

'Ben!'

'Ari!'

We kept shouting like maniacs and soon I could make out that the light was on the front of his boat. It cast a reflection across the water that seemed to stretch like a glittering pathway back to safety.

'Ari!'

'Ben!'

I could see him now, standing up in the boat with the dog silhouetted beneath him. His bony back working back and forth as he rowed with all his strength.

'Ari! I'm over here.'

'OK!'

At last he could see me, and within minutes, he drew level.

'Ah, English boy! Not so clever now, eh?' I could see his teeth gleaming in the lamplight.

He stood over me, leaning on his oars, getting his breath back. I thought of all the bad things I'd done to him. I'd taken his job, for God's sake. For one paranoid moment, I imagined him laughing and turning his boat round and leaving me there.

But he was reaching down for something. Then he threw a rope, and within minutes, I'd attached a towline and he was helping me into the boat. The dog was all over me, licking my face.

Ari threw me a filthy old sweater and handed me a bottle of water.

'Drink. Get warm,' he said.

I thrust the sweater over my head. It stank of fish but it was reassuringly warm. I found I was shaking. I took a swig from the bottle – my mouth felt as if it was lined with cotton wool. Ari had already turned the boat round and was rowing strongly back to shore.

'Ari – thanks mate – thanks,' I gasped.

'Is OK.'

'Come on. Give me an oar. Let me help row.'

He glanced at me over his shoulder.

'Siddown,' he said with that arrogant look of his. 'I not need help.'

He didn't, skinny as he was – he had no problem rowing back. I sank gratefully into the bows. The dog snuggled up beside me and I lay there savouring the feeling of warmth and security.

The light of the taverna had been drawing closer and closer. It was above us now and I could see

159

lights on the beach too and make out the movement of shadowy figures.

'Ari!' A shout came across the water followed by a question in Greek. It was Stavros' voice.

Ari shouted back and I heard him say my name. Then everyone was shouting at once. I could just see the outline of Stavros wading into the water, and suddenly his strong arms were pulling the boat up.

I climbed out and waded to the shore.

She was standing there waiting for me. Lucy. Before I knew it, her arms were round me and she was laughing and crying at the same time. We just stood there hugging each other.

It was a minute or so before I became aware of Stavros standing watching us with his hands on his hips.

'Wha's goin' on?' he demanded.

I extricated myself. 'I'm not talking to her. I haven't said a word,' I said.

'You don't be so cheeky,' he roared and then he put his great arms round us, hugging us both like a big bear.

Then suddenly everyone was joining in. That is, *almost* everyone.

In the excitement, no-one had noticed that Ari had pushed his boat out again. He was about to climb in when Stavros stopped him with a shout.

Ari paused, looking doubtful.

The two of them talked rapidly in Greek. Then Stavros waded into the water and looked straight at

Ari and asked him something.

Ari put on that arrogant look of his and shrugged. The two of them stood face to face – the skinny little lad and the great mountain of a man. More words were exchanged. Stavros seemed to lose patience – he threw his arms up in the air and turned back to the shore. Then Ari shouted something after him. Stavros turned back shrugging his shoulders.

'What's happening?' I asked.

'He bring back my windsurf. He bring back my waiter. So I ask him if he want his job back. Give him another try,' said Stavros.

'Good – that's great,' I said.

'No, this boy, he want more money. He want *double* money!'

Ari had his back to us, pushing the boat out. I helped by giving it a shove, then I turned back to Stavros. It was a risk, but I reckoned a risk worth taking.

'Well if you don't give him the money he wants, I quit,' I said. 'So you're on your own.'

'What?' roared Stavros.

'You heard.'

Stavros stood hesitating on the shore.

'Go on, Ari,' I said.

Ari climbed into the boat and started rowing.

'OK. OK! You win! He has job back – *double money*,' said Stavros.

'Thank you,' I said.

'*Yassos* – Ben,' Ari called out as his boat slid off into the darkness.

Chapter Eighteen

We had just one week left. When I look back, I realise those days together were about as perfect as life gets. Ari was working at the taverna again, so I went back to the serious business of having a holiday.

Lucy and I spent every moment we could together. I don't know whether it was my lousy experience on the broken windsurfer, but I actually lost interest in windsurfing for a while. Instead, we explored the island together. We even went to that tiny island I'd spotted. The one with the whitewashed chapel and the tree and the tiny hidden beach just big enough for two. Lucy refused to swim there, so I hired a boat and brough a picnic and rowed us over.

I think they were wrong to call that shabby old black sand beach Paradiso. Paradise itself is a bit further out and has a smaller beach altogether. At least, that's what Lucy and I discovered that day.

And I reckon ever since I've been trying to kind of replay the excitement, the exhilaration, the sheer over-the-top intoxication of a girl like Lucy. And in all the girls after her, I've in a way been trying to rediscover her. Lovely, lovely Lucy – I've found a little bit of you in all of them.

I know you want to know the obvious. Did it last? I thought it would. We rang each other a lot – but back home, we lived miles apart, practically opposite ends of the country, and we both had our heads down for exams.

We met up in London over the Christmas holidays. I bought really good seats for a show Lucy had been longing to see – they cost a fortune. I planned the *best* evening, used all my Christmas money – and I booked a restaurant in Chinatown for afterwards.

She came looking so different. She had earrings and lipstick on and she'd done her hair a different way. I felt really awkward, as if this girl wasn't really Lucy. All through the evening I kept on wondering where she'd gone, that long-legged, easy-going girl I'd met on Lexos.

We ran out of things to say over the meal. And when I saw her to her train we kissed really long and passionately. But it had gone – she knew it and I knew it – I saw it in her face, through the grimy window as the train slid out of the station.

I was so gutted I didn't have the heart to call her for days. And then she called me and we had this really grim conversation when both admitted it was over.

But I still think about her a lot, the real Lucy, the one I knew on Lexos. I like to think she's still there somehow, at the end of those footprints in the sand, staying just as she was, forever – a perfect golden memory.

footprints
in the sand

Ben's side of the story...

There was just the right amount of shade beside
the rocks – just enough for two beach towels laid
out side by side. And by my reckoning, as the sun
moved round, the area of shade would get quite
a bit smaller.

footprints
in the sand

Ben's side of the story...

CHLOË RAYBAN

Collins

An imprint of HarperCollins*Publishers*

First published in Great Britain by Collins in 1999
Collins is an imprint of HarperCollins*Publishers* Ltd
77-85 Fulham Palace Road, Hammersmith,
London W6 8JB

The HarperCollins website address is:
www.fireandwater.com

1 3 5 7 9 8 6 4 2

Text copyright © Chloë Rayban

ISBN 0 00 675303 5

The author asserts the moral right to
be identified as the author of the work.

Printed and bound in Great Britain by
Caledonian International Book Manufacturing Ltd
Glasgow G64

with grateful thanks to
Nick Price for his help with the windsurfing

Chapter One

It was brilliant, ace, legendary, *perfect*. The bay curved away in a shallow arc. Gently shelving – not too steeply – with curious black sand. It was sheltered from squalls on the north by a protective bank of cliff, but open to the sea on the south, where a stiff but steady cross-wind promised hours, days, weeks, a *lifetime* of perfect windsurfing.

'Hey, man! Look what I see!'

I'd spotted the stacked boards waiting and ready for us beside a ramshackle hut – not exactly state-of-the-art, but that was good news. They wouldn't have the nerve to charge extortionate hire fees like they'd done back in some of the plusher resorts we'd visited.

Sprout shrugged and drew his jacket up around his shoulders, blowing his nose noisily. He'd been whingeing on about breakfast all the way here in the bus. But Mick caught on, a slow smile spreading across his face as he stared in the direction I was looking. He crossed his arms and said 'Ye-ah.'

We'd arrived on the night boat and had to sit till dawn in this bus shelter – 'bout the size and cleanliness of a chicken coop – waiting for the first bus out of the port. We needed to get off the beaten track as-soon-as – didn't want to risk another tangle with the tourist police. Backpackers aren't exactly popular with the officials on the islands these days.

We'd been turned away from a couple. But nobody got turned away from Lexos.

Lexos was bottom of the pile as far as Greek islands were concerned. A resort so starved of the touristic limelight that no normal, self-respecting holiday-maker ever set a flip-flop on it. Even shabby, unwashed and unshaven backpackers like ourselves were greeted with open arms on Lexos.

As soon as our boat arrived, a load of black-clothed grannies descended on it and started squabbling over us, shouting, '*Thomatia, thomatia*'. One actually grabbed Squid by the arm and was trying to drag him towards her house.

'What's going on?' he demanded, a bit overcome by his sudden popularity.

'They want to let us rooms in their houses!' I shouted back.

I caught up with Squid and turned the lady's attention to our bedrolls, indicating sleep. She took one look at them and called over to her friends, then the old dears tutted and shook their heads and went off, grumbling to each other.

So we waited, crammed into our bus shelter, worrying about whether they'd report us to the police and whether we'd get moved on to another island. It was a relief when the first bus came rattling to our stop, good and early – even before the sun rose.

We climbed aboard feeling cold and clammy – my stomach was beginning to rebel at the treatment it'd had recently. Hadn't felt right since we'd eaten those dodgy kebabs – where was it?

Couple of islands back, anyway. So we all sat in the bus feeling green and pukey as this maniac driver negotiated the hairpin bends with one hand on the steering wheel and one eye looking over his shoulder at us. We were the only people on the bus, and he kept checking to see what effect his virtuoso driving performance was having on his passengers. As the bus climbed out of the port and switched to a narrow cliff-top road, I moved my seat to the landward side, so that I was out of eyeshot of the perpendicular drop to our left. So I didn't get much of an impression of the island on that first journey.

Gradually, the grey sky took on a warmer hue. The sun was rising, and its first rays began to catch the tips of the hills above us, tinting them golden. I felt my spirits rise as the sunlight began bleeding colour into our monochrome world. The driver leaned forward and snapped the radio on and the joyful chaos of clattering bazouki music filled the bus. I settled back in my seat. Hot sun filtered through the murky windows, warming my body. I reckoned Lexos was going to be OK.

We hadn't any idea where we were heading, so we bought tickets to the end of the route – reckoned the further we could travel from civilisation, the less likely we were to get moved on. Eventually, the bus drew into a turnaround in a kind of rough cobbled area and sighed to a halt. Outside was a ramshackle general store, a chapel with a blistered whitewashed dome, a signpost and a telegraph pole.

The driver jumped down and turned to us with a smirk. 'My friends,' he said. 'Welcome to Paradiso.'

'Is this the end?'

'Oh yes,' he said with raised eyebrows. He threw his cigarette butt down on the cobbles and ground it with his heel as if to indicate his opinion. 'This is the very end.'

So this was it.

'Where's the sea?' asked Mick as the bus rattled off again, leaving us standing marooned beside our pile of backpacks.

'Can't be far away, can it? The island's only a mile across at its widest,' I pointed out.

'Do you think that place is open? I'm starved,' said Sprout.

The general store wasn't, and a sign in its fly-spotted window indicated that it wouldn't be – until nine. Another couple of hours.

Mick was already picking his way up a rough goat track.

'Come on! We'll get a better view from further up!' he shouted. 'Maybe there's a village.'

He was already quite a way up the track, and once we'd struggled into our packs we started after him. The path was steep and rough underfoot. Mick got to the top of the rise and then he stopped short.

'What is it?' I called.

He swung round. His voice was caught and swept away by the wind.

'What?'

I drew nearer and he turned again.

'Epic,' he repeated.

With a final effort I came up next to him.

It was – quite literally – epic. We were standing on a headland which jutted out into the impossibly blue sea. On the one side, beneath us, the cliff was criss-crossed by paths and dotted with tiny whitewashed buildings built into the cliffside – half-cave, half-cottage. Nets hanging to dry outside showed they were probably fishermen's dwellings. And sure enough, down below was a jetty with a row of anchored boats. On the other side, to the lee of a further headland, I could see what promised to be good camping country. A thin wisp of smoke was already rising from between the rows of acacia trees and a ragged line of washing fluttered in the wind. Sure sign that backpackers had already taken up residence. But I reckoned, plenty of room for more, and it looked like a good sheltered space too. I knew even Sprout would be impressed. He came level, puffing and fussing about the climb. He just grunted at the view.

It seemed breakfast was still uppermost in his mind because he suddenly burst out: 'Hey, look man! Salvation! It's a taverna!'

I turned and followed his gaze. It was hardly a taverna. It was a mere apology of a place. A strange construction of tumbledown, whitewashed stone, sun-bleached driftwood and rusting chicken wire – but it did have a telltale pile of soft drink crates outside and a sign, which proclaimed proudly in Roman characters: TAVERNA PARADISOS.

Underneath this, a handwritten sign advertised:

TOST
BREUAKFAST
FRESH FISH
FRIED SQUIB

We made our way over, and found it had a terrace supported by breeze-block pillars. No great shakes in the architectural sense, but the terrace was half-shaded by vines entangled in the chicken wire and it had a view to kill for.

We decided to celebrate our 'find' with a proper sit-down breakfast. A rare luxury on our budget. Having hauled off our backpacks, we sank gratefully on to the taverna's rickety, rush-seated chairs.

Sprout was already running through the menu of his 'fantasy breakfast' – it had become longer and more elaborate as the holiday wore on.

'Eggs sunny-side up with crispy bacon rashers and pork sausages so well done they're bursting out and crunchy at the ends, with fried bread and baked beans, thick white toast and—'

'I reckon ninety-nine percent of your waking life is spent thinking about food,' interrupted Mick.

'No, man, there's drinks too...'

'Quiet!' I cut through them both. 'Listen.'

They listened for a moment. The bay was so still, you could hear the water lapping in the harbour down below. You could hear the ringing of a halyard tapping on a masthead. You could even hear chickens' claws scrabbling in the soft dust.

'What?' asked Mick.

'I can't hear anything,' said Sprout.

'Exactly,' I said. 'Haven't you noticed? It's so quiet? No cars, no roads, nothing...'

A cock crowed.

'Yeah well, I heard that all right. Reckon it's just laid an egg.'

'That'll be a first,' said Mick. 'That was a cock.'

'Well, just maybe he's got a wife. When are we going to get some service round here?' asked Sprout, rising from the table and pacing around.

'It's a bit early,' I pointed out.

'So? We might go away and they'll lose the only bit of custom they've had this decade by the look of the place. Hell-o-o-o! Anybody th-ere?'

Sprout started knocking on the closed doors.

'Shut up, you'll wake everyone.'

'That was the general idea.'

Sprout knocked harder and finally got a response. Someone was moving inside.

'Hell-o-o!' called Sprout. Anybody—'

'Yes?'

Sprout jumped back . A huge man had appeared out of the doorway. He had a head like a bull set on massive shoulders. He was wearing nothing but a worn singlet and baggy boxers and the hair on his chest thrust its way through the holes in the vest. He was a huge minotaur of a man. I almost expected his lower half to have hooves.

'Whaddyou-wan?'

'We were hoping for service,' said Sprout. 'You know, breakfast? Eggs? Bread? Coffee? Nescafé?'

'Huh,' snorted the man and slammed the door in his face.

'Well done,' said Mick.

'Bollocks,' said Sprout. 'I'm starving. I've a good mind to go into his kitchen and help myself.'

But more sounds were coming from behind the bloke's door. Sounds of thumping on an internal wall and the guy's voice raised – shouting at someone. A few minutes later, a skinny youth emerged from the door next to his.

I guess the boy was about our age. He was wearing the sort of trousers you get in charity shops – nylony material the colour of weak coffee and a thin T-shirt with an ad for Lexos printed over the front – the kind they give away as freebies. But the thing that caught my eye, the thing that made me think he was dead poor, was his shoes. They were down-at-heel, black leather slip-ons – shoes like no-one's worn in years. My eyes kept returning to them. I didn't reckon he was the guy's son or anything – the boy was too old for that.

As a waiter he didn't have a lot going for him – couldn't seem to look us in the eye. He just kind of stood there waiting to be asked for things.

'We want ham and eggs,' said Sprout, taking the initiative.

He shook his head. 'No hev ham, no ecs.'

'You must have eggs. Listen,' said Sprout. He flapped his arms and made chicken noises and indicated where the sound of chickens was coming from.

'No ecs,' insisted the boy.

'What do you have then?'

'Brekfuss.'

'Yeah, for breakfast.'

He held up four fingers. 'Four brekfuss?'

'No, three breakfasts,' said Sprout, and added in a resigned tone of voice: 'Look, just bring us what you've got, mate.'

'Nescafé? Hot, yes?'

'Nescafé, hot, yes.'

What he had was yesterday's stale white bread, a thin sliver of margarine each, and the world's lowest form of jam – it tasted like watered-down red jelly. Any relationship it had ever had to fruit was extremely distant. The Nescafé came in glasses – it was hot and strong, made with condensed milk. I drank it gratefully and dipped my bread and jelly in it.

Sprout moaned about the quality of the meal but demolished most of the bread all the same, and then asked for more.

The Minotaur emerged from his room as the boy was bringing the extra bread, and he shouted at him in Greek. The boy answered back in a sullen tone, put the bread down and disappeared along the path that led back to where the bus had stopped. We heard his hard leather shoes against the pebbles getting further and further away.

'Nice guy to work for,' commented Mick as the big fellow, who was obviously the owner, walked past us to a pump in the vineyard and filled a plastic bucket with water. He doused water over his head, shook himself like a dog, then turned to us and was about to say something when his voice was drowned out by an ear-splitting noise. It sounded like an earthquake. We all kind of ducked, instinctively. And Sprout knocked his coffee over. The landslide noise tailed off with the sound of falling debris and was followed by a thudding *chug-chug-chug* of a heavy motor revving up.

As the noise subsided, the guy stood grinning at our reaction. 'Come!' he said, beckoning to us.

We got up gingerly from the table. He led us down a path, through a hanging curtain of vines, to where we had a view that had previously been hidden by an outcrop in the headland.

Out in the bay a dredger was at work. But a dredger like I'd never seen before – pre-war, I mean pre-World War One. It looked like it was made of solid iron, and so rusted it had turned a deep encrusted ginger all over.

'Jeez! It's an antique,' said Mick.

'What a beauty!' I said. 'How d'you think they've kept it going?'

'How old is it?' asked Mick.

The guy shrugged. 'I dunno,' he replied. 'It work good. Soon we have big boats come here.'

'That'll be a shame,' I said. 'This place is so quiet...'

The sound of another slide of pebbles instantly contradicted me. As it blasted the airwaves, we watched the avalanche fall into the waiting barge.

'Quiet no good for business,' was all the guy said, and he turned and headed back towards the taverna.

We went back to finish our breakfast, and we took

our time over it, luxuriating in the warmth of the rising sun. Some time later, the boy returned with fresh bread and the menu took an upturn. We even lashed out on another round of coffees.

By the time we'd finished, the sun was well up, and I was anxious to get down to the shore and take a closer look at those boards. I wondered when they would be open for hire. I couldn't wait to get out there and have a trial sail. But there didn't seem to be anyone in charge of them right now. As the sun moved round and lit on the shack, I found I could read the peeling words painted on the side:

STAVROS HIRE
Windsurfers — Pedaloes
Good price

I went over to the taverna owner's room and knocked on the door. He was drinking coffee and smoking a cigarette, sitting on his bed.

'Yes?'

'Who is Stavros? Where will I find him?'

'You want windsurfer?'

'Yeah.'

He got up from the bed and his face broke into a smile for the first time. He held out a hand.

'My friend. I am Stavros.'

It didn't take us long to discover that Stavros ran just about everything in the village. Donkey hire, village rooms, local telephone booth, boat hire, soft drinks, ice-creams – you name it. It seemed he had the Paradiso financial empire all to himself.

He told the boy to take us down to the boards. He was dead casual – didn't ask if we had certificates or whether we'd even surfed before. He didn't seem to care.

They were pretty dated flatboards, thick and chunky, but there was a choice of rigs. The sails were rolled so I couldn't check their condition, but there were a few that looked as if they had potential. Altogether things were looking good.

I got the boy to unroll the best-looking sail and fingered the edge of it to check its weight. It was adequate, as long as the wind didn't get up too much. But as I'd noticed earlier, the bay was pretty sheltered. We'd be likely to have more problems from calms or lulls.

'I can't wait to get out there,' I said to Mick.

'You're obsessed, man. Don't you at least want to find someplace to sleep first?'

'No, look. The wind – it's perfect. It'll probably shift round later in the day,' I lied. By the feel of it, the wind direction was unlikely to change.

Sprout was fussing about stocking up on food for lunch while the store was open. We'd had a few bad scenes in the past. Greek store-keepers generally shut for a kip between one and four – and you can get pretty hungry by four.

'Relax. It doesn't need a group outing to go shopping. Or sorting out a place to sleep, for that matter. I'm happy to leave it to you. And one of us ought to check out the surfing conditions. They might be lousy. We might want to move on.'

Again, I knew they wouldn't be. I have a pretty good gut instinct for these things, and my gut was telling me they would be radical. Just enough challenge to keep the adrenalin flowing, without getting too scary.

The others seemed content with the plan. In fact, Sprout looked really enthusiastic. He even offered to take my gear for me. He seemed in a hurry for some reason, and then as I looked across the bay, I sussed why.

There they were. The three of them, picking their way down the cliff path. The three girls we'd met on the boat last night. Scandinavian types, blondes – one in particular was quite a babe. Sprout had made a bit of a hit with her. At least, that's what he thought. Girls generally take to him, not that he's that tall or anything, but he looks a bit like Leonardo DiCaprio – hence the nickname. Well, DiCaprio does look like a sprout, doesn't he? Anyway, this tag was useful for bringing Sprout down a peg when he got carried away by his infinite pulling power.

The girls had backpacks on and were obviously heading for the campsite. 'Oh I get it,' I said. I swung my pack off my back and handed it to Sprout. 'Wouldn't want to hold you up, mate.'

Mick took the bedroll with my sleeping bag in it. I was about to hand him my bumbag too, and then I thought better of it. If the sailing was as good as I thought it was going to be, I might want a second hour and I'd need enough money on me for that. But I didn't want all my money. I tried to remember how much I had in the bag. There was enough for a couple of sails and a drink or two, anyway.

Money had been a constant problem all through our trip. We'd got pretty fed up with waiting around for banks to open – one weekend we'd spent two whole days surviving on bread and tomatoes because we'd missed the opening times. So on the last island we'd cashed all the travellers' cheques we had left. I felt pretty nervous about carrying all those drachmas around. So I'd taken one of my only pairs of socks and transferred my money into it and tied it in a knot and stashed it away in the torn bit of lining in the bottom of my sleeping bag. I reckoned it would be safer than in the bumbag.

Sprout couldn't wait to be off. The girls had already spotted him and had paused and waved. So he and Mick went off in bit of a hurry.

I turned back to the boards. Lifting one of them, I tested it for weight. It was OK. Then I ran my hand over its surface. I felt a cold shiver of expectation run through me.

If we searched the entire coastline of Greece, complete with all the ins and outs and around every one of the islands, we'd never find a place to match this. We practically had the bay to ourselves.

It was sheer perfection.

Chapter Two

I was right about the windsurfing. It was brilliant. In fact, it was about the best I'd ever experienced. So good, I stayed out all morning in the end.

The boy from the taverna had been sent down with me to unlock the boards and take the money. He counted the notes carefully and put them in his pocket. Then he picked up the board I'd selected and carried it to the water's edge. I noticed that in spite of his size he was quite muscular; he carried the board easily. He took his time walking back for the rig. In fact, he did everything at such an arrogant, leisurely pace that I got really pissed off with him.

I was literally shaking with anticipation, so I waved him away, indicating that I was perfectly happy to set up the board myself. He sat on his haunches some paces off, watching me and tossing pebbles into the sea – irritatingly enough, scoring an almost perfect duck-and-drake each time.

I tried to ignore him as I tensioned the ropes. It's all too easy to get impatient setting up – you're dying to get on the water, so you rush things and make a mess of them.

And infuriatingly, when I inserted the mast foot I got sand in and had to wrench it out and start over again. The boy watched, expressionlessly, chewing on a toothpick – I was practically willing him to go away.

All through the process, he'd kept up his deadpan vigil. But then, just as I was about to shove the board out into the water, he leapt to his feet and pushed me roughly aside.

'Wait,' he said. 'I check.'

I watched as he worked fast and nimbly, checking all the knots – he really knew his stuff.

'OK,' he said. He was treating me as if I were the kid – not him.

As I set out from the shore he watched me for a while, resting back on his haunches, judging me. And then he seemed satisfied that I knew what I was doing, and he went back up to the terrace.

Once in the water, I hauled the sail up neatly and easily. There was an instant of breathless anticipation as I turned the rig to catch the wind, and then I was off. OK, OK, I'm not going to bore you with a long account of every luff and run – suffice it to say I only fell off three times; well, four if you want to be petty about it. But that last fall was more of an emergency stop, as some idiot from the neighbouring beach, on a harness that he obviously didn't know how to use, cut in on me.

Once out from the shore, I had a good look at the surfers from the next bay. I was totally upstaged – their equipment was brilliant. From their shouts to each other I reckoned the majority of the guys were German, and by the look of it, all victims of what seems to be a German obsession – the need to own the very best and latest gear. It's a trait that sends us Brits AWOL – but I reckon that's because we're just plain envious. Those German guys didn't just have

22

harnesses, they had complete ridged bodysuits that made them look like gladiators, with the harnesses built in. All in all, surfing with them made me feel like a kid in armbands who's accidentally landed himself in a poolful of Olympic swimmers.

When I'd gone out as far as I dared, I started to do some pretty neat tacking back towards the shore.My equipment might be Stone Age, but I reckoned I could still show those prats a thing or two.

It took me an hour or so to get back into the lee-side of Paradiso bay. The dredger must've knocked off for the day because it was dead quiet. In the lighter winds I could relax and enjoy the more meditative side of windsurfing. It's not something I talk about much, but when I get into that kind of mood it's like becoming part of the elements.

Just the two – air and water – I can totally lose myself in the sound and the feel of them. Water – sluicing and rushing, licking at the board, slapping and splintering into droplets; one moment refreshingly icy on the body, the next, drying saltily in the wind. The wind, the totally sensuous wind, wrapping itself around my body – cool as I head into it, and then as I come briefly into the lee of the rig, as warm as human breath on my skin.

Typically, lost in it all, I forgot all sense of time. I didn't notice until I'd beached that the bay was deserted. The boy was nowhere to be seen. I separated the rig, rolled the sail and pulled the board well up on the sand, and then noticed the heat for the first time. The sun was at its highest point in the sky. Out at sea, deceptively cooled by the wind, I hadn't realised how hot it had got.

No doubt most people were sleeping it off in the shade. I felt angry with myself. Too many people get burned sailing in a strong breeze like I'd had this morning. I'd be lucky to get away with it. I raked out my bumbag from where I'd buried it under my clothes, and smeared on some sun cream. Too late, probably.

I wondered where the others had got to. They were probably well round the bay by now, dossed down in the shade of those acacias. I faced a long hot walk along the rocky path to the far side of the bay if I wanted to join them. Not a very inviting prospect while the midday heat raged.

On the other hand, there was a welcome patch of shade between some rocks. Come to think of it, I'd hardly slept last night. After hours sailing I was all in. Too tired to feel hungry even. I took a long draft of water from my bottle and rolled my clothes into a comfortable pillow. Within minutes I was dead to the world.

I woke feeling cold and cramped. It was pitch dark. I couldn't believe it! I'd slept right through the afternoon and into the evening. I reached for my watch and remembered that I'd left it in the pocket of my backpack. And the backpack was with Sprout. And Sprout and Mick were... God knows where.

I got to my feet and strained my eyes into the darkness. The lights of the taverna were shining down on me from the headland. In contrast, the rest of the bay seemed inky black. I moved out of their range and stared into nothing but matt-black darkness. The night was moonless and starless. It must've clouded over while I'd slept – rare in the Greek islands, but it could happen. Peering into the distance, I couldn't see any campfires or anything. The wind direction had changed and it was feeling really chilly.

I considered trying to find my way along the path to the other side of the bay where I guessed they'd be. But my torch was in my backpack, and without it I risked a headlong fall from that dodgy path.

Oh thanks a lot, guys, for leaving me here. I might have drowned as far as they were concerned. I decided there was nothing for it but to make my way up to the taverna and hope the others would turn up.

On the terrace, a group of blokes I took to be fishermen were drinking ouzo and playing dominoes. They eyed me non-committally and went on playing. I sat down at a table. Stavros, the bull-headed taverna owner, was nowhere to be seen, but the boy was there, hovering in a doorway, looking arrogantly at me. I nodded to him and he came over.

'You want?'

I wanted all right. I was ravenous. I tried to remember how much money I had left in my bumbag – not a lot. But on the other hand, as soon as the others turned up, I'd have plenty. I hoped that the range of the menu had improved since the morning.

'What have you got?'

'We have ecs,' he said.

'Fish?'

'No fish.'

'No *fish*?' I said, indicating the fishermen.

'No fish tonight,' he said. He pointed at the fisherman and looked up at the sky. I stared up to see where angry clouds were gathering. It looked as if we were in for a storm.

So I settled for egg and chips. When I'd finished the plateful I settled for another plate. As I wiped the second plate clean with my bread the wind really started to get up. Thunder rolled in the distance and with the total predictability of Greek electricity – all the lights went out.

The sudden eclipse of their game was greeted without comment by the fishermen. There was a lot of scraping of chairs and Greek farewells and they made off into the night. The boy brought a lantern, which was immediately blown out. It was some storm. I could hear the sea raging on the shore below. We were in for a rough night. What a bummer. No sleeping bag and only the shirt, T-shirt and jeans I was dressed in for warmth. I didn't even have my sweater. My sunburned skin felt hot and shivery at the same time. There was no way I could sleep out in the open on a night like this.

'Do you have a room?' I asked the boy. 'Cheap room?'

'Room? Sleep?'

I nodded.

He beckoned and I followed.

It was a pretty good room from what I could tell. Big, with a good dry concrete floor. And since the windows were covered by shutters it had retained the heat of the day. I felt my way across and found a bed. It had a mattress and a pillow and what felt like clean starched sheets.

The boy had gone ahead of me and was opening a further door.

'Private facilities,' he said in the first perfect English I'd heard him speak.

'Lush,' I said.

I leaned in and groped. It was a proper flush-down and there was a basin too – I turned a tap. Hot water! This was the ultimate in luxury. If I could scrounge a bit of soap I'd have a proper fresh-water shower and a hairwash.

'Soap?' I asked hopefully.

'Wait,' he said.

I sat on the bed luxuriating in the warmth and comfort. My full belly gurgled gratefully. I was starting to feel deliciously sleepy. I'd stopped caring how much it cost, I'd economise somehow later. The boy came back with soap and two threadbare towels.

I had the shower of a lifetime. And then I climbed into bed feeling warm and relaxed. Outside the wind howled and its sound was joined by torrential gusts of wind-blown rain. It was a good feeling to be in there, safe in the warm, listening to the sound of the weather raging through the thin roof. The sheets felt clean and wholesome against my bare skin. I even smelt good, a kind of soapy smell. Made me feel dead sexy, which started me wondering if the others had made any headway with those Nordic babes. Whether they had or not, Sprout would be bound to make a big thing of it. Sprout had elected himself the expert of our trio on sexual matters. I reckoned it was mainly boasting. I bet he hadn't got much further with a girl than Mick or I had. But I could hear him now, telling us in minute detail how one, or maybe even two, of those girls had begged to get into his sleeping bag with him because of the cold and the rain. And how epic the night had been. Good thing Mick was with him to give me a truthful account.

But then on the other hand, maybe they were all crouching under some shelter somewhere, freezing their backsides off, and dodging cold rivulets. Rain always finds a way in somehow when you're sleeping out. Huh! Serve them right – going off with my stuff like that and not even coming back to check on me or tell me where they were, or anything.

As the storm raged, I drifted in and out of sleep.

The next morning, I woke up gazing into whiteness. In the few seconds it takes the brain to readjust and recall the current situation, I thought I was back at home and it was my bedroom ceiling I was looking at. I leaned over for my watch, which wasn't there, of course. And then it all came back to me.

By the light that filtered through the cracks in the shutters I could now see that the room was large and bare. It had two narrow wooden beds, each covered with rough, homespun striped sheets, and there was an oval rag rug on the floor. Besides the beds, there was just one rickety table, a typical Greek rush-seated chair, and a bare electric light bulb hanging from the ceiling, a fly-paper sticky with corpses attached to it.

I sat up on the bed and inspected my skin condition. Luckily, I wasn't too burned from the day before. Over the two weeks we'd been in the islands, I'd built up quite a protective tan. With any luck, if I kept my shirt on for a day or so, I'd get away with it.

I went into the bathroom. It was a lot less glamorous than it had seemed the night before. The drain was a rough hole in the floor and the whitewash was flaking off the walls. My morning shower wasn't as luxurious as the night before, either. I reckoned the taverna's standard form of heating water was the sun on the tank on the roof.

Washed, dressed and back on the terrace again, I found there was little sign of last night's storm. The boy was sweeping up a few leaves with a rush broom. The wind had blown itself out in the night, and the sky was pale and clear apart from a few streaks of high, windblown cloud.

'What time is it?' I asked the boy, indicating where my wrist watch should be. He shrugged and looked at the sun.

'Six – seven?'

I'd no idea it was so early. I gazed over in the direction of the campsite. Now it was daylight, it would hardly take more than half a hour to reach it by the path. But if the others had had a rough night they wouldn't take too kindly to an early morning visit from me.

I sat down at one of the tables. I was famished again – egg and chips don't stay with you for long.

'Brekfuss?' the boy asked.

'Good idea.'

'Tost? Ecs?'

'Even better.'

'You want?'

'Anything you've got, mate.'

He brought me an ace breakfast. Two fried eggs with some slices of salami. A couple of pieces of toast, and the inevitable thick, sweet Nescafé.

I'd finished the bread and wanted more, so I walked with the plate to look for the boy. He was sitting in a room the size of a broom cupboard. He had a worn-out mattress in there. It was the sort of place you'd hardly keep a dog in.

'Could I have more bread please?'

He jumped to his feet. 'No bread. Come soon.'

'Can I have another coffee, then?'

'Coffee, yes.'

I was just finishing the second coffee when I heard the crunch of heavy footsteps. Sounded like Stavros coming back. Sure enough, he appeared from the direction of the goat track. He was carrying a loaf of bread – and I could smell its lovely fresh-baked smell. It must've still been hot from the oven.

'Ah, bread!' I said, meaningfully.

Stavros ignored me. He took one look at the plates in front of me and roared for the boy. There were some quick exchanges in Greek and the boy looked nervous. He backed away into the kitchen, and Stavros followed, slamming the kitchen door behind him. Then I heard him shouting at the boy – some kind of serious argument was going on.

I was just finishing the dregs of my coffee when Stavros strode past me again. He picked up his red plastic bucket and walked through the vines to the pump.

The boy came to me. 'He want you pay now,' he said.

'Ahh-hh,' I said, and made a big act of delving into my bumbag. I knew I was practically out of cash. At most I had five hundred drachmas or so – barely more than a pound.

'How much?'

The boy handed me a paper napkin with some rough biro calculations on it. The total came to ten thousand drachmas, a whole week's budget! My heart sank: Mick and Sprout sure had something to answer for. I was going to give them hell when they showed up.

'I pay later,' I said.

'No, now!' said the boy, looking anxiously over his shoulder in the direction of Stavros.

'I do not have money now. My friends...'

Stavros joined us at this point and caught this phrase.

His face seemed to turn black. Fire didn't actually come out of his nostrils but pretty nearly.

'You have no money?' he roared.

'No, you see, my friends...'

'What friends? Where?'

I pointed in the direction of the backpackers' camp.

'Those your friends?' He turned to the boy and shouted at him in Greek again. The boy flinched and edged away, almost falling backwards into his broom cupboard. And then Stavros swung round to me. 'No money! You pay or I get police.'

'No, you see, my friends—'

'You sit here. You eat dinner. Big brekfuss, sleep in my rooms and you have *no money*...'

'If you'd just let me go over there and get my money from my friends, I could pay you...'

'My friend,' he said, putting his face very close to mine. 'You are not leaving here. Oh no. Not leaving until you have paid.'

Oh, I got it now. He thought I was planning to do a runner. Clearly, he wasn't going to let me out of his sight until he had the money in his hand.

'OK. You'll get your money. I'll just have to wait here for my friends to come here.'

'OK,' he said, and shot me a look of total disbelief.

Chapter Three

Mick and Sprout didn't show up until around midday. I had the most awkward morning of my life – sitting feeling like a virtual prisoner while Stavros and the boy worked around me. My eye kept on sliding down to the boards. The wind had settled back into its usual direction. If this whole stupid situation hadn't come about, I'd be out there right now, gliding across the water having the *best* time.

The dredger started up around nine, and the sound of it added to the edginess of my nerves. I can tell you, by the time I sighted those two familiar figures picking their way along the path, I was pretty glad to see them.

I stood on the edge of the taverna terrace and waved both arms. I saw Mick look up, shade his eyes from the sun and then turn and say something to Sprout, who was behind him. There was something odd about the way they were moving. They looked pretty dejected. But I guess they'd had a rough night. And I wouldn't be surprised if Metaxa had come into it somewhere – Greek brandy, absolutely lethal – I never touch the stuff.

As they came within earshot, I shouted: 'Boy, am I glad to see you!'

Neither of them responded. They just climbed up the final flight of rock steps that led up on to the terrace.

'Had a good night?' I asked sarcastically as I saw the expression on their faces. Boy, did they look green.

Sprout exchanged glances with Mick, but Mick didn't say anything.

'Look, for God's sake. Where were you last night? I think at least I deserve an explanation!' I burst out.

'Listen!' said Sprout. 'Stay cool – OK?'

'Cool! If you'd like to know, I'm being held prisoner here because I didn't have my gear with me—'

'That's the thing,' cut in Mick. 'You see... our gear. It's gone.'

'Gone? Where?'

'Last night, we were having a bit of a party when the storm blew up. We would have come to get you, mate, but...' Sprout was being unusually nice to me.

'What do you mean? *Our* gear? Where's *my* gear?' I demanded.

'Look chill, man – it's probably fine. There were these guys who kind of cut in on the party and then, when the storm came, everyone split up and tried to find shelter. That's when our gear went missing... They've probably got our stuff...' said Mick.

'What d'you mean, *got our stuff*? Where the hell are they?'

'We've been searching the beach all morning...' said Sprout.

'What about my sleeping bag?' I demanded.

'Look, mate. That sleeping bag of yours. It was festering. It's no big deal!' said Mick in an exasperated tone of voice. 'At least you've got your dosh...'

I shook my head.

'You've got your bumbag – that's more than we've got,' said Sprout.

'Don't tell me they stole those too. Oh, *Jeesus*.'

'We don't exactly know they've stolen them – they may still turn up,' said Mick.

'Yeah. They're probably looking for us right now,' agreed Sprout. But I could tell from his voice that he didn't have much faith in the idea.

'Fat chance!' I said.

'Yeah, well. You may have to tide us over. Till we, like – catch up with them.'

I spoke very slowly: 'My dosh – was in my sock – and my sock – was in the bottom – of my sleeping bag.'

'I think I'm going to throw up,' said Sprout.

Mick sank down on to a chair.

The dredger slid another earsplitting torrent of stones into the sea, tactfully blotting out the puking noises Sprout was making behind the vines.

'Wha's goin' on?' demanded Stavros, who had arrived in time to shoo Sprout further away from the terrace. 'Where's my money?' he added, slamming a fist down on the table.

When I explained to Stavros what had happened, and it had become clear to him that he wasn't going to get his money, he called the police. Well, that saved us the job anyway – we needed to report what had been stolen. After that, Stavros disappeared inside. We could hear his voice through the walls as he interrogated the boy. The boy replied in monosyllables. He didn't sound arrogant any more. He sounded as if he was practically crying. I felt really bad about it. It wasn't the boy's fault.

I went and hovered by the open door, wondering if I should intervene.

Stavros looked up and demanded: 'What you want?'

'You can't blame him—' I blurted out.

But Stavros slammed the door in my face.

Later I heard the sound of the boy's hard leather shoes on the steps going down to the harbour. I got up and looked over the side of the terrace. He had a bundle with him – looked like clothes. With a sinking feeling, I reckoned he'd been fired. If he had, it was definitely my fault. God, I felt a heel.

We sat miserably waiting for the police to arrive, ranged in an irritable group around a table. As we sat there, I managed to extract from the others a half-hearted account of the night before.

For once Sprout didn't try and make out that he was the world's greatest gift to womankind since Casanova. He admitted that the tall blonde – the one he'd thought fancied him – didn't want to know when he tried to make a move on her. He reckoned she was in with the guys who'd cut in on them. It was a set-up job. The guys had arrived on mopeds and they seemed to know their way around. Then later, in the confusion, when Sprout discovered our stuff had been nicked, the girls were nowhere to be seen. Mick reckoned they'd gone off on the back of the scooters and got away along the coast road, in spite of the storm. They could even have caught the night boat out of the port.

'But you must know something about them?' I said.

'They were blonde. One was tall and pretty and the other two were average,' said Mick.

'You didn't ask their names, even? Where they were from?'

'When you're chatting a girl up, you don't ask for her passport,' said Sprout. 'I think the big one was called Anna. The others could have been called anything. They were bad news, anyway.'

When I realised I wouldn't get any more information out of them, we lapsed into silence. Sprout had one hell of a hangover and kept going over to the garden pump to douse his head with water. Mick just sat there, twanging the elastic which held the paper tablecloth down – he was driving me crazy.

At around two in the afternoon, a rich smell of some kind of stew came from the kitchen. I avoided the others' eyes. We were all ravenous. Stavros appeared, tantalisingly standing in the kitchen doorway wiping his mouth on the back of his hand. He must've seen our hungry expressions because he came back a few minutes later with a round loaf of stale-looking bread and a bottle of mineral water, and slammed them on the table.

'You eat – OK?' he said without smiling or anything.

Ignoring his charity, I got up from the table. 'Where's the boy gone?' I asked.

'What boy?'

'The Greek boy who said I could stay here.'

'He not Greek boy. He Albanian,' said Stavros, and he held a finger up to his temples and added dismissively: 'Stupid Albanian.'

Well, I don't know that much about politics but I'd seen enough in the papers to realise that the Albanians had had a pretty rough time recently. I thought Stavros was totally out of line.

'You shouldn't have fired him. It wasn't his fault,' I said.

'You tell me how to do my job?' demanded Stavros. He loomed over me.

The others looked on.

'Cool it, Ben,' whispered Mike. But I stood my ground.

'How was he to know I didn't have any money?'

'You listen,' said Stavros, bringing his face uncomfortably close to mine. I got a waft of the garlic from his stew straight in my face. 'I tell him, any boy, any man, any woman, want to sleep here, I want to see money first — or passport. That is the rule. He break it. He stupid. No good. See?'

'Yeah, but... I mean, the storm...'

'No *but*. He stupid. No good. He gone.'

Stavros shook his head dismissively and went back into the kitchen.

I slumped down on a chair and tore off a bit of bread. I'd done what I could. Hadn't done a lot of good. Hadn't done *any* good. But I wasn't exactly in a bargaining position.

I chomped thoughtfully on the crust. It tasted great — must've been the loaf he'd brought back with him earlier. The one I'd smelt while it was still hot... the one

I'd smelt a lifetime ago when I was carefree and on holiday… when I had money and a passport and mates who didn't look as if they'd just been kicked in the stomach… and the prospect of weeks of perfect windsurfing ahead of me…

God – to have our stuff nicked like that – it made my blood boil.

We travelled back to the port in style. Police escort. They didn't actually put handcuffs on me but they looked as if they'd have liked to.

We sat forever in their stuffy little office making statements. And then we waited even longer while they filled out endless forms and got us to sign them. Dad had told me never to sign anything I hadn't read – but Greek script? I don't think he'd anticipated a situation like this.

They photocopied all the forms and gave us copies to keep. Then they handed each of us an official piece of paper which would stand in, temporarily, for our stolen passports.

Darkness had fallen by the time we walked out into the open air, free men.

'What do you think happens about that Stavros guy at the taverna?' asked Mick. 'Do you think he'll get compensation?'

I shrugged. 'Doubt it.'

I didn't care about the guy – didn't matter whether he got the money or not. It was what happened to the boy that bothered me.

'So...' said Mick. 'What now?'

'S'pose we'd better ring home and get the olds to bale us out,' said Sprout.

Mick looked really pissed off. His dad had a fearful temper – he'd give him hell.

I wasn't looking forward to calling my parents either. Not that they'd fly off the handle or anything, but they'd be so disappointed – for me as much as anything. I'd worked my arse off to earn the money for this trip. Six weeks on double shifts in a fast food kitchen. I'd only just managed to wash the smell of the place out of my hair.

'All I want is to get shot of this place,' said Mick.

Sprout nodded. 'Likewise. Doesn't feel like a holiday any more.'

'What you thinking of doing – hitching a lift home?' I asked sarkily.

'Get the olds to send out some money and fly back,' said Sprout.

'That'll take days,' I pointed out. 'What do we do in the meantime? Drink tap water, suck stones? We don't even have our sleeping bags.' I kicked at some rubbish in the gutter and stubbed my toe.

'Uh-uh,' said Sprout. 'I've just had a brainwave! Mum's Barclaycard! I've got a second card on hers.'

'You don't mean to say you've had it in your pocket all along?' groaned Mick.

'Not exactly. The card's gone, too. But I've gotta report it. And remember all those commercials?' He did a quick impression of Rowan Atkinson making sucking noises. 'If I call the Helpline, they should send us some dosh.'

'Genius! Where? How? What do they have – carrier pigeons?' demanded Mick, getting to his feet.

'They send it to a bank, stupid,' said Sprout.

The banks were closed, but the Tourist Office was open and it had a Visa sign outside and a notice which said they changed money.

The tourist people pulled out all the stops. They let Sprout use their phone to ring the Helpline, and by some sort of telegraphic magic, faxes started to roll out of their machine. Eventually a wadge of money was handed over.

'So,' said Sprout as he counted through the notes. 'What say we get on the night ferry? We could even get a decent kip if we sleep inside.'

'And we can get a hot meal,' said Mick.

I didn't say anything.

'And beers – they're on me by the way,' said Sprout. He slapped me on the shoulder. 'Cheer up. We'll be in Athens by the morning. Nice brekkie at the airport and then we'll get a flight home. You can be tucked up in your own bed with your teddy by tomorrow night.'

I shook my head. 'Let's have a beer first and think about it.'

'What's there to think about? The ferry leaves in half an hour. We can have a drink on board.'

Both of them started walking in the direction of the jetty. The ferry was waiting there with all its

41

bright rows of lights shining invitingly.

I hung back. 'Wait,' I said.

'What's up?'

I shrugged. 'Maybe I don't feel ready to leave yet.'

Mick looked me up and down. 'What you gonna do, mate? Take up begging?'

The island bus had arrived. It was standing at the terminal. I could hear the faint jangle of bazouki music coming from the driver's open window. It had its engine running, waiting for the last late passengers of the day.

'Look, guys – give me some of the money,' I said suddenly. 'I mean, lend it to me...'

The bus was hooting, preparing to make off.

'You mad? What you thinking of, man?' demanded Sprout as I stripped ten thousand drachmas off his roll.

'There's something I've got to do. Look, I'll see you, OK? Tell my parents I'll ring – not to worry – I'll keep in touch.' This last phrase was delivered at a run.

The bus driver was closing the doors. I forced my body through as they slammed shut.

My last view of Mick and Sprout was their two figures standing in the road looking bemused. Mick held up a hand and Sprout put a finger up to his head indicating that I was screwy.

I grinned out of the rear window, then sank into a seat.

I was the only person on the bus.

The driver turned the joyful clatter of the music up a few notches and turned to me with a slow smile. 'My friend. Where you go?'

I handed him a note.

'To the very end,' I shouted over the music.

'Ahhh,' he said. 'Paradiso.'

Chapter Four

Paradiso – paradise.

The place was in darkness when I arrived. I peered at my wrist and then remembered that my watch wasn't there – but it must be pretty late.

I made my way quietly down the rough track to the taverna. The ragged row of coloured light bulbs that decorated the frontage was turned off, but there was a light on in the little kitchen and I could hear sounds coming from inside. I crept up to the window and peered in.

Stavros was washing up. At least, there was a great pile of dirty glasses and dishes beside him and he was thrashing stuff about in a plastic bowl. He swung round and his elbow caught a teetering pile of plates. They smashed to the floor and broke into a thousand pieces. Stavros swore emphatically and unintelligibly in Greek. There was a bottle behind him – he turned, filled a glass and drank. I realised he was pretty drunk. Not happy drunk but mad, furious, raging drunk – frightening – he was such a big bloke. Anyone could see that right now was not the best time to approach him.

I crept further round and looked in from the other side, wondering if the boy was back or whether I'd been right in assuming he'd been fired. There was no-one about. But there was a light showing under the door of the room I'd slept in the night before and a murmur of voices coming from inside. And then laughter. A girl's laughter. So someone was staying there.

I remembered the warmth in that room and the comfortable bed. I hugged my arms around me. Greek nights could be chilly, even in midsummer. I'd have to find somewhere sheltered to sleep. I decided to leave it till morning to tackle Stavros.

I spent a terrible night. I don't think the chickens enjoyed it much, either. Having a large unwashed male in their shack must've made the poor old biddies uneasy. They'd all get off to sleep, perched side by side with their feathers fluffed out, heads under their wings, then one of them would suddenly remember and shout: 'Oh-my-God-there's-a-man-in-here' – or the chicken equivalent – and they'd all flap and shriek and cluck disapprovingly until they settled down again.

But I must've fallen into a heavy sleep around dawn because when I finally got up, the sun was already quite high in the sky. Luckily no-one had come to feed the chickens. As I emerged into the warm sunlight I wasn't sure which of us smelt worse – but the chickens seemed pretty glad to see the back of me.

I made my way around the headland to the beach – a swim was definitely in order. Stripping off to my shorts, I hid my clothes under a rock. Maybe I was getting paranoid but I didn't want to get robbed again.

The water was that perfect temperature – just cool enough to make you hesitate going in, cool enough for a good brisk swim. I walked in to waist height and then dived under. The sea closed over my head and rang in my ears, and I swam forward underwater and opened my eyes. I could see the surface above me like a second sky, and then I broke through it, shook the water out of my hair and swam as hard as I could out into the bay. I'm a pretty strong swimmer. I got my two-kilometre certificate early on, and the olds had insisted I did a life-saving course when I took up windsurfing. I've never been able to understand people who are scared of water. It seems like a natural habitat to me.

I swam out for about half an hour and then turned and looked back, treading water. The houses in the village had shrunk to the size of those little china models you get in Greek gift shops. Now I could make out the shape of the hills. I knew the island was volcanic. But from out where I was, I could see that the cliffs must have been part of the edge of a crater. That explained why the sand on the beach was black. The cliffs looked red and scorched, burned to a dull clinker grey in places, like the inside of hell. They made a pretty dramatic contrast to the sunlit blue of the sea. Paradise – that's what they called the place. Ironic maybe.

I could just make out the terrace of the taverna. Barely discernable human shapes were moving on it – people reduced to the size of ants. Bright clothing, so females most probably. One of them might be the girl who'd been in my room the night before. I remembered the laughter – she'd sounded quite young… Nice young laughter. Hmmm… I wondered who she was with. I wondered what she looked like. Slowly and easily I started to breaststroke back to the shore. By the time I reached it, I was going to be in need of breakfast. I wondered if the girl would still be there, on the terrace.

I dragged my T-shirt over my head and shoved my jeans on over my wet shorts.

Now for the confrontation. I hoped that Stavros had recovered from his mood of the night before. It would be just my luck if he had a blinding hangover. I made my way up the steps to the terrace, walking firmly and trying to look confident.

There was no-one there. The people I'd seen, whoever they were, must've left. No sign of the boy either. Stavros emerged from the kitchen with a grubby looking tea towel in his hand. He scowled at me. He did look pretty hung over, actually.

'You back again!' he said. 'What you want?'

I stood my ground. 'Where's the Albanian boy?'

'Why you wan' know?' Stavros came a few steps closer.

I took the notes out of my pocket, counted out the money I owed him and placed it on the table between us.

'Would you take him back if I pay you what I owe?'

Stavros looked at the money and then back at me, obviously hesitating between the urge to pick it up and the climb-down that implied.

'That boy no good. He poison my guests.'

'Oh come off it!' As an excuse, this sounded somewhat excessive.

'Yes, I tell him. You make café frappé – always use

bottle water. Boiled water OK hot coffee. Frappé always bottle water. He think he know better. American peoples very sick – they leave.'

'Well, OK. But a guy can make a mistake.'

'Then you come. Backpackers, I say, always money upfront. Otherwise, *pouff*!' Stavros made a gesture like a backpacker disappearing into a cloud of dope-scented smoke. 'Gone in morning, never see money, never see nothing.'

'Yeah, but that night – the storm. You wouldn't've sent a dog out in it.'

'Backpackers worse than dogs,' said Stavros angrily, eyeing the money again.

I just lost it at that point. There was this greedy, over-fed bastard about to pocket my money and he wouldn't even give the poor little guy a second chance.

'Take it then,' I said. 'Take the money. I hope you're satisfied. You don't deserve to have anyone working for you. I hope you have to do all the washing up and sweeping up and... cleaning the lavatories and... and...' I ran out of ideas.

Stavros picked up the notes and counted them carefully with his back to me.

'...and make brekfuss?' he asked, swinging round to face me.

'Yeah, that too...' I said.

I hadn't noticed the twinkle in his eye.

'You want brekfuss?'

'That's all the money I've got.'

'Siddown,' he said.

He was crashing around in the kitchen for a while.

I sat down, feeling dizzy from hunger. I hadn't eaten the night before – and what with the swim and everything...

Stavros re-emerged with breakfast for a king! A huge omelette, plenty of bread, a tub of yogurt and a glass of milk.

'On the house,' he said in answer to my expression.

Then he went and sat at the next table with a tiny cup of gritty Greek coffee, and watched while I wolfed the food down.

'Hungry, eh?'

I nodded and continued eating. The omelette was brilliant – reckon it might have had something to do with my hostesses of the night before... Really fluffy, golden yellow and full of flavour.

'Where your friends?' Stavros asked after a while.

'Gone back to England.'

He nodded thoughtfully, swilling his coffee round and taking sips.

'What you do now?'

'What d'you mean?'

'You got no money. You got nothing. Nowhere to stay.'

'I dunno. Maybe I'll go home like the others. Maybe I'll stay – look for work...'

He stared into the dregs in his cup.

'You want work here?' he asked abruptly.

'For you?'

He nodded.

Suddenly, there it was – the answer to everything. To stay at the taverna – work for my keep – it was such a tempting thought. But the idea was lousy. I couldn't do that – and live with myself.

'You mean... do the Albanian boy's job? No, I'm not taking his job from him.'

'I no take that boy back anyway,' he said.

I paused and took another sip of milk. 'What will happen to him?'

Stavros shrugged. 'He find something. Albanians – they find work. Albanians do anything.'

'Yeah, but it doesn't seem right. He lost his job because of me.'

Stavros leaned forward. 'Listen, my friend. Ten, twenty years ago – Greek men, no work in farming, no work in fishing – we go everywhere. Everywhere in the world you find Greek men, wait at tables, wash dishes, clean floors. In America, Australia, England – every country. Then, when tourists come – Greeks have plenty money. All change. Now it's the Albanians – their turn, go work for everyone – everywhere...'

Those last words were delivered with some satisfaction. After Stavros' little lecture on world economics I felt worse, if anything. But I had the sense to realise there was no way he was going to take that boy back. If I didn't take the job, someone else would get it.

'What would I have to do?' I asked. I couldn't help my eyes sliding round to the windsurfers, piled up there, idle on the beach.

'First thing, make brekfuss, clean tables, change beds, maybe. Then morning, sit on beach, take money for windsurfers – watch surfers not drown and lose boards. Evening, serve drinks, more clean tables.

No cooking. I do cooking. Nice job, free food, free bed.'

'In there?' I asked, indicating the broom cupboard where the boy had slept.

''Is good room,' said Stavros. 'Warm, clean, dry.'

'Yeah,' I said with a grin. 'Well equipped.' Still, my standards had gone down somewhat since the accommodation of the night before.

'Good room! Better than beach,' protested Stavros.

'I can't stay long. I have to get back by September.'

'Fine. Now is August – is now I need help – in high season.'

I had to suppress a smile at this. Some 'high season' – Paradiso wasn't exactly teeming with tourists.

'So how much will you pay me?' I asked, leaning forward and looking him in the eye.

'Four thousand drachmas a day.'

According to my lightning calculations that was less than ten pounds. 'That's slave labour!' I said.

'Is what?'

'Not enough.'

'My friend – take it, or leave it.' Stavros sat back in his chair and stared into the distance.

My eyes slid back to the stacked windsurfers. 'What about using the boards?'

'Windsurfers? I seen you, I watch. You good sailor. In afternoon, when cabin is closed, you surf – all you like.'

'For free?'

'My friend... who will be there to take the money?'

'It's a deal!'

I couldn't believe it! I couldn't believe my luck. A job

and a roof over my head and food and FREE
WINDSURFING!

Oh boy, wait till the others heard about this!

Chapter Five

Stavros let me use his phone to call my parents. They'd already heard the news of the theft through the parental bush telegraph. Dad sounded pretty fed up with me.

'What did I tell you about sticking to travellers' cheques?'

'Yeah, we did to start with. But we kept missing the bank...'

'Well, it's your money, Ben...'

'Don't remind me.'

I could hear Mum trying to grab the phone from him.

'He's fine...' Dad's voice was reassuring her.

'When's he coming back?' I heard her ask.

Stavros was frowning at me.

'Listen, Dad. I can't talk for long. It's someone's phone. I've got a job. I can earn enough to pay my way. And I'm sorting out a refund on my air ticket.'

'A what?'

The line was lousy.

'Look. I'm fine. I'm staying. I'll call you again from a better phone, OK?'

The line gave up entirely at that point and there was a deafening buzzing sound. I hung up.

'OK?'

'OK.'

Stavros looked as though he thought I ought to

pay him for the call. So I started work right away by doing my own washing up. Then I had to clean down the tables and hose the terrace. Stavros watched critically from a comfortable vantage point, on a chair in the shade. From time to time he made the odd comment.

Once the terrace was spotless enough to eat off, he took me round the back and showed me how to sort through the empty bottles and stack them in crates for collection. The delivery lorry was coming that evening – a fact which might have helped him come to a speedy decision about employing me. It was OK carrying the crates of empties down the track to the square, but something told me the full ones would be a different matter. No wonder the Albanian boy had muscles – this job was going to do the world for my pecs.

As soon as I'd finished, Stavros took me down to the beach. He unlocked the shack and showed me how to fill in the hire books for the windsurfers. A glance down the pages told me that it wasn't exactly going to be a hectic job. I was the only person who'd hired a windsurfer in the past three days.

Stavros saw me looking.

'The surfers – they go round next bay. Big resort, Germans, plenty money – only want new windsurfers...' he said with a grimace.

'Really?' I wondered if they had funboards.

'These good boards – strong,' said Stavros, catching my expression and slapping the top of the pile. 'I buy the best.'

'Yeah, sure,' I said. I noticed the look of hurt pride

in his eyes and didn't have the heart to ask: 'When?'.
Things move so fast in board design, a small guy like
Stavros wouldn't have the cash to invest in the latest
technology. Progress had simply passed him by.

I spent the morning sitting on a decaying canvas chair
beside the shack, waiting for the would-be
windsurfers to show up. I knew no-one would. At one
point, a group of bearded hippy-type backpackers
ambled up and looked at the boards and said a few
patronising things. One of them tried to beat me
down on the price of a session. I had the impression
he'd tried this before, because Stavros had drummed
into my head that this just wasn't on. So the guys told
me to 'get a life' and went off, laughing and throwing
the stubs of their roll-ups into the sea. I didn't like the
look of them. They reminded me only too vividly of
how I'd got ripped off. Every time I glanced at where
my watch had been, I felt a wave of futile anger.

For the first couple of hours the wind was perfect.
The pain of it! I sat tormented by the thought of how
brilliant the windsurfing would be out there. Every
muscle in my body ached to be on the board, feeling
the water under my feet, moving, alive – like riding
bareback on something wild. Harnessing the strength
of the wind and taming it. Not forcing it – but going
along with it – my whole body totally into it... Yeah
well, I can get a bit carried away at times.

The longing to sail was like a dull ache inside. How
could I just sit here until the afternoon? What if the
wind dropped? It was so frustrating. I tried to move

my mind off the subject and started fantasising about how I would run the place if I were Stavros...

The first thing I'd do is set up this workshop in one of those old fishing huts – the derelict ones I'd seen from the terrace. We'd make these custom boards which were epic – legendary – speedboards and needleboards or totally revolutionary waveboards, or maybe boards tunnelled out underneath like catamarans – something totally radical anyway – all made to my own unique designs. I could see the logo for the company now, *Ben-B*, embossed in a funky way. Yeah, it would be brilliant, we even had the next bay where those speed freaks could test them. We'd get TV coverage and everything. Maybe stage a Windsurfer Olympics here.

Sure, I'd need a workforce. And that was best thing about it. I'd fill the workshop with Albanians and pay them really good wages. And all the Greeks would be dead jealous. That way I could make it up to the boy. I'd use him to recruit the workforce – he'd know where to get the guys, and he could interpret too. Man – the idea was foolproof!

I was so carried away with the whole concept that I was even trying to work out how much profit I'd make and what I'd do with it...

Slowly, I came to my senses and wondered what the time was. My stomach was suggesting it was around lunchtime. In the absence of a watch, it was going to be tricky knowing when to knock off. I searched the horizon for signs of surfers from the next bay. There wasn't a sail to be seen. The sea had turned to a limpid turquoise, the kind of colour you see on tourist postcards and never believe possible. And I realised why, with a hollow feeling – the wind had dropped.

It was totally unlikely that any would-be windsurfers would come now, so I locked up the shack and made my way up the steps to the taverna.

Everything seemed to be closed up. I went towards Stavros' door and was about to knock when I was greeted by the sound of deep and very impressive snores. Not a good idea to wake him. But he'd promised food –'bed and food', that's what he'd said. I went into the kitchen and found some bread, a cold meat ball, and a tomato.Then I took a Fanta from the fridge and carried everything back to a table.

Sounds were coming from the room the women had taken, voices. I remembered the girl, the girl who I'd heard laughing the night before. I still hadn't set eyes on her – well, not close up anyhow. She wasn't laughing now. I could hear her voice rising and falling and another lower, older voice cutting in. They were having some sort of argument. Women, eh!

I sliced the tomato and the meatball thinly and made a kind of sandwich. Greek country bread doesn't take too kindly to this kind of treatment and it was a two-handed job eating it. And yeah – the tomato did spurt out right down my chin. Just as I was groping for something to mop up the damage, I heard footsteps coming from inside the women's door. I shot into the kitchen – didn't want my first introduction to this potential love-goddess with my face covered in tomato.

But it wasn't a girl who came out. It was an older

woman. She had a sunhat on and a bag under her arm and a very determined look on her face. She strode across the terrace and headed off in the direction of the bus stop. I waited for the girl to follow, but nothing happened. Their door stayed closed.

I glanced at my reflection in the spotted mirror Stavros kept above the sink, for the purpose of shaving by the look of it. I was unshaven and still salty from this morning's swim – my salt-caked hair was standing on end the way it used to when I was a kid – the way I hated. I looked a joke. I turned on the tap and it made some half-hearted coughing noises. No water came out. Typical, just when I could do with a wash!

I slunk back to the terrace, eyeing the girl's door, hoping that she wouldn't come out now. Not with me looking so wrecked. Then I went across to my broom cupboard. I ripped the sheet off the bed and noted the unsavoury nature of the mattress. But in my present state I didn't have too much to boast about in that direction either. So I took a clean sheet off a pile on the shelf and wrapped it round the mattress with a silent prayer that nothing would leap out and bite me. Then I dossed down for an illicit afternoon snooze.

I don't think I could've slept for long. I was woken by a shutter rattling irritatingly back and forth. I sat bolt upright. The wind had got up again!

No fireman could have rushed to the scene of a fire with the speed at which I hit that beach. I literally abseiled down the steps to the waiting boards. I held up a hand in the wind – yeah right, the direction was perfect. Brilliant! I could see the surfers from the neighbouring beach already heading out to sea. *Ideal* conditions, by the look of it.

They were. I had an epic afternoon. Went out much further to the left of the bay this time – I wanted to investigate the harbour side. Came across this island. Well, you could hardly call it an island really, it was hardly more than a rock. I tacked past it a couple of times to get a better look. It had a chapel with a tree beside it for shade and a minute beach – it was a *wicked* place.

Rounding the island once more, I glanced back towards the shore to check my direction. Hang on. There was someone there, on my beach, stretched out on the sand. A girl. I came to the end of a tack and gybed. Yeah, a girl in a bikini, long hair. Nice! Laid out on a towel, sunbathing not far from the shack.

What was she doing on my beach? I gybed again. Yeah, as I grew closer I could see she was definitely a babe – very nice indeed. She wasn't looking in my direction. At least, I didn't think so. She had sunglasses on, so it was hard to tell. I gybed again and felt convinced she was looking my way this time, which made me lose my concentration for a moment. I nearly did the most humiliating thing that can possibly happen when you're being watched – a catapult fall. I regained my balance with an awkward wobble.

Once I'd got my equilibrium back, I tried to get a better view of her without being too obvious, by peering through the sail window. A water-spattered sail window is fine for checking your general direction, not so hot on assessing the potential of a

59

female. I gybed again. Nice long legs, by the look of them, and reddish hair. I felt convinced now – it must be the girl from the taverna – the one who'd laughed. But where was the other one? The older woman – her mother maybe – she'd gone off on the bus somewhere. That's why the girl was alone.

I gybed again. I was getting really near the shore now. Still couldn't be sure whether or not she'd seen me. I now could make out that she had a Walkman on – she might have her eyes closed – she might even be asleep, for all I knew. I wondered how long she'd been there. She looked pretty red actually. Maybe when I got to the shore I should warn her to get out of the sun.

I did a last gybe – I had to be really, really careful not to make a fool of myself coming into the beach – always a tricky manoeuvre. Step off too far out and you can find yourself upside down, or up to your neck. Leave it too late and you can run aground – or even break the skeg.

I made a dream landing, although I say it myself – straight out of the book – stepped off the board really professionally. I glanced casually over to the girl to see if she was impressed.

She'd turned over. *She hadn't even been looking*.

I had to walk past her several times as I stacked the board and stowed the rig. She was lying sunbathing face down, so I got a good look at her. Really nice body. Fabulous legs, nice smooth back, kind of modelly look about her shoulderblades. Skin not so sunburnt this side. So I didn't really have the excuse to start up a conversation – not without admitting I'd been staring at her from the sea at any rate.

As I locked the shack, I sneaked another glance. Lovely shiny hair. Wonder if she was such good news on the front side. She'd looked fine from out at sea but that was a long way off. I kind of willed her to turn over. But no such luck.

I spent more time than absolutely necessary securing the boards. But she seemed intent on whatever she was listening to on that Walkman – or perhaps she'd fallen asleep again. Maybe I should wake her? What would I say? Maybe I should warn her about getting burned? Not exactly the coolest introduction. Let's face it – did she really want to get woken up by a guy saying something as pathetic as that?

In the end, I just left it and set off up the steps to the taverna, telling myself in no uncertain terms: 'Forget it, Ben Bernard. That girl is gorgeous. You don't stand a chance in hell. She wouldn't even want to know.'

Chapter Six

Stavros was standing waiting for me at the top of the steps with his arms folded. 'Where you been?'

'Not late back, am I?' I asked innocently.

He pointed at his watch. 'Six o'clock. Peoples come maybe for drinkses.'

'Sorry, I don't have a watch. Anyway, I can't see anyone.'

'I say *maybe*,' said Stavros. 'And I want you to go, get bread.'

'Look, there was no water at lunchtime. Can't I at least have a shower first?'

'Shower, OK. Good idea,' said Stavros. 'Get clean up before you serve guests.' He leant into the kitchen and handed me a bar of soap and a clean but worn towel.

'So where's the bathroom?' I asked.

He beckoned to me to follow him and led me down a concrete path between the vines. At the end of the path there was a building that had the unmistakable architectural style of an outdoor khazi. It had some sort of tank on the roof, and a hose leading from it disappeared through the gap above the doorway.

'In there,' he said.

I was dead right in my identification. It was a lavatory – one of those ingeniously economical Greek ones – a ceramic tray with two worn boot shapes indicating where your feet should go, and an evil smelling hole in between. The 'shower' was another masterpiece of economy. When you took the bung out of the end of the hose, water from the tank above shot out all over your body.

It took a few minutes to master the intricacies of the plumbing. Bung out for water – which was scalding hot incidentally (the sun had been on the tank all day). Bung in: soap body and head. Bung out again: wash off soap. All this was done in a flash and the 'bathroom' was sluiced out – all at the same time.

I emerged into the open again, towelling myself down. I could see plenty of advantages from Stavros' point of view. As a staff cleansing system it was economical on time, too – showering was not something I was going to take long over.

However, I did feel a lot happier once I was dry and clothed again. I decided to give shaving a miss for another day – in fact, in the absence of a razor I didn't have much choice in the matter.

Back up at the taverna, I leaned into the kitchen and asked Stavros: 'So where do I get bread from?'

Stavros chewed and swallowed. He was having a little snack and a glass of ouzo to tide him over until his next meal. A frequent habit by the look of him. He didn't offer me any, though.

'My friend,' he said, taking me by the shoulder. 'You see that path, through the olive trees?'

I nodded.

'The bakery is that way. Just keep going and you get there.'

'Right – OK.'

As I set out, the sun was already low in the sky. I could see it was going to be an epic sunset. The heat of the day had reduced to around blood heat; the temperature had come to a perfect balance between the inside of my body and the outside. The air had that wonderful Greek smell, a mixture of thyme and pine with an odd dry sweetness underneath, faintly musky, like cat's fur. I swung my arms loosely in it, savouring the sheer pleasure of the moment. The end of the day, a body tired but clean, a meal of some kind to look forward to and then tomorrow – *more windsurfing*. But something else was adding a background rosy glow to my sense of anticipation...

Oh yes – the girl! Maybe she'd be there when I got back.

I decided mentally to record this walk and add it to my select list of 'Very Best Moments of my Life'. I'm making a kind of memory bank of these. So that later, one day when I'm past it, say, I can call them up and enjoy them all over again. Kind of a nice alternative to photography and you don't have the bother of carrying a camera around with you.

The bakery was quite a walk, a mile at least, but a mile with views that made me want the walk to last forever. The building was at the very edge of the next bay, the highest in the village. It was just a rough, whitewashed house like the others, and its faded blue washed door was propped open with a stone. It didn't have a sign outside or anything. It didn't need one. The delicious fresh bread smell that wafted out through the doorway served as sign and poster and TV commercial all in one.

Inside, it was brightly whitewashed. The oven itself was the traditional kind – just a semi-circular hole cut into the thick wall which closed with a heavy iron door. The kind of oven they'd most probably baked bread in since Ancient Greece. It was open and I could feel the heat of the furnace on my face. There was a bustling movement from a further room and a woman came through carrying a set of iron bread pans filled with uncooked dough.

'*Kalispera*,' she called to me as she deftly slid the pans into the oven and slammed the door shut.

She was a big woman, with a bosom of the kind that had always puzzled me – just one piece that went straight across like a massive shelf. I always wondered what women like this could be like, underneath.

'What you want?' she asked with a smile, catching up a stray curl of her dark hair and slipping it back into the net that must've been designed to keep her hair out of the way while she was baking. There was something almost flirtatious about the way she turned and held a hand out to her shelves of plump round golden loaves.

'They're for the taverna – the Paradisos?' I said, as I'd been directed by Stavros.

In an instant's hesitation she looked me up and down. Immediately, I thought she must be wondering what had happened to the Albanian boy. It must have been his job to fetch the bread.

'I'm new – I work for Stavros.'

'Ah!' she said and smiled again. 'For Stavros.'

She walked over to a further shelf where two loaves were waiting. I could tell by the way she walked that she was proud of her one-piece bust, and as she turned her back on me I noted that she had a one-piece bottom shelf to match. But what really caught my eye were her feet. Her legs kind of tapered off to tiny little feet. She was wearing shiny black shoes with dumpy heels and on the back of each heel there was a seductive little bow.

She caught me looking and smiled again. She obviously thought I was impressed by her little feet. And I suppose I was, in a way – they looked far too small to support a woman of her size.

She wrapped the bread in sheets of white paper and handed me the two loaves.

'For Stavros,' she said, showing off her dimples. She was really quite pretty for such a big woman.

'Thank you.'

'*Yassos,*' she called after me. It was the old Greek greeting, the equivalent of 'God bless you'. Not something you'd ever hear in England these days.

I took the path back, hugging the warm loaves to my chest. The smell was so tantalising, I was tempted to tear a piece off and eat it. But I didn't want to push my luck on my first day.

Walking back through the olive grove the crickets were making a terrific racket – quite an evening concert. The sun was really low now, it had turned the sky a flamingo pink and olive trees stood out

66

against it – gnarled silhouettes like so many witches out of a Walt Disney movie.

Quite suddenly, a shadow detached itself from the trees.

'Pssht! Hey! English boy!'

It was the Albanian. I came to a halt not knowing what to say. I wondered if he knew I'd got his job. Maybe he was thinking of attacking me. He was a skinny boy but he had plenty of muscle on him.

I waited as he came towards me along the path.

'What do you want?' I asked. I was on my guard.

'Nothing,' he said.

He wasn't going to attack me. He looked dejected, beaten. He stood there, avoiding my eyes.

'Look,' I started. 'I feel really bad about what happened...'

He stared at me uncomprehendingly. Maybe his English wasn't so good.

'I only came back to give Stavros the money I owed him,' I started again.

He still didn't seem to understand. His eyes kept sliding back to the bag of bread I was carrying.

Oh my God, I suddenly realised the boy was hungry. Without a job he probably hadn't had anything to eat all day.

I tore open the paper. To hell with Stavros. I broke off half of one of the loaves and handed it to him. He took the bread and just stood there holding it. He didn't say thank you or anything. He was obviously too proud to eat it in front of me.

I paused, uncertain about what to say next, and then I blurted out: 'Look, if you want bread, come here again tomorrow, same time.'

He shrugged as if to say 'maybe'.

Now I felt embarrassed, as if I'd offered charity. 'OK. I'd better be off. See you.' I started off again down the path.

But he whispered again: 'Pssht, English boy. You find my knife?'

'Knife, no. What knife?'

'Knife. In my room. You find it. Give me, yes?'

'OK,' I said, and turned and walked on.

So he did know I'd got his job. He'd probably been watching me all day from some hiding place on the cliff. He wanted his knife – what for? Some chilling thoughts ran through my brain. Maybe he was planning to knife me in the back. Then I put them right out of my head. He was only a boy for God's sake. I wondered where he was sleeping tonight and remembered my night in the chicken coop. Well, it wasn't my problem. The nights weren't *that* cold at this time of year. He'd be OK.

But I still felt bad about it.

My mind was still going over this awkward encounter as I approached the taverna. But that evening there was a brilliant sunset. The sky was putting on a royal command performance – all bloody behind a ridge of thin grey cloud. As I covered the last few hundred metres, I tried to put the boy out of my mind and regain a bit of the euphoric mood I'd had earlier.

Beneath the vines the terrace was flooded with amber light and the chairs and tables cast long...

Hang on – there was someone sitting at one of the tables.

She was in silhouette. She was gorgeous, even better than I'd imagined her. She had one of those slightly turned up noses like that girl I fancied like crazy in *Neighbours*, and she must've just washed her hair because it was half-wet and clinging to her but stray strands of it were drying and curling...

She turned and caught me looking at her.

'Hi,' I said, trying to sound super-casual.

'Hello,' she said back.

I made my way down the last few steps and dumped the bread in the kitchen. Then I bolted into my room and shut the door. Had she been aware of me staring at her like some pervert? I scraped my fingers through my hair and wondered if it was still sticking up on end. Oh for some gel or something. How to make a cool impression? Not in my sagging salt-stained shorts for a start. I slid into my jeans and had a tentative sniff at my shirt. The shirt was not good news, but it was better than my T-shirt, which had been crying out for a wash for over a week. Did girls notice that sort of thing? Not if you didn't get too close, maybe.

Having repaired the worst of the damage I slipped into the kitchen. How should I break the ice? I cast around for inspiration – simple. I'd stroll out and ask if she wanted anything to drink. Then I'd open up the conversation...

I grabbed a tray and swung out of the door.

That was odd. Where'd she gone? The table was deserted.

'Lucy... Lucy!' It was a woman's voice calling.

The older woman must've just come back – she was leaning into their room looking for her.

'Lucy'. Funny old name – sort of girly, but it kind of suited her. 'Lucy'. Yes, it definitely had a nice feel to it.

I went back into the kitchen and observed them through the kitchen window.

The girl must've walked out on the headland, to watch the sunset maybe. But she was back now and the two of them were hesitating, deciding which table to choose. They settled for one overlooking the harbour.

'Lucy, what's going on?' I heard the older woman ask.

I lost the rest because Stavros appeared in the kitchen window completely blotting out my view. He looked furious.

'What happen to the bread?' he asked, pointing at the massacred loaf.

'Oh that. I got hungry,' I lied. 'You know fresh bread. It smelt so good.'

'Now we not have enough for meals if peoples come. For brekfuss,' he stormed.

'OK, OK. I'll go again in the morning,' I said.

'When you go get bread, you get bread – not eat bread,' said Stavros sulkily. 'Understand?'

'Understand,' I said. I was still straining to hear what was going on outside.

'You go clear tables. Ask if they want drinkses.'

'Right.' I didn't need asking twice.

Now was my opportunity to make a favourable impression on the mother. Always a good move.

I made my way over to their table and picked up the girl's glass and an empty plate.

'Hi,' I said to the mother. 'Welcome to the Paradisos. My name's Ben. Can I get you anything?'

I'd made my presence felt, I could tell by the way she half-smiled up at me. And I could tell that the girl 'Lucy' had noticed me too.

'I'd love a glass of white wine. Chilled white wine?' the mother asked.

'Coming right up.'

Chapter Seven

So next morning, I faced the cross-country hike to the bakery again. I didn't mind that much. I often used to go for an early morning run at home, before school. I tried to pace myself so that I could keep the same speed for more or less the whole run. My trainers weren't up to much and I didn't want them to give out altogether.

When I reached the bakery I found the doorway was blocked by a queue of Greek women standing and chatting. Most of them were carrying big metal dishes full of what looked like *dolmades* or stew or stuffed tomatoes.

The women nodded to me and let me overtake them and go in ahead to the counter. I stood inside enjoying the warm wholesome smell of the room – today it had some sort of sweet smell too, kind of like toffee or caramel. I couldn't quite place it. The double-shelved bakery lady was taking one of the women's metal dishes and giving her a ticket in return. She slid it into her oven while I waited to be served. And then I remembered something I'd read in Sprout's guide book, about how Greek bakers used to let people cook their dinner in their ovens while they were cooling. I didn't think that kind of thing went on any longer, but obviously it did in this village.

The bakery lady was still wearing her funny little

shoes with the bows. She turned and caught me looking at them again.

'Three loaves, for Stavros please?' I said.

She smiled at me brightly. 'He has guests?'

'Yes. Two English people – a girl and her mother.'

'Good,' she said: 'Say "*Yassos*" to Stavros – from Maria, OK?'

'OK.'

And she added a little sweet sesame-topped bun to the loaves as she wrapped them.

'For you,' she said.

'Thank you,' I grinned.

'*Yassos.*'

'*Yassos,*' I replied.

I didn't eat the bun, although I was pretty hungry. I wedged it in the cleft of the tree where I'd seen the Albanian boy. Maybe he'd find it, maybe he wouldn't. But I'd get breakfast at the taverna anyway.

Then I started to sprint again. Before it reached the taverna, the goat track crossed the square where the bus stopped. As I reached the top of the rise, I could see that the first morning bus was already standing there waiting.

And then I saw – Oh no... The older woman had a suitcase with her and the girl had a backpack on. It was Lucy and her mother – they couldn't be leaving. They'd only just arrived. What was going on?

My heart sank as I heard the bus give a last

warning hoot and start up. It lumbered across the square and then picked up speed as it turned the bend.

I slowed to walking pace and made my way back into the taverna.

Stavros was sitting at a table fiddling with his worry beads. He looked depressed. The door of the girl's room was open and the key was in the lock.

I slammed the bread down in the kitchen and came back, to be confronted with the remains of their breakfast left on a table outside. Stavros' miserable packaged jam was untouched and the measly slivers of margarine had melted into greasy yellow pools.

'Where have the English people gone?' I asked.

Stavros sighed and shrugged. He took a flat pack of cigarettes out of his pocket, shook one out and lit it. 'They say they stay one week, maybe more. Then this morning, they get up – want leave – go – gone.'

'Why? What happened?'

He exhaled heavily. 'You tell me?'

'Maybe because you gave them such a horrible breakfast,' I said bitterly. I felt furious with him. There was no need for him to be such a penny-pinching bastard.

'What you mean?'

'You could give them fresh bread, sweet buns. Maria has brilliant ones. Honey, good decent coffee, proper orange juice...'

'You tell me how to run my business?' Stavros flared up.

'Yes, maybe I do,' I said. I felt so pissed off I didn't care at this point if he fired me.

He got to his feet and towered over me.

'I know why they leave,' he roared. He pulled down an eye with his finger. 'I see...'

'Oh yeah?'

'I see how you look at the girl with big cow eyes.' He made a hilarious face like a sick cow, rolling his eyes. And then he leaned forward and pulled down his eye again. 'And I see how the mother sees. And she no like it. That's why they leave.'

'Rubbish. I never even spoke to the girl.' But I could feel my face going hot all the same.

'And the girl. I see her when she look at you...'

'Really?'

'The mother, she sees. She say she leave because of the girl. Young peoples, she says, and she looks at me like this...' Stavros gave another hilarious impression, this time of the woman raising her eyebrows suggestively.

'Look, Stavros. We're English. We don't live in the Dark Ages like...'

'Young peoples the same everywhere.'

'Sure, but—'

'Waiters and guests. Is not allowed.'

'But—

'No but. You listen to me. If peoples come here. You no talk to guests. You no look at guests. Specially girlses. You no do nothing with guests, never, OK? Understand?'

Stavros had come out with so many negatives that I reckoned they made a positive – but I got his point.

'Yeah well, OK, I guess so. But I still don't think they left because of me.'

'You do as I say or you finished, OK?'

'OK.'

'First thing you clear their room.'

'Can't I have breakfast first?'

'Brekfuss?'

'I've just *run* all the way to the bakery and back—'

'You bring bread?'

'It's on the table... Oh, and Maria says "*Yassos*" to you.'

'Maria?'

'"*Yassos*."'

Stavros unfroze a little. He shrugged. 'Brekfuss yes. Help yourself.'

'Do you mind if I have an egg?'

'You want ruin my business?' he asked abruptly. But I caught a glint in his eye. I could see he wasn't serious this time. 'Egg yes, go on. But *only one.*'

After breakfast I set to work on the room. I realised I'd never really cleaned a room before. Not properly. Occasionally, when my room had got into chaos-mode I'd stacked things up and vacuumed, under threats from Mum. But something told me Stavros wouldn't have a Hoover. I helped myself to a broom from my 'bedroom' and made for their room, closing the door behind me, so that Stavros couldn't witness my total lack of domestic know-how.

The shutters were closed to keep out the heat of the day. With the door shut too, the room was in semi-darkness. It smelt slightly perfumy, a sweet spicy smell – of herbal shampoo, maybe. I went over to the bathroom. It was still warm and damp from the shower and a rim of white froth had been left on the blue tiled floor. I had an illicit thought at that point – of the shower washing the froth down from Lucy's hair. Of how it must have slid down her body, then on down those long sleek legs to end up washed into that little rim that still stood there like a ridge of white surf on a blue sea. I could almost feel the presence of the girl, behind me in the room.

The sound of Stavros moving chairs around outside brought me back to my senses.

The room – cleaning. Where did I start?

The beds. I hesitated again. Which one had Lucy slept in? The far one or the nearer one – the one I'd slept in, the night of the storm?

I started to strip off the sheets. And then stopped...

There was one long silky hair on the pillow. A dark hair with a glint of red in it. So she'd slept in the same bed, my bed. I leaned down and picked it up. The hair curled and clung around my finger as if it had a life of its own. It brought on a totally uncalled-for rush of excitement and my heart pounded.

I heard an echo of Stavros' voice in my mind: 'And the girl. I see her when she look at you...'

How had she looked at me? I didn't see her looking at me. But she must have. She must have been pretty interested for Stavros to have noticed. Lucy. Lovely, lovely Lucy. Oh smegging hell – why did she have to leave like that?

But then I had another thought. Maybe she was still on the island? They were obviously right at the start of their holiday – they'd both been dead white.

Yeah, that's right, they'd probably just moved on to the next beach, where there was more life. They couldn't have gone far. How many beaches were there on the island, anyway? I'd search them all. I'd find her somehow. Stavros must give me a day off sometime or even an afternoon off? Why hadn't I thought to ask?

Stavros threw open the door and found me standing there like a moron still clutching the sheets.

'How you doin'?'

'Fine, nearly finished.'

'Good. I want you wash the terrace, before peoples come.'

Jeesus, I had to get a move on or he'd throw a wobbly again. I ripped the sheets off and dumped them in a pile outside on the terrace. Then I went at the floor with the broom like a maniac. Trying to catch up. Trying to calm down.

'Peoples' didn't come of course. By mid-morning I'd finished all my chores and the room was made up ready for more guests. Stavros had wandered off somewhere up the goat track, leaving me in charge.

I went and sat at a table at the edge of the terrace looking out over the bay. The dredger was putting on a five-star performance, working double time. It had crept just a few metres further out to sea. From this side of the terrace there was a panoramic view of the village. It was built in a totally arbitrary way, the tiny whitewashed houses clinging to any available scrap of land, some of them perched so precariously they looked as if they were about to tumble down into the harbour. I could see now that some of them had tiny terraces, built out like ashtrays. No, more like boxes in the theatre, all facing towards the bay, as if a performance was about to take place. Maybe with the dredger as the star.

One terrace in particular caught my attention. A woman had come out on to it. She threw a cloth over the table and started laying out dishes of food. She was wearing skin-tight white cycle shorts and a skimpy black T-shirt and had sunglasses pushed back into her blonde hair. Certainly not one of the locals.

A guy joined her. He had his arm possessively around her waist. Cool-looking guy – and he knew it by the look of him – wearing tight black jeans and a white T-shirt that must've showed off every muscle of his torso, the kind of guy girls went for. Well she did, anyway, you could see by the way she pressed her body against his. I felt a frisson of envy. They stood there for a moment, clamped together, gazing out to sea.

I got up and fetched myself a Fanta at this point. Watching them like this was really getting to me. I still hadn't quite recovered from making, or rather unmaking, the girl's bed – my bed. When I came back the two of them weren't on the terrace any longer. But their breakfast was still there, waiting, untouched.

I took a long draught of my drink. They were probably inside making the coffee or something. It was then that I noticed I wasn't the only one observing this breakfast. Three sleek bodies detached themselves from the shadows and went stalking down towards the carefully laid table.

Cats. Young cats in the absolute prime of life. That perfect age between late kitten and adult cat status. A white one, a tabby and a perfect ginger cat. All of them long-legged, lithe and hungry.

I looked on with a snort of amusement as they homed in with ever-decreasing circles towards the breakfast. Serve Lover Boy right. A slight clink of a spoon on china could be heard as the first cat landed with a bound on the table. The others joined it, knocking over a yogurt pot. Three hungry heads bent over the creamy pool and I expected the couple to come out and shoo them off. But nothing happened. They were going to be so mad when they found out... Why didn't they notice?

And then it occurred to me that maybe they had something more important than breakfast on their minds. I got up and paced around the terrace. I had some censorable thoughts about what was going on in that house – lucky guy.

Chapter Eight

I had plenty of time to observe the bay over the next couple of days. Stavros managed to think up endless lists of useful jobs for me to do around the taverna.

And frankly, anything he wanted me to do, I did. I was trying to build up enough goodwill to ask him for the time off I needed, and maybe an advance on wages. I was going to need money to fund my search for Lucy. It was pretty difficult being penniless, although I'd solved the shaving problem. I'd found an old disposable with some life left in the blade in one of the rooms. So I wasn't totally without possessions.

Being without a watch was more tricky. But on the second morning, I'd discovered an utterly brilliant natural alarm clock. My room had a tiny window high up over the door. As the sun rose, it shone in through the window, casting a square of sunlight on my wall. By positioning the mattress in precisely the right place, the square would move round to shine on my face, waking me up at bang on seven o'clock – neat! Never had I been woken so pleasantly. No violent shrill alarm clock, no murmured threats from Mum, just a glorious golden warmth on my face – magic!

So that third morning I was up early and keen to get down to work. Which was more than I could say for Stavros. He never came round till at least ten o'clock. He just sat drinking tiny cups of Greek coffee and calling out commands to me. I'd quickly learned to ignore his moods. I just tried to pace myself and get on with the job.

First task of the day was always to stack the chairs on the tables and sweep and hose the terrace. This was on the village side, so while I worked I could observe the activities of Lover Boy and Blondie. It made a pretty stark contrast to my current way of life. They spent most of the time sunbathing on their balcony. The guy had really creepy Speedos that were so small they were indecent, and she had one of those bikini bottoms that get kind of swallowed at the back so she looked as if she had nothing on. They lay so close together you couldn't slide a credit card between them. By the look of it, their holiday was the nearest thing you could get to taking up residence on a double sunbed.

That morning, when I'd finished the terrace and was about to take a breather, Stavros decided that his vines were looking sickly and I had to spray them with an evil-smelling noxious substance that turned them white.

Stavros, meanwhile, was 'hard at work' down below, sitting by the shack, reading a newspaper, waiting for windsurfers to show up. I expected to take his place when I'd finished the vines. But no such luck. He had a better idea. He found me a pail of whitewash, a brush and a bucket. He took a long time instructing me on that particularly Greek obsession for painting everything white. First, I had to paint a load of empty olive-oil drums so that he could use them as plant tubs. When I'd finished turning the drums into garden ornaments he wanted me to climb on to the roof and paint under the eaves with a brush on a long pole. And finally, just in case I should get bored or something, he told me that he wanted all the white lines repainted down the steps that led down from each side of the taverna. There were literally thousands of them. There was enough work to keep me occupied for a lifetime! Repainting the Forth Bridge was a doddle compared with this.

I stood there with the brush and the bucket trying to find the right way to phrase my request.

'Look, Stavros...'

'Hmmmm?'

'I was wondering if... I mean, before I start a job like this, I've really got to go into town and sort out my travel arrangements. And I ought to ring my parents again...'

'Your parents? You ring from here...'

'Yeah but it's expensive, you know, calling England.'

'You don't talk long – OK?'

'But I still need to go to the Tourist Office, to re-book my air ticket.'

'What you saying?'

'I need a bit of time off. And I don't have any money, Stavros. Remember, I gave it all to you. Everything I had.'

'You want time off. AND you want money?'

'Er... yes well... only an afternoon or so... and an advance maybe?'

'Advance. Hmm. How much?'

I managed to screw about twenty quid's worth of drachmas out of him. The time off was a bit more of a struggle. But, in the end, he relented. So that afternoon, I found myself on the two o'clock bus out of Paradiso.

I realised as the bus took off that I didn't really know where to start looking for Lucy.

'Where are the good beaches?' I asked the driver as I bought my ticket.

'What you want? Jet ski? Para-gliding? Water-ski?'

'Maybe?'

'My friend! You must go to Skiathos then.'

I grinned back. 'No. OK. Nothing fancy. Just a nice beach with a taverna perhaps.'

'Next beach, best beach. No taverna. But plenty backpackers and windsurfers.'

'OK. I'll try that then.'

So I got off at the next bay. It was like I thought. A place entirely given over to posers. Those guys had equipment that brought tears to my eyes – must've cost a fortune. I scanned the beach for any sign of Lucy and her mother. If they'd been there they would have got trampled underfoot. Everywhere you looked there were these gladiator types competing with each other to be the best dressed and best equipped this side of Malibu.

I walked along the row of shops that fringed the seafront. There was a flashy modern café plastered with posters of windsurfers, a number of smartish restaurants with brash new tables and umbrellas set out on the sand, one glossy air-conditioned shop selling boards and accessories which were so out of my price range I didn't even dare look inside. And at the far end, a scrubby sort of enclosure surrounded by trellis that called itself the VIP Club. I peered through the trellis. Inside, there was a circular slab of concrete that was intended to serve as a dance floor flanked by a couple of dusty amplifiers – the whole place looked pretty run down. The tables hadn't been cleared from the night before, empty beer bottles and cigarette packs littered the place. So this was the local night life. Some VIPs...

I soon gave up on that beach and went back to the bus stop and waited for the bus to come round again. When it arrived, it disgorged its entire cargo of passengers and I was the only person to get on.

The driver grinned widely as he saw me climb in again.

'You no like?'

'The beach is OK. Not wild about the inhabitants.'

He rubbed his fingers together. 'Plenty money, eh?' And he whistled through his teeth.

'Yeah.'

I slid into a seat and we set off for the next bay.

Altogether, I checked out six beaches. Apart from the windsurfers' beach, the others were about as popular as the Paradiso. If Lucy had been on any of them I would have seen her. But she wasn't.

I was pretty downhearted by the time I got to the port. I was beginning to feel convinced that Lucy and her mother must have left the island, or were just about to.

I scanned the crowd waiting to board the ferry just in case. But there were only locals, waiting patiently with their bundles and suitcases. Not a sign of a tourist among them.

The Tourist Office was just opening up after the afternoon siesta.

Lurid T-shirts swung from the door-frame bearing the message: *You'll learn to love Lexos*. I smiled grimly to myself. Maybe I should consider moving on.

It took ages to sort my flight out. A fax was sent to the airline and then I had to wait around for a reply. The girl in there rang the airline three times. In the end she told me to come back in a few days.

All through that journey back to the taverna, I scanned each village for a sighting of Lucy or her mother. Once I saw a girl who looked like her and I leapt to my feet, hitting my head hard on the luggage rack. I was about to stop the bus, but as we drew nearer I realised, no, she was nothing like her. It was useless – they could be anywhere and they'd hardly be standing by the roadside, would they?

Feeling really depressed, I disembarked from the bus at Paradiso. The square was catching the last of the evening sunlight – in the olive grove the trees cast long shadows, and the crickets were tuning up for their evening performance. The whole place smelt like pure magic. What a waste it all was without Lucy.

I hesitated before going back to the taverna. If I did, and Stavros saw me, he'd probably present me with his blasted brush and bucket of whitewash. So instead I crept round by the cliff path and made my way down the steps to the beach.

In the twilight, the sea looked thick and inky. A single fishing boat was being rowed out. The slow, rhythmic creaking of the oars sounded ridiculously clear in the silence. The rower was standing upright, leaning on the oars in that curious Greek way. The boat was heading out to where a ring of makeshift floats showed that a net had been set. I'd thought the floats were garbage when I'd seen them at first. They were a colourful collection of mis-matched plastic bottles, some still bearing their labels.

Now the fisherman had come level with them, and I watched as he leaned forward and hauled in the net, tossing the occasional bit of seaweed back into the water. At last, as the final length of net came up, I saw the flash of a couple of fish as they fell into the boat. Such a meagre reward for so much work.

The boat turned now and started heading back towards the harbour. I suddenly realised, there was something familiar about the figure rowing. I heard his voice, hardly more than a whisper in the darkness, coming over the water to me.

'Hey – English boy. You find my knife?'

I realised guiltily that I'd totally forgotten about it.

'Hi!' I called out. 'No, not yet. I'll look tonight.'

The shadow of the boat moved a little closer.

'What're you doing with that boat?' I called.

'I work – for a fish,' the boy held up one of the fish by the tail. He spat dismissively into the water. The fish was barely fifteen centimetres long.

I remembered the fishermen, their salt-hardened hands playing at dominoes. They had little enough to live on themselves, without helping the boy. And there was Stavros, no doubt sitting on his terrace with a glass of ouzo and a nice little plate of something to go with it. And here was I, just passing through, working for the luxury of a few hours' windsurfing. It put things in a new perspective.

'I'll find your knife,' I called back.

He nodded, then leaned on the oars again and resumed rowing. I watched him round the headland. Then I turned and went back to the taverna.

I searched my room from top to bottom, but there was no sign of the knife. I thought of the one I'd had in my backpack. It was a real Swiss army knife, one of the more expensive ones, with scissors and everything. If I ever caught up with the scum who'd nicked our gear – I'd... I'd... I don't know what I'd do.

Chapter Nine

The next morning I went about my routine tasks dutifully. No robot couldn't have worked more systematically or with so little emotion. Even Stavros noticed my glum expression.

'Was wrong? You OK? You sick?'

'Didn't know you were paying me to smile,' I said.

Stavros hesitated, looked at me again and then went off, shaking his head.

OK, I was in a foul mood, I admit it. I kept telling myself I was crazy. I didn't even know the girl. I should put her right out of my mind. Why the hell should she spoil my holiday? Windsurfing – that's what I was here for. Yeah, windsurfing – what did a mere girl matter when I had a bay like this to myself?

That afternoon, the wind was perfection again. I felt the cool breath of it on my face as I swabbed down the tables after lunch. It made me feel a lot better. A good long sail – that's what I needed. The sooner I could get out there, the better. Stavros muttered something and lumbered off for his siesta. As soon as his door closed I was down with the boards.

I sailed round the headland into the windsurfers' bay this time. My heart was in my mouth as I came out of the lee of the headland and caught the wind full on.

Even the German guys in their windsurfer power-dressing were keeping in to the shore. I had some pretty hairy minutes tacking in towards them but then, once I was into more sheltered waters, I could see what attracted them to this particular bay. It was much wider than Paradiso. There were no rocks or shallows, just an endless silver expanse of glittering water, a windsurfer's paradise.

Time after time I tacked out and took long satisfying runs back with the wind into the shore. I was starting to feel that I was getting some respect from my fellow surfers – in spite of my antiquated equipment.

After an hour or so, my body told me it had had enough. It was tempting to go on, but I knew the dangers of surfing too long and finding yourself in a tricky situation without the strength to cope. So reluctantly, I braved the headland again and rewarded myself by one long seamless ride into the shore.

I climbed off the board neatly and drew it up the beach. I was about to dismantle and stack it when I paused. Someone else had been on my beach. There were footsteps leading down from the shack to the water. I wondered guiltily whether I'd actually missed the one potential piece of trade to come Stavros' way this side of Christmas.

The footprints were small. They certainly didn't belong to Stavros. They were even too small for the Albanian boy. I measured my foot against them. They were definitely a girl's footprints. I felt a quite manic rush of interest at this point. Another girl, maybe she'd be equally gorgeous? No – not equally, not possible, but she could be OK. The footprints changed direction at the water's edge and then led off down the shoreline beneath the taverna. I was intrigued. There was absolutely nothing of interest down that way.

I stacked the equipment, puzzling over this, and then came back to the footprints. Where had whoever-she-was been going? Maybe there was another path leading upwards. One I hadn't found yet. A shortcut to the taverna.

I'd be a fool not to check, wouldn't I?

They were nice little footprints – they made me think of someone light and lithe. My progress was checked briefly where a wave had swept inland and washed the tracks away. But no – there they were, leading off again towards a group of rocks. I was almost at the rocks when I was stopped dead.

'Looking for something?'

I jumped so hard I think she must've noticed.

It was *her*. Unless she was a mirage, of course. No, it *was* her. It was Lucy. But it couldn't be. I'd searched the whole island for her. And here she was... Right back where I'd started.

Hang on, I was standing looking like a complete *idiot*. I had to say something. Inspiration please!

'Yeah... a flip-flop.'

'A flip-flop?'

'Mmm.'

'Want some help?'

'Help?'

'Finding it.'

It occurred to me at that point that a fictional flip-flop might be quite hard to find. A nice opportunity to get to know her – so I said: 'Oh yeah, thanks. Why not?'

'Right. What colour was it?'

(Jeesus, I don't know. Think! Make it up!) 'Umm. Blue... Blue and white.'

She started searching round her group of rocks. I concentrated my efforts on an area a bit further back along the beach. I tried to stay cool but my mind was racing. Where had she sprung from? What was she doing here? How long was she staying?

'So you came back?' I called over to her. (Please don't tell me you're just here for the day.)

'Mmm. Mum liked it here. So I had to give in, in the end.'

'Ohh?'

I waded into the water, pretending to search through some weed. She'd climbed down and was leaning over some kind of rock pool. She suddenly straightened up and beckoned to me.

'I've found it!' she called out.

'*Have* you?'

'Yep. But I don't think I can reach it.'

I went over to where she was standing staring down into a rock pool. Would you believe it? There in the water was a blue and white flip-flop. It was really manky-looking.

'You could probably reach it if you climbed down. Your arms are longer than mine.'

'Yeah, guess so.'

We both stood gazing at it. I wasn't in too much of a hurry to poke around in the rancid-looking water so I changed the subject.

'You staying back at the taverna?'

'Yes.'

'How long for?'

'Not sure. Depends...'

'On what?'

'Oh I don't know. Mum's always getting ideas. She'll probably want to go off and delve about in some boring old ruin or something.'

'There's an interesting site on the next island.' (Oh why had I said that? They'd probably want to go there instead.)

'Is there?'

'Well, it's not up to much – mainly Roman but...'

'Whatever you do, don't tell Mum about it.'

'You going back to the taverna now?'

'Mmm... sun's going down.'

'Maybe I'll walk back with you.'

'Aren't you going to get the flip-flop?'

'Yeah, guess so.'

The things we do for girls! The sides of the pool were caked in green ooze. I semi-slid, semi-clambered down into it. It'd be just my luck to stand on a sea urchin. I reached down and located the flip-flop. The rubber was perished, wrinkled to the touch, felt like ancient skin. Felt as if it'd been under water as long as the Titanic.

'How can you tell it's yours? You'd better try it on.'

I turned to her and caught her expression. She was sending me up – the minx.

'Here, catch,' I said.

She did a typical girl's scream-and-duck and held out her hands in protest.

I was tempted but I restrained myself. Instead, I hurled it as far as I could out to sea.

'What a waste,' she said.

'Yeah, well. What's the use of one flip-flop anyway?'

So, she was back!

I didn't actually walk all the way to the taverna with her. Remembering Stavros' little lecture, I let her go on ahead and followed after a decent interval.

Her mother was up there already, waiting for her. Closer up, I could see she wasn't bad-looking for a woman her age. What Sprout would've called a yummy mummy – probably followed up by some crude innuendo. I wondered why there wasn't a dad around.

I served them drinks and chatted for a while. I would've liked to sit down and join them. But in my current status of waiter-cleaner-gardener-decorator I was forced to stand at a 'respectful' distance. I wondered if I could sneak off during the evening when Stavros wasn't looking and find Lucy on her own, so that I could at least *talk* to the girl.

Stavros appeared a few minutes later. He had my brush in one hand and a new full bucket of whitewash in the other. He had other plans for my evening's entertainment. The 'khazi' hadn't been whitewashed inside for ages, it seemed.

So I spent an 'unforgettable' evening, stripped off to my boxers, standing on a broken stool, improving the facilities. It was nearly midnight when I finished.

Chapter Ten

The next morning I went down to my masterpiece of interior decor and had a good long shower. The place was rather more acceptable now it was white inside.

Well-showered, I set off down the goat track for the bread. I'd make sure our guests got a good breakfast – didn't want them taking off again.

It was another brilliant morning. The crickets were chirruping away fit to bust. It was on the way back that I got around to wondering what they were so noisy about. I came to the conclusion that on a morning like this, with the sun beating down on them, and the air so clear it went to your head, they were probably a load of male crickets feeling dead randy and showing off like crazy to attract the best females. Well, that was the usual stuff animals were up to, wasn't it?

Then I started wondering whether it was the biggest and best male cricket with the deepest voice who attracted most females, or whether it was the leanest and fittest who got them rubbing their back legs together over him. I had some rather sexy thoughts at that moment.

That's when I saw her. As if my thoughts had materialised into real life! The lovely Lucy – she was coming along the path towards me. Well, this was a turn up...

I slowed to a trot as we came face to face.

'Hi. You're up early.'

'Mmm. Seemed such a waste of time. You know – staying in bed.'

Staying in bed, her bed – my bed. I couldn't help remembering the strand of her hair, how it had curled and clung around my finger like that. 'Here, look. Hold this a moment? ' I blurted out.

I had to bend down and pretend to re-tie my shoelace while I recovered.

She hadn't noticed. She was saying: 'Fresh bread! Smells good, I'm starving.' She'd broke off a bit of crust and was nibbling at it.

'Don't! Stavros'll kill me.'

'Blame it on me.'

'I can't. I'm not meant to speak to you, remember?'

'Crazy,' she said and smiled. There were tiny crumbs on her lips and for a moment I imagined leaning over and... licking them off.

I pulled myself together and said something about hurrying to get back for breakfast while the bread was hot.

She turned and started walking back with me.

'Where were you going?' I asked.

'Just wanted to see what was along the path.'

'Another village.'

'Oh, right.'

We continued in silence for a while. I racked my brains for something interesting to say. Anything to keep my mind and eyes off those wonderful long legs of hers swinging along beside me. The crickets, yes – they'd just stopped. All together. Suddenly. In that weird way of theirs. I wondered if she had the same theory about them as I did.

'Listen.'

'What?'

'They've stopped. The crickets. One moment they're all going for it like crazy, giving it everything they've got, chirping or whatever they do. And then suddenly, they all stop. All at once. Why do you think they do that?'

The crickets started up again.

'I don't know.'

Oh my God, I couldn't start telling her what I really thought. That there was this incredibly sexy kind of massive insect orgy going on all around us. That they were playing a totally pornographic insect version of the Rite of Spring. So I said instead: 'Maybe there's one of them – like the boss. A kind of bumped-up orchestral-conductor cricket who's in charge.'

(Naff, I know, but it got me off the hook.)

She laughed. 'No, I think it's more likely to be because of predators.'

'Predators?'

'Yes. If you really listen, there comes a point when they're all starting to go quiet. Imagine you're a cricket and you suddenly become aware of it. You don't want to be the last one to chirp, or you'll get noticed and nabbed... by a predator.'

'You think?'

'Mmm.'

'Then why do they start up again?'

'Maybe it's a mistake. Perhaps some inexperienced cricket kind of can't stop himself. You know, like when you're singing at school and you come in at the wrong moment and all eyes turn on you...'

(The thought of Lucy, singing at school, with loads of gorgeous girls around her. Oh man – it was too much.)

I tried to keep my mind on the crickets. 'And then all the others feel – like it's safe to join in?'

'Exactly.'

And she wasn't just pretty, she was really bright, too. There are some girls you try to talk to – you make some witty comment and it kind of lands with a thud like a dud tennis ball and nothing comes back. But everything I said to Lucy came back – with bells on.

'No. I think you're wrong. It's nothing to do with predators.'

'What is it then?'

She was looking at me. Her lips were slightly parted – expectant. There was no way I was going to be able to explain my cricket sexual serenade theory with her looking at me like that.

'There it is again. They've stopped,' I said.

We had both come to a halt. We were standing on the path listening and staring at each other – the way you do when you're trying to hear something. But clearly, neither of us had our mind on crickets.

For one crazy moment I was about to take the initiative – to lean over and just kiss her. I could see she wanted me to. She wanted me to – really badly.

But a single cricket started up nearby, distracting her. Damn it.

I backtracked. 'There it is. It's in that tree.'

'So you see what I mean?' she said, looking me in

the eyes again. (Yes, I was definitely going to kiss her.)

I think I said something like: 'When there's only one you can kind of *home in* on it.' I moved a step closer, hoping she'd take the hint.

'Mmm,' she agreed and took a step back.

(Nope, not now, too soon.)

The other crickets started up, joining in louder than before – like cricket laughter.

I came back to my senses. What was I thinking of? There was no way I should think of making a move at a moment like that. Standing there in the middle of a goat track. For God's sake – there were even goat turds lying around. Had I gone totally insane?

Chapter Eleven

We split up in the square and I let Lucy go on ahead. When I reached the taverna, I found Stavros was standing waiting for me with some money in his hand.

'Good – bread. Now I want you go to shop. Buy honey and... What you think they like?' He was obviously dead keen to keep them happy.

'Proper orange juice... but the shop won't be open yet.'

'No worry – knock on window. Say you want honey for Stavros.'

'OK.'

The little old lady who ran the shop got the shock of her life when I knocked on her window, but she opened up and let me in and I selected some local honey and orange juice, and I actually found some decent butter in her fridge too. She took the notes and smoothed them out and put them in her till as if they were pure gold. By the look of it, she didn't get much custom.

The honey, it seemed, was the thin end of the wedge. My job at the taverna took on a totally new aspect now Lucy and her mother were back. Stavros had got it into his head that the whole bay needed a make-over. Well, it did. But unfortunately it was my job to do the making-over. Stavros sat in the sagging chair beside the windsurfers, reading his paper and waiting for customers, while I worked like a galley slave tidying up the stuff that had been allowed to accumulate on the beach during the last millennium.

That morning, Stavros told me to take down all the beach parasols and carry them up and stack them in the square. He'd decided to dump them. No-one ever sat under them anyway. They were stained with black mould, and most of them had broken ribs so that they opened into weird irregular shapes.

While I was occupied with this chore, Lucy and her mother came down to the beach. As I worked, I could keep half an eye on Lucy, who was stretched out on the sand. She was wearing that bikini again, the pale blue one, the one I'd seen her in the first day. Nice. Strangely enough, I didn't really mind the work that morning – I even found I was whistling to myself at one point and I *never* whistle.

From time to time, Lucy would climb to her feet and go in for a swim. She didn't go out far. I wondered how well she could swim. I wondered if I could tempt her to swim with me, the half a mile or so to that tiny island I'd discovered. The one with the chapel and the hidden beach with just enough room for the two of us...

I worked down the beach, pulling out the pegs that tethered the parasols to the ground. The last one didn't even have a proper peg – the rope was attached to some old knife or something. I pulled it out of the sand. It was a kind of primitive penknife – just one curved blade that closed into a rough wooden handle – almost looked handmade. But the hinge had been carefully oiled so that it slid open and closed with ease and the blade had been sharpened to a lethal cutting edge.

The boy's knife – of course! It could only be his. Nothing Stavros ever owned would be cared for like this. I closed it and thrust it into my pocket.

Stavros meanwhile had moved up to the terrace and was sitting in the shade, 'under the tree of idleness'. He wasn't totally idle of course – he could still use one arm to raise a glass of beer to his mouth and the other to reach out towards a plate of little snacks.

As I passed him on the umpteenth trip he said: 'You watch what you's doing. No watch peoples on the beach – OK?'

'OK,' I said and then added: 'Look, Stavros, give me a break. I'm all in.'

'OK, OK,' he said. 'Go siddown. Take over at the shack. But no talk to girlses.'

'Sure. Even if a coachload of them come to hire windsurfers. I won't say a word. I'll just let them walk away.'

'What? You don't be cheeky – OK?'

On my way back down, I noticed Lucy's book. She'd left it open, face down on a wall where it could easily blow away. I stretched out and picked it up.

My Family and Other Animals. I'd read it as a kid, it had been one of my all-time favourite books. One of the reasons I'd wanted to come to Greece as a matter of fact. So Lucy was reading it now. I'd take it down to her. Maybe I'd say some cool and knowledgeable things about it. Let drop that I'd read it ages ago.

I continued down the steps and had a better idea. Maybe I'd use the book as a decoy. Get her to come over and ask for it. While Stavros was out of the way, it could start up a conversation.

Lucy and her mother were sunbathing some way down the beach. I moved the deckchair to the further side of the shack, hidden from view from the terrace. Then I settled down with Lucy's book.

I'd forgotten what a good read it was. That crazy family with the nicely dotty mother – and the way Gerald sent his brothers and sisters up. I was so engrossed in it that I hardly noticed Lucy had got to her feet.

Sure enough, she was making her way over.

'What are you reading?' she asked.

'*My Family and Other Animals.*'

'Where did you find that?'

I looked up innocently. 'Someone must've left it on the wall.'

'They did – *me.*'

'Oh, look, sorry – take it – I had no idea.'

'No honestly – you borrow it. I've hardly started it.' (Lies – she'd left it open a good half way through.)

'No really – take it back.'

'No, I don't want it. I'd like you to have it. Mum's brought plenty of other books.'

(OK – reading between the lines this was real bonding. A kind of literary equivalent of the way people lend each other sweaters and CDs and stuff.)

'Is it any good?' I asked.

'It's about this boy living on a Greek island and the animals he finds and his family and it's really funny.'

'Sounds great.'

'Just let me have it back when you've finished.'

'Thanks.'

She looked as if she was going to make off at that point. Don't go, don't go, I begged silently, racking my brain for some way to prolong the conversation.

She turned to go, and then swung back and asked: 'Do you know that boy?'

'What boy?'

I looked past her to where the Albanian boy was running up the beach. He had a rough-looking dog with him – looked like a stray. The two of them were having some kind of game with a stick, rushing in and out of the water like kids. Well, he was hardly more than a kid anyway.

'Oh him, yeah – kind of.'

'Is he Albanian? Mum says he is.'

'Yeah, she's right.'

'He's always hanging around. Hasn't he got anywhere to live?'

'Search me. Why do you want to know?'

I felt for his knife, it was still in my pocket. But I didn't want to call him over and risk a confrontation.

'He carried our suitcases. He's really thin and he looks dead poor. I just wondered...'

It made me feel really guilty the way she said that, so I answered in an off-hand way: 'There are loads of Albanians around. The Greeks use them as cheap labour.'

'No-one's using him. He doesn't seem to have anything to do.'

'No.'

I cast a glance up at the taverna, wondering where Stavros was. She took this as a hint.

'Oh I'm sorry, I forgot. I wouldn't want to get you into trouble.'

She looked straight at me with those lovely sea-blue eyes of hers. The wind was catching a stray frond of her hair and it was blowing across her face. She scraped it back behind her ear and turned to go. Before I knew quite what I was saying I blurted out:

'I was thinking of trying out a club in the next bay tonight. It's not much of a place but it might be good for a laugh.'

'Really?'

I waited, hoping she'd say she'd like to come along, but she didn't.

Instead she said: 'Well, have a good time. Let me know what it's like.' And turned and walked back to where she'd been sunbathing.

After half an hour or so, Lucy and her mother collected their things and walked past me up to the taverna.

As they passed, her mother said cheerily: 'You've got a nice job, sitting there in the sun.'

'It has its good points,' I agreed.

But Lucy said: 'Come on, Mum. The sand's broiling. It's burning my feet.'

When they left I cast a sweeping glance over the

beach for the boy. He was nowhere to be seen, but I could make out the place where I'd last spotted him with the dog. I walked down to where the sand was churned up from their game.

'Hey – English boy!'

The voice came from behind a group of rocks. I made my way over to where the boy was crouching near a rock pool, the dog laid out beside him, panting.

'Hi – I've been looking for you. The name's Ben by the way.'

He stared at me, frowning. He didn't seem to want to be friendly.

I pointed to myself. 'Ben,' I tried again.

I held out a hand but he ignored it. I wondered whether I should try again to explain about his job – force him to listen – but what with his lack of English I knew I'd mess the whole thing up. So instead I said hurriedly: 'Look, I think I've found your knife.'

I held it out to him.

He leapt on it and opened the blade and examined it as if it was the most precious thing in this world. Then he looked me in the face for the first time – he didn't smile or anything.

'Thank you – English boy.'

'Ben,' I said.

He pointed to himself. 'Ari.'

'Harry?'

'No – Ari.'

I held out my hand once more and this time he shook it.

Then he beckoned to me. 'Come,' he said. He was

already making his way back to the rock pool with the dog panting at his ankles.

He leaned over the pool once more, staring down into the water. I bent over beside him. All I could see was our reflections in the water.

'Look,' he said. As my eyes focused through the water, I noticed the rocky sides were encrusted with evil-looking black sea urchins.

'Urgh,' I said. 'Horrible, aren't they?'

'No, good, eat,' he said.

He already had his knife in the water and was scraping one off. He balanced it on his hand very lightly, so that the prickles didn't pierce the skin, then he deftly split it open and offered it to me. It had a kind of grey oozing jelly inside.

'*Eat*?'

He nodded.

I backed away. He laughed and threw back his head and swallowed the contents of the sea urchin like someone eating an oyster.

Then he split another open.

'Now you eat,' he said, offering it to me on the tip of his knife.

It was one of those invitations that is very difficult to refuse without giving offence. He split the urchin further and held it up for me.

There was nothing else for it. Closing my eyes and trying very hard to think of something else, I let him slide the urchin into my mouth. For a moment I experienced a nauseous taste difficult to describe – somewhere between rancid car tyres and mucous sea water. Then I felt the brute slide down my throat.

I opened my eyes and wondered how long it was going to stay down. The dog looked at me with its head on one side.

'Good? Yes?' said the boy.

I nodded and swallowed hard. 'Interesting,' I said.

'You want more?' he asked, holding up his knife.

I backed away, declining with both hands. Ari laughed in a superior kind of way. Then he leaned over the pool and scraped with his knife, intent on gathering his harvest.

'I'd better be off,' I said. 'See you.'

'See you – English boy,' he said without looking up.

Chapter Twelve

I was out windsurfing again that afternoon. The wind had shifted to an off-shore, so it took an age to tack back. Afterwards, I made my way up to the taverna, caked with salt and sweat – dying for a shower.

As I padded my way over to my 'bathroom', I heard a deep bass humming coming from it. Surprise, surprise, Stavros was in there. He must be having his once-in-a-lifetime shower. And using all the hot water by the look of it – I could see the froth gushing out from under the door.

I went back and sat on the terrace to wait. Ten minutes later, Stavros emerged with a towel round his waist, rubbing his hair with another. I must admit, I was quite impressed by the stature of the bloke. Without his singlet he looked even more like a minotaur. He had a great mat of black hair growing across his chest, and as he turned I saw it went right down his back too.

I had a pathetic cold shower. When I re-emerged, Stavros was dressed and standing on the terrace. He was wearing clean, newish-looking trousers and a shirt that had actually been ironed – you could see the creasemarks down the sleeves. But most surprising of all was his face – he must've had his weekly shave because his face was now as soft and smooth as a baby's bottom.

'Hey Stavros, you off out somewhere?'

'Tonight my friend? Yes. I go out. And you – you are in charge of taverna.'

'Oh?'

'You have problem?'

'Errm, well... I was thinking of going out myself, maybe.'

'Where you go?'

'Nowhere.' (There was just an offchance of persuading Lucy to come along and I didn't want Stavros cramping our style.)

'That's OK then – you stay here. Mind taverna. Serve peoples when they come.'

'*If* they come.'

'You don't be cheeky. You take rubbish, stack everything in square. Right?'

'Right. Do I have to work all night?'

'You work till midnight, OK. If no-one come, you shut up, go to bed. Sleep.'

I was longing to ask Stavros where he was going. But it didn't seem to be appropriate somehow.

'What if people come for rooms?'

'Take money up front, understand?'

'I think I've gathered that one.'

'What?'

'Yes.'

'Good.'

Stavros gave his belt another hitch and took a sidelong look at himself reflected in the glass of the kitchen window. Then he leaned towards me.

'How I look? What you think, eh?'

'Very smart.'

'You think ladies like, yes?'

'Oh yes, absolutely.'

'Good.' Then he went off into the kitchen humming to himself.

So much for my big night out. I sat on the terrace feeling well pissed off.

After a while, Lucy came out of her room with her hair all wet – the way it was the first time I saw her. She went to hang her swim things over the balcony rail. She caught me looking and flashed one of her smiles at me, then went back in.

I could hear Stavros preening himself. The smell of some dire kind of hair-oil wafted out, ruining the pure scented air of the evening. Stavros going out on the pull, what a laugh!

The lights were coming on in the village below. I could see the 'lovers" terrace illuminated by some sort of wavering light. Blondie came out carrying a candle and placed it on the table, and Lover Boy came out behind her. He leaned on the balcony with her body caught between him and the rail, giving her a good long snog – lucky man.

I was distracted by a funny kind of buffing sound coming from Stavros' room, I crept over to look through his door. Believe it or not, he was shining his shoes!

'What you doin'?' he demanded.

'Er, – just on the way to shift the rubbish.'

'Good.'

There was more rubbish than I would have believed. Alongside the standard kitchen stuff, there was loads more to lug up from the beach. As the path was narrow, I could only take so much at a time, so the job took the best part of an hour.

When I'd finished the terrace was deserted. I checked Stavros' room. He'd left already. There was no light on in Lucy's room, either and their key was hanging from the hook in the kitchen, so they must've gone out too.

I made myself a meal of some warmed-up pasta I found stewing in a saucepan. It tasted pretty vile but I guess better than the Albanian boy was having. The very thought of those sea urchins – yukk!

As I predicted, no-one came to the taverna. I washed up, swept up, cleaned the tables and then sat looking out to sea.

One by one the lights of the fishing boats traced their way out into the bay, each shrinking to a tiny shimmering dot in the ink-black sea, then disappearing. The night was so still. It really was a legendary place. I sat there drinking a beer and savouring the cool of the evening.

The only sound was the occasional drip of water from Lucy's swimming things. I glanced over – her pale blue bikini was hanging over the railings. Just a few tiny triangles of cloth. This brought such unbidden thoughts, I had to turn my chair round and look the other way.

I tried to think of something else. I got another beer and read Lucy's book as a distraction. In fact, I finished it. As I turned the final page, the lights were going off in the village down below – and Lucy and her mum still weren't back. Where on earth were they?

The club. I bet you anything they'd gone to the club after all. Typical! Here was I, chained to the taverna, bored out of my skull, while they were all out enjoying themselves. Even Stavros!

I imagined him surrounded by plump, seductive Greek girls. And Lucy. What about all those gladiator types on the next beach? The guys who looked so damn loaded – looked like they flew off to their dad's place in Monte Carlo for the weekend – had a new Porsche delivered every birthday. The thought of them having seen me surfing on my crummy board looking like a total loser! Maybe, right now, they were having a laugh at my expense with Lucy.

And I was stuck here till midnight. After that, I'd been told to go to sleep in my 'broom cupboard' like some dog. I sat raging against the unfairness of it all.

But hang on. Who would know if I was asleep in there on not? Stavros was hardly likely to check, was he? So what would it matter if I slipped out for an hour or so? I could walk over the top of the hill, through the olive grove, easily. Stavros would never be any the wiser.

By the time I got to the club it must've been well past midnight. The place was seething, man. There was a queue outside – mostly guys. They were handing notes over into a booth. I hovered, wondering what the damage would be. I still had a couple of thousand drachmas left from the money Stavros had given me as an advance. It might get me in, but it sure wouldn't buy me any drinks.

Since the club was an open-air affair, I decided to do a recce round the perimeter, just in case there was a short-fall in their security.

Making my way round to the darker side, I caught sight of Ari. He'd set himself up behind a low wall which he was using as a kind of counter. In front of him was a pile of some sort of fruit – shaped like grenades but pinkish in colour. He was splitting them open with his knife and offering them to the passers-by. Several people had gathered round, others joined them as I watched – by the look of it he was doing a roaring trade.

It was ironic really. There they were, all these German giants, most of whom owned enough top quality sports equipment to stock an average leisure centre, queueing up for this little guy whose only possession in the world was a pocket knife.

When there was a lull in the trade, I called out, 'Hi Ari! *Yassos*!'

'English boy,' he called back, with that arrogant look of his. 'Come – have some. On the house.'

'What are they?'

He said something unintelligible in Greek. They were the fruit I'd seen growing on the cactus by the roadside, but he'd stripped the prickles off. God knows how. I used to keep cactus when I was a kid and I remember the pain of a single prickle in my finger – it was too small to see, but it stayed with me for days. Typical kid, I'd made a great fuss about it. And there he was, handling the fruit as if he was immune. Watching him split one open, I realised why. His hands were work-roughened to a kind of hide.

They weren't like a boy's hands at all – they were more like an old man's.

I reached out gingerly but he shook his head. He made me eat the fruit from his hand. It was sweet, juicy and somehow gritty at the same time.

'Good, yes?'

'Better than the sea urchins.'

'You no like?'

'I like these better.'

He looked at me in a superior manner and patted his pocket. 'Make plenty money,' he said.

'Good on you,' I replied. 'See you round.'

'See you, English boy.'

I continued on my investigative tour. Yep, sure enough there was a group of shifty-looking guys hanging around the back of a low building to the rear of the club. One of them was keeping watch, and as he gave a low whistle, a couple of them were given a lift up and slipped in over the roof. It was pretty dark out here. I heard them whispering – they were English. I reckoned, if I played my cards right I could join in – gate-crash the gate-crashers, as it were. I picked up a loose stone and threw it hard into the bushes behind them. As I anticipated, they all swung round, thinking they'd been sussed.

In the confusion I slipped into the queue.

'Move. I'm next,' I said to the boy giving the leg up. And before I knew it, I was up and over the roof. It was a doddle the other side. Just a short drop down and I dissolved into the crowd – magic.

❁

The place was absolutely jam-packed – heaving with bodies – mostly backpackers by the smell of them. I shouldered my way through to the bar and asked for a beer.

A Heineken was handed over and the guy demanded two thousand drachmas, more or less all I had. Extortionate – no wonder they were pretty lax about people waiving the entrance fee. Cradling my bottle like it was vintage champagne, I made my way from the bar. This one drink was going to have to last the night.

Now to find Lucy. Not an easy task in the pulsing disco lights. I retreated into the shadowy outskirts of the club. They were playing pretty predictable dance music – the kind of stuff that was passé in Britain but still popular in the clubs on the Continent. I'd come across a lot of it inter-railing. It was a pretty international scene here tonight. I reckon I overheard every language from Gibraltar to Malmö in just two square metres.

As I'd noticed at the gate, there were loads more guys than girls. So the girls were very much in demand. I could see a couple of them in really short sawn-off shorts, dancing together with a hungry-looking male audience waiting to break in on them – practically had their tongues hanging out. But still no sign of Lucy – or her mother for that matter.

I shouldered my way through the massed ranks of blokes and then caught sight of the guys I'd gatecrashed with. They were pretty rough-looking types, but I guess everyone looks rough when they're backpacking. I considered making my way over, thanking them for the leg-up, making a joke of it. I could do with a bit of company. I edged closer and tried to eavesdrop on their conversation. Not easy, with music playing club-pitch.

I eyed them carefully, trying to judge what sort of guys they were. Watches – they're always a dead give-away. Hang on – that guy with the triple nose-ring had a watch just like the one I'd had nicked! An Omega with a black face – pretty unusual. I suddenly broke out in a hot sweat of anger. *This must be the bastard who'd nicked my stuff*. There were three of them together. Sprout had said something about three guys. They were acting in a dead suss fashion – they'd come over the wall for a start, without paying, hadn't they?

Conviction flowed into every vein. I strode over to him.

'Hey, mate!' He swung round. 'Where d'ya get that watch?'

'What?'

'I was asking where you got that watch.'

'Why d'ya wanna know?'

'Had one like it myself, that's all.'

I waited for this to register. He didn't flick an eyelid. In fact, he moved his face closer to mine.

'Oh yeah?'

'Yeah – but it went missing.'

'Meaning?'

'Meaning – I'd like to know where you got yours.'

He exchanged glances with his mates and shoved his hands in his pockets.

'My auntie gave it to me, for passing GCSE maths –

that make you happy?'

'That's a coincidence, because so did mine.' (Not true but I thought it sounded like a cool response.)

'Oh yeah – so how many watches d'you think they made like this?' He moved closer. And his mates took a step closer, too.

'Dunno.'

'Have a guess. A thousand – coupla thousand?'

His leering face was really getting to me. With a totally misjudged flash of anger, I burst out: 'I think you nicked it – along with all my other stuff.'

I didn't see it coming. One of his mates wrenched me by the shoulder, and before I knew it, I was down on the ground. Suddenly, there were feet all round me. I was staring helplessly up into a forest of legs bearing in on me. In a reflex action, I put my arms up over my head to stop being trampled on. With a hard thud a trainer kicked into my shoulder – pain shot down my back – another landed on my cheek, glancing off my eye..

Oh my God – they were going to kill me. I tried to get my body into a kind of ball with the smallest possible surface area. I lay there waiting for the thuds to multiply...

But they didn't.

Gingerly, I opened my eyes.

Standing above me, outlined against the disco lights, was the great bull head of Stavros.

'Wha's goin' on?' he demanded.

I looked around. The thugs had somehow dematerialised. Suddenly, arms were reaching down, helping me to my feet. A girl was dabbing my eye.

119

Someone else was suggesting I should've stayed where I was and another guy kept saying we ought to call an ambulance.

'No – I'm all right. It's OK.' The club reeled for a moment and I felt as if I was going to puke. 'I'd just like to sit down, that's all.'

Stavros shoved me down on a chair and someone handed me a glass of water. I took a long draught and felt better. As everything came back into focus, I found Stavros had an arm round my shoulders. His big baby face was a picture of concern.

'You tell me who done this,' he said. 'I kill them!'

'No, it's all right,' I said, stretching myself and finding to my relief that all my limbs still seemed to be in working order. 'It's just bruises, I think. And they've gone, anyway.'

Stavros insisted that I went back to the taverna in a taxi. He even paid the guy to deliver me to the door.

'Aren't you coming?' I asked as he handed the notes over.

'Me? No. Maybe come later,' he said.

Chapter Thirteen

The key to Lucy's room had gone from the hook in the kitchen and the light was off in their room, so I presumed they were back and asleep.

I lay down on my own bed feeling all in. The bruise on my shoulder was throbbing and I could tell from the tight feeling around my eye that I was going to have a nice ripe shiner in the morning.

I couldn't get to sleep at first, it was almost impossible to find a comfortable position – the bruise was on the side I generally lie on. I realised now what an idiot I'd been. That guy was right, there must be thousands of watches like mine in circulation. I'd made a total prat of myself.

I woke late next day. The little square of sunlight must've passed right across my face without waking me. It was there on the wall, slanted into a golden trapezoid, way over to the right. I wondered how late it could be. And then I remembered my watch, and the total berk I'd made of myself the night before.

My shoulder was stiff and when I put a tentative hand up to my face, I could feel the skin was tight and swollen. If Stavros hadn't stepped in, it could have been a lot worse.

I climbed out of bed and dragged on my clothes. And then emerged half-blinded by the bright sunlight.

There was no-one around. I wondered what time Stavros had got back. Surely he couldn't still be asleep? I went down the couple of steps between his room and the kitchen and peered in through the gap between his makeshift curtains. His room was empty and the bed didn't look as if it had been slept in. Odd.

I went back to the kitchen and helped myself to a big glass of orange juice – without Stavros around, I could enjoy the luxury of a peaceful start to the day. Lucy and her mother must be sleeping in. Their swimwear, now stiff and dry in the morning sun, was still hanging on the balcony rail.

I wondered whether I should go for the bread right now or whether I ought to stick around in case they got up. On balance, the idea of waiting conscientiously and peacefully, sitting in the sun with my orange juice, was a lot more attractive than pounding through the olive grove. My eye throbbed. And there was still some of yesterday's bread left in the kitchen.

As I was weighing up the alternatives, I heard footsteps crunching up the path to the taverna – heavy footsteps, unmistakably Stavros.

'*Yassos,*' he said as he rounded the corner.

He beamed at me. I'd never seen him looking so pleased with himself. He wasn't in his normal grouchy morning mood at all. He positively exuded well-being. For God's sake – he even *smelt* good for once – he had this wonderful wholesome... what was it? Something vaguely familiar. Yeah – this *fresh bread* smell about him.

He produced two round loaves from under his arm

and placed them between us on the table.

'You OK?' he asked, sitting down opposite me.

'Yeah, fine. Only bruises, I'll live.'

'Good.'

'I don't know what those guys would have done to me if you hadn't been there. I really can't thank you enough, Stavros.'

'They see me, they run – eh?' he said, flexing an arm.

'Yeah.'

'Your eye bad?'

'Not too bad. Thanks for getting the bread.'

'Bread? Oh bread, yes...'

It occurred to me then that he might have had better things to do last night than scrape employees off the floor...

'I hope I didn't spoil your night out,' I added.

He looked down at the two round loaves on the table with an unreadable expression on his face.

'Night? My friend. No. No worries,' he said with a contented smile.

I stared down at the bread. It smelt so good. It reminded me of Maria, plump and smiling, and I thought of those little feet of hers which she was so proud of...

Stavros' eyes met mine. Hang on a minute... Where had he been all night? No way! Maria? The old devil!

Stavros and Maria! Of course – they were custom-made for each other. The thought of them was kind of touching and ridiculous at the same time – like trying to imagine giant turtles getting off together... I mean you think of all that love stuff being between people who are young and beautiful – like you see in the movies – but Stavros and Maria – *Stavros and Maria*. I had to work hard to keep a straight face.

'Hm-hm,' I cleared my voice. 'I think I'd better make a start on breakfast.'

'No!' he said holding up a hand. 'Today – I make brekfuss. You go check windsurfers, shower, put cold towel on eye. OK?'

'Thanks Stavros, you're a mate.'

He got up and slapped me on the shoulder – my bad shoulder as it happened, but I forced a smile anyway.

Later, as I emerged from a long shower, I found Lucy and her mother had already finished their breakfast and gone back to their room.

'Good now?' asked Stavros.

'Much better.'

'You sit, eat, then I have job for you.'

'Fine. What?'

'Windsurfing lesson.'

'Hey, now look. I'm not qualified or anything. I can't give lessons.'

'Only beginner. Show her how to get up sail, balance. Keep windsurfer on a rope. Easy.'

'*Her*?' I asked.

Stavros cast a glance over his shoulder towards Lucy's room. 'Yes, *her*. And remember my friend,' he pulled down an eye. 'I'm watching, OK?'

'It's going to be difficult teaching her to windsurf if I can't speak to her,' I pointed out.

'You speak to her. Only about windsurfing, OK?

Nothing else.'

'Sure,' I said with a grin.

I caught up with Lucy on the terrace.

'I hear you want a lesson,' I called to her.

She nodded. 'I'll probably be hopeless.'

She was twisting her hair up into a knot at the back. I'd never seen her with her hair up. She looked really cute – I could see the shape of the back of her neck – it was lightly flecked with baby hair.

'What time?'

'When it suits you.'

'How about in half an hour? That'll give me time to get a board set up.'

She moved a step or two closer. 'What happened to your eye?'

'Had a bit of a disagreement over the ownership of a certain possession.'

'That's awful. Who with? What happened?'

Stavros came out of the kitchen drying a cup on a tea-towel and frowned at me.

'It's a long story, see you on the beach – OK?'

I'd never taught anyone to windsurf before. I tried to remember how I'd started. I selected the smallest rig and the most stable board, but I didn't assemble them. Instead, I built a mound of sand to act as a kind of makeshift simulator, so that Lucy could get the feel of balancing on the board without all the business of falling off into the water.

125

About half an hour later she came down on to the beach. She was wearing a one-piece swimsuit this time. Bit of a pity, but obviously more practical for windsurfing.

'Hi,' she said. 'Where do we start?'

'Right here,' I said, indicating the board.

'What? Not even in the water?'

'It's better this way. Step on and get the feel of it.'

She made quite a fuss about the lesson on the sand, kept jumping off with little shrieks every time I tipped the board too steeply. I had the feeling that teaching Lucy to windsurf could turn out to be an uphill struggle.

Hearing her, Stavros came over to the edge of the terrace a few times and looked down, but I nodded to him and he nodded back.

'I'm sure I'd be much better on the water,' she said at last.

'No, it's better to master the basics on dry land.'

She fell off a few more times and then lost patience entirely.

'Oh, this is crazy. I've had enough,' she said. 'Let me try in the water.'

'Well, if you really think you're ready.'

She wasn't. Nowhere near. She insisted that I inserted the rig. She kept saying that once she had something to hold on to, she'd be able to balance. I tried to point out that it didn't work like that. If you hang on to the wishbone for support you're more likely to end up on your backside in the water. But she wouldn't listen. We had a bit of an argument about it. She got quite cross in the end so I gave in. Why not let the girl learn the hard way if she wouldn't take my advice?

I tethered the board securely and stood in the shallows watching her and calling out advice. She couldn't get the hang of judging the wind direction, which is essential if you're ever going to get the rig up.

I kept on shouting: 'Get the rig to the lee of the board.'

'I am!'

'No you're not. You're about five degrees off.'

'How can you tell?'

'By the way the board's acting. And you should be able to tell by the feel of it.'

'OK, I've only just started – give me a chance.'

'I am. Why don't you come back on the shore like I suggested in the first place, and learn to keep your balance?'

'Why don't you just let me be? I can't concentrate with you criticising the whole time.'

'I'm not criticising, I'm trying to teach you.'

'If you'll just leave me alone, I know I'll be able to do it.' Her face had set into a determined expression. Once again she let the board slew round so that the rig was out of alignment.

'Look, Lucy...' I said. My patience was running a bit

thin as she fell off backwards for about the twentieth time.

She stood up in the water, looking wet and cross.

'Don't you "Look Lucy" me!'

'Look, the thing is, I don't think you're really trying to do what I...'

'*Trying*! I don't think you really know how to teach windsurfing.' (She had a point there.)

'How can I teach you when you won't listen?'

'How can I learn when you're telling me three different things at once?'

'OK – have it your own way. I won't say another word.' I crossed my arms and waited.

She scrambled on to the board again. Thrusting the wet hair out of her eyes, she managed to balance with an enormous effort. How she did it beat me. I could see she wasn't bending her knees enough – she'd be off into the water again any minute.

Carefully, she eased the board round until it was at right angles to the wind.

'Right – cast the rope off. I'm ready,' she said between gritted teeth.

'No way!'

'*Let go*!' she shouted over her shoulder.

'Oh Lucy, be realistic...'

'Who's paying for this lesson?'

'Who's giving this lesson? Look, you haven't got the faintest idea...'

'Stop being so bloody superior,' she snapped.

'Superior? Right! OK. Have it your own way – here goes.'

I untethered the rope and let out some slack. Of

course I had no intention of letting her go out to sea on her own.

By some sort of magic, the rig actually lifted out of the water. As the sail caught the breeze and bellied out, the board started to move forward. Lucy cast a triumphant smile over her shoulder at me. And sure enough, within seconds, her over-confidence was rewarded by the most dramatic over-the-top catapult fall I've ever witnessed.

I cracked up. I couldn't help it. She went in head-first, bottom-up, right into the middle of a great big sludgy clump of weed.

When she surfaced, she had weed tangled in her hair and running down her body – she looked like some grotesque kind of sea-creature. She rubbed the water out of her eyes and caught me laughing.

'*You did that on purpose,*' she said.

'No I didn't.'

'You pulled on the rope. You must've done.'

'No I did not!'

'Liar!'

'Look Lucy...'

'You enjoyed every minute of that, didn't you...?' She was wading out of the water now, sounded near to tears.

'Honestly, Lucy. You did just about everything in the book totally wrong...'

She stood in front of me, dripping weed.

'If you weren't so *bloody arrogant*, you might be able to teach...' she stormed.

I felt angry at this. I'd really been trying to help her. I just blew my top.

'If you weren't so bloomin' *pig-headed* you might be able to learn...' I called over my shoulder as I went to retrieve the board.

'*Pig-headed*!' she retorted. '*Who's talking*?'

'Oh, Jeesus – women!'

I waded through the water. 'Come on,' I said. 'You can at least learn how to get the board out on to the shore.'

With as much dignity as anyone covered in weed can muster, she stretched to her full height.

'You can get the damn thing out of the water yourself,' she said. And she stomped off up the beach.

Chapter Fourteen

I didn't see Lucy for the rest of the day. I think she must've gone off to another beach or something.

It was a pretty lousy afternoon – my head ached and I didn't want to risk windsurfing with my shoulder feeling so rough. So I just continued painting the white lines down the steps. I was making headway. I'd only got another hundred or so to go.

It was hypnotic work, dipping the brush in the can, brushing it along the step, dipping and brushing, brushing and dipping. As I worked my way down the steps, the sun gradually rose higher and higher in the sky, burning the back of my neck. My head throbbed and the dredger marked time with an intermittent deafening cascade of stones.

Jeez. I felt like someone in a penal colony doing hard labour. Everything had gone bloody wrong. I'd had my gear nicked. I'd been beaten up. I had a lousy, ill-paid job. And I'd messed up any chance of a relationship with the only decent female around. Yeah well – it was her fault, too. She didn't have to be so pig-headed.

My mind kept going over everything that had been said. Had it been my fault? No way! She was behaving like a right little prima donna. Who did she think she was? '*Who's paying for this lesson*?' Huh!

That was when I accidentally kicked the paint pot. I looked on in horror as a long slow slick of white paint formed a sort of waterfall down the steps. Oh bloody hell. Help! Disaster.

I dragged off my T-shirt and staunched the flow. It came to a halt in an oozing pool of white. Slowly and painfully I mopped up. Two steps were ruined and so was my T-shirt. My T-shirt? My one and only T-shirt. Oh smegging hell! This had to be the worst afternoon of my entire life.

I went to clean up in the shower. Stavros emerged from his siesta and caught me at it.

'What happened?'

'Had a bit of an accident with the paint. But it's OK.'

He looked on as I wrung white paint out of my T-shirt. It was useless, it was totally trashed.

Stavros took one look at it then ambled off through the vines. He reappeared holding a plastic bag with a T-shirt inside.

'Take this – on the house,' he said.

I opened it. It was one of those gross give-away T-shirts I'd seen the Albanian boy wearing. It had a garish picture of blue sea and geraniums on the front and bore that killer of an advertising slogan: *You'll learn to love Lexos.*

'Thanks.' I dragged it over my head and slumped down on a chair.

'You not happy?' asked Stavros, perceptively.

'No – not very,' I said.

Stavros sucked his breath through his teeth and considered me. 'Windsurfer lesson, no go well?'

'That's the understatement of the year,' I muttered.

'What?'

'No, it went very badly.'

'Lucy, no like learn from you?'

'Not exactly.'

'Ahhh! Women.'

'Mmm.'

'You want time off? Tonight maybe? Feel better?'

I thought of standing round like a lemon, serving Lucy and her mum drinks in this crummy loser's T-shirt. Yes, I would like tonight off – very much.

'Thanks Stavros. You're a mate.'

'No worries,' he said.

As the sun set, I walked over to the surfers' beach. Stavros had paid me for the week and I thought I might as well blow the money. I'd buy myself a decent T-shirt for a start, have a few beers, maybe a meal. Anything to get the thought of Lucy out of my mind.

The only place that sold T-shirts was the exorbitant windsurfers' shop. I had a mosey through their selection and found they all cost a small fortune, so I decided I'd have to bear the humiliation of being a walking advertisement for Lexos for the evening.

I sat alone in a bar on the seafront watching the sunset as the last of the surfing gladiators came into shore with the maximum of show – one guy even hurled his rig up over his head, giving the admiring crowd the treat of a shower of seawater. Jeesus, what a saddo. Mind you, sitting there in my hand-out Lexos T-shirt, I guess I didn't have much to boast about.

When I'd drunk a couple of beers I started to feel in

need of something more solid. So I walked down the front studying the menus: King Prawns in Seafood Sauce – Steak Tartar – Lobster. And the prices! Like everything else on this beach they were designed for people with more money than sense. I tracked down to the very end of the front where a shabby little shack advertised doner kebabs. There was a ragged queue of backpackers lined up outside. This looked more like my scene.

Inside the envelope of cardboard bread, the meat tasted like warmed-up cat food. All in all, it was probably one of the worst meals I've ever experienced. But I was hungry, so I wolfed it down anyway and then I went back to the bar for another beer to take the taste away.

The sun had set by this time and couples were starting to wander up and down the front, hand in hand, enjoying the cool of the evening. Predictably, my thoughts turned to Lucy. Still, she wasn't the only girl on the planet. I took another swig of my beer and studied the talent, giving the girls points out of ten on the standard system that Sprout and Mick and I had devised. None of them came anywhere near the 9.9 Lucy rated.

When I finished my beer I walked home. It wasn't the greatest evening of my life.

Next morning I awoke to serious internal rumblings. And then it hit me. Gut rot, Delhi Belly, Montezuma's Revenge, The Curse of the Pharoahs – it goes by many exotic names, but whatever the nationality, the effects are identical. I spent most of the morning in the khazi, vowing that I'd never ever let a doner kebab pass my lips again.

Stavros fussed around tutting like an old woman and made me drink loads of fizzy water, which helped a bit. Eventually, when the worst of the symptoms subsided, I crawled into my bed and was lost to the world.

When I emerged, I could tell by the height of the sun that it was well past midday. I started to make my way towards the vineyard for a wash and teeth-clean and then I stopped in my tracks.

Lucy was sitting there, at a table in the shade of the vines, writing postcards.

'Hi,' I said.

She looked up and frowned. 'Hello. What are you doing here?'

'I work here – remember?'

'I thought you'd be out *windsurfing*.' She said the final word with the emphasis of sarcasm.

'No, I er...' It struck me that gut rot isn't exactly the most charismatic topic of conversation, so I said: 'I... er – had other things to do.'

'Oh.'

I made off for my wash. As I splashed cold water on my face I considered tactics. What should I do? Pretend to ignore the whole row, treat it as if it hadn't been important? Or hold my ground and show the girl that it was all her fault – you know, '*Treat 'em mean. Keep 'em keen*'. Or maybe apologise. Yeah, maybe it would be best to get a quick apology in and then move on – fast.

As I walked back to the terrace I still hadn't made up my mind. I paused at the end of the path. Maybe I should start on something neutral and feel my way.

'So... How's things? What are you up to?'

She didn't look round. 'Writing postcards.'

'Yeah I know, but – apart from that.'

'Nothing.' (She still sounded pretty narked with me).

'I'm er – going to get a drink. Do you want anything?'

'No... thank you.' She finished a postcard with a flourish and added it to the pile in front of her.

I came back with a lemonade and sat at a table some way off.

'Lot of postcards,' I commented.

'I've got a lot of friends,' she said, picking up the stack and tapping them to get them to line up as if they were playing cards.

I took another sip of lemonade. Lucy took up another postcard and started writing.

'Do you want me to post those for you?'

'No... thank you.'

She leaned over her card, ignoring me.

'Look Lucy...'

'You're distracting me. I can't write while you're talking.'

'Oh right. OK. I won't say another word.'

'Thank you.'

I took another swig and felt in my pocket, I couldn't remember what I'd done with the room keys.

'You're still distracting me.'

'No I'm not.'

'You are. You're rattling things and you're looking at me.'

'I am not.'

'Yes you are.'

'You can't possibly tell! Unless you've got eyes in the back of your head?'

'I can feel it.'

'Rubbish. Look here... Lucy...'

She swung round, 'What?'

Her nose was peeling badly. Made her look absurdly like some sort of fluffy toy. I cracked up: 'Whatever happened to your nose?'

She ignored my comment and licked another stamp – oh those lovely lips and that little pink tongue! I couldn't help noticing she'd stuck the stamp on upside down.

'Why don't you just *go away*!' she said.

'Oh come on – loosen up – I've got just as much right to be on this terrace as you have.'

I meant to stand my ground – be really assertive. But at that moment the lemonade must've met up with whatever was awry in my plumbing system and I was forced to get to my feet and make a hasty exit through the vineyard.

When I returned she was still sitting there, with those lovely legs of hers – one tucked up under her – the other dangling, long and gorgeous...

She obviously thought she'd achieved a minor victory getting me to leave the terrace like that. There was a triumphant little smile on her lips as she turned and looked full at me. Her eyes were so blue, they were exactly the same colour as the sea behind her...

There was nothing else for it. I'd have to go for the apology route. I stood at the end of the path and took a deep breath.

'Look, I mean... Listen, Lucy... I'm really sorry about losing my cool with you yesterday.'

'Are you?'

'Mmm – really, truly.' (Absolutely damn truly – it was the worst mistake I'd ever made in my entire life.)

'Well, maybe I was a bit... er…'

'No... no, it was my fault. It's difficult enough learning to windsurf, without...'

'Well maybe, you know... I shouldn't have flown off the handle like that.'

'Oh, it was understandable...'

She was almost smiling now. 'Listen, Ben...'

My stomach interrupted with simply appalling subterranean rumbling noises.

'You OK?'

'I think maybe it was something I ate last night.'

'Oh you poor thing, there's nothing worse.' She actually looked sympathetic. 'Look, Mum's got some tablets somewhere. They're brilliant.'

You wouldn't have thought that discussing the symptoms of gut rot was the ideal way to chat up a girl. But her mother had an arsenal of tablets, and as we checked the instructions on the back of the packets all the resentment of the day before seemed to dissolve.

I selected what looked like the strongest and took a couple, then asked: 'Why aren't you on the beach?

Where's your mother?'

'I really overdid it yesterday. Mum got a lift to the port with Stavros to change money.'

'So it's just you and me, marooned here?'

'Mmm.'

'Nice.' I drew my chair up to her table.

'Mmm. But you better not sit too near. Germs, you know.'

'Oh yes, right.' (Curses!)

She took another postcard and started writing.

And then I heard the distant *phut phut phut* of Stavros' three-wheeler coming back – oh bollocks!

Chapter Fifteen

I had to go into the port the next day to pick up my ticket from the Tourist Office. Lucy's mother caught me just as I was leaving.

'If you're going in, would you mind picking up Lucy's film? The place is just next door.' She handed me the stub and the money.

'Sure. No worries.'

My ticket had arrived, amazingly enough, so I collected the film and got on the next bus back. The port was not a place you wanted to linger in long.

It was on the bus that I started wondering about the photos. I mean, photos, they're not really private property are they? And the envelope was coming open a bit... Maybe they were the ones her mum took of that famous windsurfing lesson!

I slid them out. There were some pretty standard views of the village and some photos of the local cats – typical girly stuff. Then a few of that disastrous windsurfing lesson. And then – hang on. These were all of *me*. Ten at least, no, more like fifteen of them!

I was looking pretty good in some of them, although I say it myself.

Now I don't want to sound big-headed – but how would you interpret this? A girl, taking lots of photos of a guy? There really was no other conclusion I could come to. Lucy fancied me. She fancied me like crazy.

So she'd been playing hard to get all along!

My head was swimming. My heart was pounding in my ears. Why was the bus being so damn slow?

It took forever to get back to Paradiso.

Lucy wasn't around when I got back, so I left the photos in her room. I didn't meet up with her until the afternoon when everyone else had gone off for a siesta.

'Did you get your photos OK?'

She didn't react, just said: 'Yes, thanks for picking them up.'

'No trouble. I was going in anyway. Any good ones?'

She still didn't react.

'Aren't you going to show them to me?' I asked, putting the pressure on.

'No.'

I could see the start of a blush spreading up from her neck.

Her eyes met mine and she bit her lip. She was just so unbelievably gorgeous. There was a silence which seemed to last forever and then we both started speaking at the same time.

'Listen...'

'Listen...'

'After you.'

'No, after you.'

I leaned towards her. I could hear sounds coming from inside Stavros' room. So I asked in an undertone: 'What I was going to say was – I should get a whole day off soon. Maybe we could do something...?'

'What did you have in mind?'

'Oh I don't know. Perhaps we could go for a swim at another beach or something…'

'Do you know one where there's no weed?'

If it had been any other girl, I guess I would have thought 'pathetic'. But at that point a totally unbidden vision entered my mind. I was lifting Lucy up, carrying her over the weed and sliding her down into the water.

'Does it really bother you?' I asked.

She looked at me archly. 'It did the other day.'

I grinned.

'You shouldn't have laughed, it was cruel,' she said – but in a jokey way.

'It won't happen again. Promise.'

'In that case – I'll come,' she said.

I managed to negotiate a whole day off the following Saturday. Until then, Lucy and I kept a polite distance from each other. Whenever Stavros was around I behaved like the perfect waiter and she put on an big act of ordering me around – I think she rather enjoyed it. She even left me a tip once – a very small one.

I woke early on the day of our trip. The square of sun was still weak and watery-looking way over to my left. What had woken me? Voices. Yes, voices arguing in Greek – it was Stavros and some woman. She was practically shouting at him. The Greek came out in great bursts. I lay there listening to their voices bantering back and forth – his a low conciliatory rumble, hers a shrill accusatory torrent of words.

I crept out of my room. Whoever it was, she was in Stavros' room. No, not in it – her lower half, dressed in a tight black skirt, was sticking out through it. I recognised that bottom – I recognised those shoes with their little stubby heels and the bows on the back. Maria!

What on earth was she doing here? She should be at the bakery at this time. It must be something really important.

She backed out and I shot out of sight behind my door.

Stavros came out of his room dragging his clothes on. He was shrugging his shoulders and gesticulating as if whatever they were arguing about wasn't his fault. But by the look of her, Maria wasn't having any of this. She let out another furious torrent of abuse and lifted up a hand and cuffed Stavros on the cheek. Stavros kind of swayed and held his hand up to his cheek in shock. Both of them stood there in silence for a moment, glaring at each other.

And then suddenly everything changed. Stavros put out a hand and took Maria's little chubby hand in his. He said something quiet and low. Maria burst into tears. I watched, intrigued. This was hardly some row about an unpaid bread bill.

And then he threw his arms around her. They stood there for a moment in the doorway like a couple of wedged bears, and then they moved as one into his room and the door slammed behind them. *Well!*

From inside the room I could now hear gentle

voices and the squeak of bedsprings as something landed heavily on the bed. This was too much. I dragged on my clothes and headed off down the goat track, not knowing whether to feel shocked or amused.

There was a big queue of women outside the bakery, at a loss to know quite what to do without Maria there. I pushed past them and helped myself to two loaves and left the money on the counter.

Halfway back along the goat path I met Maria. She was coming as fast as her short little legs would carry her.

'*Yassos*,' she shouted to me.

'Hi,' I called back.

'*Yassos*, Ben,' she called out again, waving her handkerchief at me. She was half-crying and half-laughing. All her anger seemed to have disappeared. She had this look on her face. Honestly, this may sound crazy, but this little fat lady looked almost beautiful.

'*Yassos*, Maria,' I called to her.

Back at the taverna I approached the terrace cautiously, wondering what mood I'd find Stavros in. Quite obviously, he'd lost the argument.

He was sitting with his back to me, gazing out to sea. His fingers were busy with his worry beads. He hadn't heard me approach.

I coughed politely.

'I've brought the bread.'

'Bread?' said Stavros, and he got to his feet.

He walked over to me, took the loaves in his big hands and just stood there with them. He looked as if he was in a state of shock.

'Everything all right?' I ventured.

'OK? OK? Is OK yes. Ben. Is OK...'

'Well good. I'm glad to hear that.'

'You see... I'm getting married,' he burst out and slapped me on my bad shoulder.

'Well, that's fantastic!'

'Yes, big surprise eh? Stavros married!'

'To Maria?'

'Yes. How you guess?'

'Well you know. I notice these things.'

'Good woman eh? Beautiful.' His hands drew a kind of Grecian vase in the air.

'Very nice.'

'Bakery – makes good money.' He rubbed his fingers together.

'Yes, sure – everyone needs bread.'

'Everyone needs bread. Good! Fantastic! Stavros married. Maybe father soon.' He rocked his arms as if cradling a baby.

A baby! Well yes, I suppose it was *just* possible. Maria couldn't be that old.

'Everyone needs bread!' said Stavros again. He threw his head back and roared with laughter – I think maybe he was a little hysterical. He was already opening bottles and shouting greetings down the cliffside, inviting various members of the community to come and join him in a celebratory drink.

Chapter Sixteen

I nearly missed the nine o'clock bus. Lucy was standing in the square pleading with the bus driver not to shut the doors. We climbed in and took the last two free seats at the back. I told her about Stavros and Maria – she was really chuffed.

'Why are there so many people on the bus?' Lucy suddenly asked.

I looked around, I guess it was a bit unusual.

'Oh, I don't know. It's Saturday. I suppose a lot of people get the day off.'

'Oh, right. Is it Saturday? I'd totally lost track of time.'

She stared out of the window and then a weird stricken expression came over her face.

'What's wrong?'

'I've just remembered something…'

'Do you want to go back?'

'Not that sort of thing. And it's too late now.'

'It can't be that bad?'

'No, it's OK.' She scrabbled for something in her bag, then brought out a tissue and blew her nose.

'Lucy? What is it?'

I could see now that her eyes were brimming with tears. She bit her lip and said: 'It's just that my dad's getting married today, that's all.'

'Your dad? Didn't you want to be there?'

She shook her head and looked away. I didn't know quite what to do or say. I'm no good with girls

Chapter Sixteen

It was a curiously quiet evening. I leaned over the rail, gazing into the bay, thinking about what Mum had said.

I wondered what Dad was doing. The reception would be over by now. It wasn't going to be a big affair, just a party in a room over a pub – but with loads of people we knew. They'd probably be driving to the airport – right now. Dad and Sue were going to have a really lush honeymoon in a proper hotel with a pool in the Seychelles. I felt the familiar frisson of envy.

But Mum had got over it. Why hadn't I?

The sun was setting with its usual swiftness. I watched as the horizon took the first chunk out of the bottom of it. The low light was turning the harbour that ridiculous over-the-top copper colour. Hang on – something was missing – the dredger. It had gone. It must've been towed away during the day. I'd got so used to seeing it there, the bay looked somehow empty without it.

I remembered my first impression of the place. I'd thought it was so run down. What a dump! But I'd really got fond of the funny old village. If you looked closely, you could see that each house had its own little path and gate, a balcony to sit on, a blue or green-washed window, a flowering pot plant, a birdcage, or a rag rug outside its door. As if however small or humble the house might be, someone was taking pride in it.

I wandered down the steps to the beach; each step with its neat white line and then the flight of wobbly ones which Ben had painted.

His windsurfer wasn't stacked with the others, so he must've still been out there. I decided to wait on the beach for him. On the rock, at the tip of the headland – the place where we'd first met. I wanted him to come back and find me waiting there for him, so that I could make up somehow for this afternoon. But how would he know I was there? Simple!

I slipped off my shoes and laid a neat trail of footprints along the beach for him to follow. Then I settled in the shade, expecting any minute that his sail would come darting towards me across the bay.

Shading my eyes against the low light, I scanned the sea. I couldn't see him anywhere. The gloom was gathering fast. It would be dark soon. He should be back by now.

After another ten minutes or so I was starting to feel really worried. I stood up and searched the sea from one side of the bay to the other. He must be ever so far out if I couldn't see him.

Could people windsurf in the dark? They didn't have lights or anything so how could they see where to go? And more to the point, how could other boats *see* them? It must be dangerous, sailing out there at night. Really dangerous.

There *were* lights in the bay. Two of them moving in unison. I strained my eyes into the gloom and could make out two figures standing up rowing. They must be fishermen rowing their boats out to check their nets. I went to the very edge of the water and called to them.

'Hello...!'

'*Yassos*,' the call came back.

'No! Please listen... Have you seen Ben?'

The fishermen leaned on their oars and said something to each other in Greek.

'A boy... on a windsurfer... Have you seen him?' I tried again.

A stream of Greek came back. They obviously didn't understand a word of English.

'Please... listen. Will you look for him?'

I pointed out to sea and tried to make the shape of a windsurfer with my hands But it was no use, I couldn't make them understand. I was starting to feel desperate. What should I do? Ring for the coastguard? What number did you ring? Did the coastguards speak English? It was like one of those terrible nightmares where you're running against time and not getting anywhere.

The fishermen were shouting to a boat further out. One I hadn't noticed before. I could just make out the skinny outline of another figure. There was a dog in the boat too, I could see its silhouette against the water. It was Ari – the Albanian boy. He spoke English – *he'd understand...*

I shouted for all I was worth.

'Ari! Have you seen Ben?'

He rowed closer inland. 'Ben? No.'

'He's out there, on his windsurfer. He hasn't come back. We've got to do something...'

'How long is he gone?'

'I don't know. Two hours. Maybe more.'

Ari shouted in Greek to the fishermen. They responded. They were going to help, I could tell by their voices. They were already turning their boats and starting to row out to sea.

Ari shouted back to me. 'Go tell Stavros. Ask him, ring for help. We look.'

'Thank you, Ari. Oh thank you...'

'Don't worry. I will find him.'

I felt panic rising as I ran breathlessly up to the taverna. Stavros was standing at the top of the steps.

'I hear,' he said. 'Help is coming. I made the call already.'

The hour that followed was the longest of my life. I stood on the shore going through all the events that had led up to this one impossibly horrifying moment...

If only he hadn't gone out windsurfing so late in the day... If only I'd tried to stop him... If only I hadn't remembered that Dad was getting married at three... Then we'd have spent longer together on the beach... And he wouldn't have gone off like that – so far and so late. If anything happened to Ben it would be my fault. If only I'd stayed there instead, with his arms around me, so warm and so strong. I kept going over and over it in my mind. And all the other 'if onlys' that led on from that.

Mum came down on to the beach with a blanket and Stavros brought a bottle of Metaxa. Mum looked tense and frightened and I could tell Stavros was trying to put on a brave face, but his fingers shook as he fiddled with his worry beads. We built a fire of driftwood and stood there in a miserable little huddle, waiting round it.

I kept wandering away from the fire trying to make out the lights of the fishing boats through the darkness. I could hear the engines of speed boats setting out from the windsurfers' bay. They were obviously taking the search really seriously. I kept telling myself, nothing as horrible as this could possibly be real.

I stared out to sea. That same sea that had appeared so dreamily inviting – such a vivid turquoise during the day, now turned black and oily and threatening.

Time passed impossibly slowly. As slowly as sand passing through an hourglass, grain after grain after grain. My whole being ached for this all to be over and everything to be back to normal. Why did this have to happen to me? Why did it have to happen at all?

And then I saw it.

One tiny light. I was sure it was moving towards us – approaching the beach.

I went and grabbed Stavros's arm. 'Look!'

He moved down to the edge of the water and stared intently in the same direction.

'Look, there!' I pointed it out to him.

'Yes,' he said. 'You are right. A boat is coming back.'

What had they found? I hardly dared imagine. My mouth went dry. My knees were weak with fear, my hands clammy with a cold sweat. An eternity seemed to pass before we heard his shout. It was Ari's voice, very faint in the distance.

Stavros waded out into the water and shouted back in Greek. I studied his face as the reply came back again.

'Bravo!' roared Stavros, and he turned back to me, splashing through the water.

He lifted me up and was hugging me, nearly squeezing the breath out of me, before I could get any sense out of him.

'Is OK. Ben's OK. He's found him!' he said at last.

Suddenly I was laughing and hugging Stavros back and Mum came and joined us. So we were all standing in the water laughing and hugging each other like a load of loonies.

All I could think of was that Ben was alive. The nightmare was over. I don't think I've ever felt so happy in all my life, or ever will again. Within ten minutes we could make out the boat coming towards the shore with the windsurfer dragging behind it. Stavros waded in waist-deep to meet it.

And then Ben climbed out and made his way through the water. He walked straight past the others. He just came to me and put his arms around me without saying a word. We forgot about everyone else. We just stood there clinging to each other.

Everything was a kind of blur after that. All I can remember is that everyone seemed to be talking at once and fussing about blankets and water and hauling out the windsurfer and that Ari got left out somehow. Before anyone noticed, he'd started pushing the boat back out to sea. Ben tried to stop him and then Stavros waded in after him.

Some kind of discussion was going on between Stavros and Ari, and then Ben was joining in. The dog was leaping round in circles, barking with excitement, drowning out what they were saying.

The three of them stood knee-deep in the water, arguing. At last Ben waded back shaking his head as if he didn't believe what he'd heard.

Chapter Seventeen

Looking back on the week that followed, I realise now I was living in a sort of haze. Everything fell into place. Ari had his way – he had his job back, with double money. So, Ben was back on holiday. Which meant, of course, that we could spend as much time together as we wanted. And we wanted all right!

We explored every inch of the island. We even found places like Dad had told me about. Where the sea was an endless limpid blue and you could see down to where the fish swam metres below.

One day, one perfect day, we hired a boat and Ben rowed me out to this tiny island with a chapel and an olive tree and a beach just big enough for two people...

And no – I'm not going to tell you *everything* that happened there.

I can hardly bear thinking about the day we had to leave. Ben came to see us off on the ferry. I can remember him standing on the jetty, watching the boat go out. And how he got smaller and smaller as we headed out to sea, until he was just one tiny dot among all the people waving from the shore. And then I lost sight of him.

I thought it would last forever. Love like that had to. And although we lived miles apart, it did at first. For those first few weeks we rang each other every night and talked for hours.

But after a while, there wasn't so much to say. He didn't know any of my friends and I didn't know his. And it's a bit boring hearing stuff about people you don't know. But we planned to meet up in the Christmas holidays and I thought it would all come right then. We'd get back to where we had been.

We both wanted it to be a really special night out. The best. We argued for hours about what we would do. In the end Ben rang Mum and then secretly bought tickets for a show I'd been dying to see.

I had a brand-new outfit and I actually lashed out on proper haircut for our big night out.

Ben met me at the station. He looked *so* different. I'd never seen him in normal clothes and he had this jacket on that was new and didn't really fit him and was, well – a bit naff. He wasn't tanned any longer and his hair looked darker. And I don't know why I'd ever thought his eyes were blue-green, they were really quite a dull sort of grey.

We had a meal after the show and it was so obvious that he was making a big effort to keep the conversation going. I wanted to say – loosen up, it's OK, it's me, Lucy. But I couldn't find the right way to say it. And then it was too late – it was time to leave the restaurant, I had a train to catch.

When he kissed me goodbye on the station platform, I knew it was the end. We didn't mention seeing each other again. I think both of us knew there was no point.

When I got home that night, I went straight up to my room and I took out the pebble he'd given me that afternoon on the beach – the little piece of serpentine that was the colour of his eyes. The pebble wasn't blue-green any more. As soon as I'd got it home it had turned a plain dull grey. I'd kept it all the same. But even when I'd soaked it in water, that wonderful magical colour hadn't come back.

Where had it gone – the love we thought we had? Could it actually have been love, if it could disappear like that? It was back to that same old circular argument again.

That's when I got to thinking about Dad and Mum. I realised I'd been blaming them for not loving each other any longer. Deep down I'd been really resentful. But it wasn't really Dad's fault. And it wasn't Mum's fault either. They couldn't help it, any more than Ben and I could.

I walked slowly back downstairs. Mum had been waiting up for me. She was sitting in her dressing-gown in front of the electric fire.

'Oh dear,' she said when she saw my face.

'Don't ask,' I said.

'I wasn't going to.'

I settled down in the warmth of the fire and leaned against her knees.

'I think maybe I might go over and see Dad and Sue tomorrow,' I said. 'Would you mind?'